超級英語閱讀訓練

SUPER READING TRAINING BOOK 1

FＵＮ學美國英語課本精選 二版

Michael A. Putlack &
e-Creative Contents_著
Cosmos Language Workshop_譯

1

MP3
寂天雲 APP

MAIN BOOK

如何下載 MP3 音檔

❶ 寂天雲 APP 聆聽：掃描書上 QR Code 下載「寂天雲－英日語學習隨身聽」APP。加入會員後，用 APP 內建掃描器再次掃描書上 QR Code，即可使用 APP 聆聽音檔。

❷ 官網下載音檔：請上「寂天閱讀網」（www.icosmos.com.tw），註冊會員／登入後，搜尋本書，進入本書頁面，點選「MP3 下載」下載音檔，存於電腦等其他播放器聆聽使用。

Preface 前言

用美國教科書來學習英語,是目前甚受歡迎的英語學習風潮,就像美國兒童學習母語一樣,透過教科書中各科的知識來奠定英語基礎。本書的所有內容都是美國教科書最基本的課程,對於非英語系國家的我們來說,是非常有用的英語學習書。

美國的教育過程著重統合教育,將各個科目彼此連結,本書並配上生動的照片圖解,幫助學生提高學習效率。透過這種精心編寫的內容與編輯方式來學習英語,除了能幫助學習正確的英語,也能夠在各個科目的教育過程中,自然而然地熟悉與運用英語。讓你不用出國,也能體驗美國課程,全面提升英語能力!

1 本套書完整收錄美國一年級到六年級的各學科核心內容，並依文章長度與難易度，共分為兩冊。

·超級英語閱讀訓練 1：FUN 學美國英語課本精選
·超級英語閱讀訓練 2：FUN 學美國英語課本精選

2 每一冊皆精選 90 篇文章，分析美國最多人使用的四大教科書內容，文章範疇遍及各個學科與領域。

3 依據美國教科書的英文單字和閱讀文章，並穿插上百張的照片資料，精心編寫與設計，幫助學生以最輕鬆的方式，達到最大的學習效果。

4 讀完課文之後，隨即有題目練習，測驗讀者是否能抓出文章的「主旨」（main idea）和細節（details），並有字彙能力（vocabulary）測驗。這些題型是各種英文考試最常見的出題型式，透過這些簡單的練習，除了能幫助理解文章，也能幫助培養日後參加各種英語檢定考試的能力。

　　本套書旨在幫助讀者打好紮實的英語基礎，朝向高等的英語能力邁進。書中羅列各種範疇的主題，幫助讀者熟悉各種學科和領域的背景知識和用語，培養能進一步閱讀《時代》、《紐約時報》的能力。無論是求學、參加英文檢定或是在職場工作，亦或是想參加多益、托福等各種英文考試，或者想到國外留學、在國際企業或跨國公司工作，本書都可以幫助您一圓美夢！

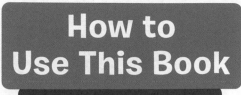

How to Use This Book
本書的使用步驟

本書設計有「課本」（Main Book）和「訓練書」（Training Book）兩大部分：

課　本 精選各學科範疇的菁華，全書以全英文呈現。

訓練書 針對字彙、閱讀和聽力做設計，並特別標示出英語的句子
　　　　結構，幫助理解句意與文法結構。

STEP 1　閱讀課文

首先，先閱讀搭配了各式照片和圖片的課文。在這過程中，如果出現不認識的詞彙或片語，先不要看翻譯，也不要查字典，而是藉由在閱讀的過程中，培養由上下文掌握內容的能力。在這階段，要參考文章所穿插的照片或圖片，這些圖片具有「圖像字典」的功能，能幫助理解文章內容。如果有無法推知的詞彙或片語，就把它們圈出來，在回答文章下方的題目之後，再查看「訓練書」。

STEP 2　做文章下方的題目

讀完課文之後，隨即有題目練習，測驗你是否能抓出文章的「主旨」（main idea）和細節（details），並有字彙能力（vocabulary）測驗。這些題型是各種英文考試最常見的出題型式，透過這些簡單的練習，除了能幫助理解文章，也有助於培養日後參加各種英語檢定考試的能力。

STEP 3　查看訓練書

訓練書除了附有答案和翻譯以外，還標示了文章的句子結構，根據文法和片語詞組來斷句，以幫助理解句意與文法結構。透過這種斷句的練習，除了能提升英文的理解力，也能加強詞彙和句型的掌握能力。

STEP 4　對照課本與訓練書

接下來，要一面看訓練書，一面確認課文中不認識的詞彙或片語的意思，並完全了解課文內容。首先，先把〈Words to Know〉的詞彙掃視一遍，然後一邊讀英文課文，一邊對照中文翻譯。

STEP 5　自己練習翻譯與斷句

接下來，不要看翻譯，試著自己翻譯英文課文。這時，你可以練習斷句，這會對文章理解有很大的幫助。如果有無法掌握的，就再一次確認英文詞彙、片語的中文意思，直到充分理解。

STEP 6　邊聽音檔邊閱讀

熟悉英文的發音，比用眼睛看英文，來得更為重要。本書的課文皆由專業的母語人士所讀誦，每一篇文章最少反覆聽兩遍，以熟悉正確的發音和音調。在聽課文的誦讀時，可以參考訓練書的斷句處，並注意聽母語人士的發音、音調和連音等。你也可以在訓練書上標示出音調和連音的地方。然後再聽兩遍，並大聲地跟著唸。這時，要盡量去模仿母語人士的唸誦與發音。在本書中，西方歷史的地名和人名很常出現，這些發音要特別留意，並盡可能熟悉。

STEP 7　不聽錄音，自己大聲唸出課文

再接下來，暫時不要再聽音檔，自己練習把課文大聲讀誦出來，並且盡量模仿母語人士的發音與語調。發音或語調不順暢的地方，要再多聽音檔來練習，直到熟練為止。

STEP 8　重新再閱讀英文課文

現在再次回到課本，仔細閱讀英文課文，並再做一次題目。這一次要要求自己能夠充分理解文章內容與句法結構，要能完全掌握文章與題目。

The Introduction of Training Book
訓練書特色說明

透過「斷句」掌握「即讀即解」的竅門

　　為了能更快、更正確地閱讀英文，就需要能夠掌握英文的句子結構。而要培養英文句子結構的敏銳度，最好的方法就是以各「意義單元組」來理解句子，也就是將英文句子的「意義單元組」（具一個完整意義的片語或詞組），用斷句（chunk）的方式分開，然後再來理解句子。只要能理解各個「意義單元組」，那麼再長的句子，都能被拆解與理解。

　　聽力也是一樣，要區分「意義單元組」，這樣能幫助很快聽懂英文。例如下面這個句子可以拆解成兩個部分：

> I am angry at you.
>
> I am angry / at you
> 我生氣　　　對你

　　我們會發現，這個句子由兩個「意義單元組」所組成。不管句子多長多複雜，都是由最簡單的基本句型（主詞＋動詞）發展而成，然後再在這個主要句子上，依照需求，添加上許多片語，以表現各式各樣的句意。

　　在面對英文時，腦子裡能立刻自動快速分離基本句型和片語，就能迅速讀懂或聽懂英文。在讀誦英文時，從一個人的斷句，大致就能看出個人的英文能力。現在再來看稍微長一點的句子。經過斷句以後，整個句子變得更清楚易懂，閱讀理解就沒問題了：

> Leonardo da Vinci painted / the most famous portrait / in the world: / the Mona Lisa.
> 里奧納多達文西畫了　　　最有名的肖像畫　　　全世界　　（就是）蒙娜麗莎

一個句子有幾個斷句？

一個句子有幾個斷句？有幾個「意義單元組」？這是依句子的情況和個人的英語能力，而有不同的。一般來說，以下這些地方通常就是斷句的地方：

★ 在「主詞＋動詞」之後
★ 在 and、but、or 等連接詞之前
★ 在 that、who 等關係詞之前
★ 在副詞、不定詞 to 等的前後

另外，主詞很長時，時常為了要區分出主詞，在主詞後也會斷句。例如：

Your neighbors / are the people / who live near you.
你的鄰居　　　　是人們　　　　住在你附近

In our community, / people help each other / and care about one another.
在我們社區　　　　人們互相幫助　　　　　並彼此關心

對初學者來說，一個句子裡可能會有很多斷句的斜線，而當閱讀能力越來越強之後，你需要斷句的地方就會越來越少，到後來甚至能一眼就看懂句子，不需要用斷句的方式來幫助理解。

本訓練書因為考慮到初學者，所以盡可能細分可斷句處，只要是能分為一個「意義單元組」的地方，訓練書上就標示出斷句。等你的英文實力逐漸提升，到了覺得斷句變成是一種累贅，能夠不用再做任何標記就能讀懂課文時，就是你的英文能力更進一階的時候了。透過斷句的練習，熟悉英語的排列順序和結構，你會驚訝地發現到，自己的閱讀能力突飛猛進！

The Structure of Main Book
課本架構

11 National Parks

The United States has many national parks. These are protected areas. So people cannot develop or damage them. The first national park was Yellowstone National Park. It is an area with stunning scenery and many wild animals. The Grand Canyon is also a national park. It is one of the largest canyons in the world.

Every year, millions of people visit these parks. They tour the parks and go hiking. Some even camp in the parks. They learn about the land and how to preserve it, too.

課文
藉由閱讀課文，培養掌握上下文的能力

Some National Parks in the U.S.

▲ Yellowstone National Park

▲ Grand Canyon National Park

▲ Yosemite National Park

1 **What is special about the Grand Canyon?**
a. Many wild animals live there.
b. It was the first national park.
c. It is a very large canyon.

2 **Answer the questions.**
a. What was the first national park? _____
b. What is one of the world's largest canyons? _____
c. What do people do at national parks? _____
_____

文意理解測驗
透過主旨 (main idea) 和細節 (details)，測驗是否讀懂課文內容

3 **Write the correct word and the meaning in Chinese.**

canyon	damage	stunning	go hiking	preserve

a. _____ : a deep valley with steep rock sides and often a stream or river flowing through it
b. _____ : to go for long walks in the countryside
c. _____ : to save; to conserve

字彙能力測驗
確認是否理解英文詞彙片語的真正意義

32

The Structure of Training Book
訓練書架構

01 Good Neighbors 好鄰居

Your neighbors / are the people / who live near you. In our **community**, / people help **each other** / and **care about one another**. If you want / to have a good neighbor, / you **have to** / be a good neighbor / first. There are / many ways / to do this.

First, / you can be nice / to your neighbors. Always **greet them** / and say, "Hello." **Get to know** them. **Become friends** / **with them**. Also, don't be noisy / at your home. And **respect** / your neighbors' **privacy**. If they have / any **problems**, / **help** them **out**. They will help you / too / **in the future**. If you do / all of these things, / you can be / a good neighbor.

單字提示
· 藉由文中重點單字畫記，理解字彙如何運用

課文斷句
· 透過分離基本句型，迅速讀懂英文
· 反覆聽音檔，練習把課文大聲唸出來

你的鄰居 neighbor 就是住在你家附近的人。在我們的社區 community 裡，人們會互相幫忙 help each other、彼此關心 care about one another。若是想要有個好鄰居，你必須先成為一個好鄰居 be a good neighbor。要做到這點有很多方法 many ways。

首先 first，你可以對鄰居表示友好 be nice。要經常和他們打招呼 greet，並且說「你好」。去認識他們 get to know them，和他們成為朋友 become friends。還有，不要在家裡製造噪音 don't be noisy，並且要尊重鄰居的隱私 respect privacy。他們若是遇到問題 problems，你可以幫助他們 help them out，將來 in the future 他們也會幫助你的。如果這些你都做到了，你就是個好鄰居 good neighbor。

中文翻譯與重要字彙片語中英對照

Words to Know

· **community** 社區　· **each other** 互相（兩者之間）　· **care about** 關懷
· **one another** 互相（三者以上）　· **have to** 必須　· **greet** 打招呼
· **get to know** 認識　· **become friends with sb.** 與某人做朋友
· **respect** 尊重　· **privacy** 隱私　· **problem** 問題　· **help out** 幫助擺脫困難
· **in the future** 日後；未來

單字學習

6

Table of Contents

Chapter

2

Science

Life Science

Earth Science

Chapter

3

Mathematics

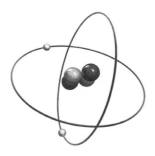

Chapter 4

Language •
Visual Arts • Music

Chapter

1

Social Studies

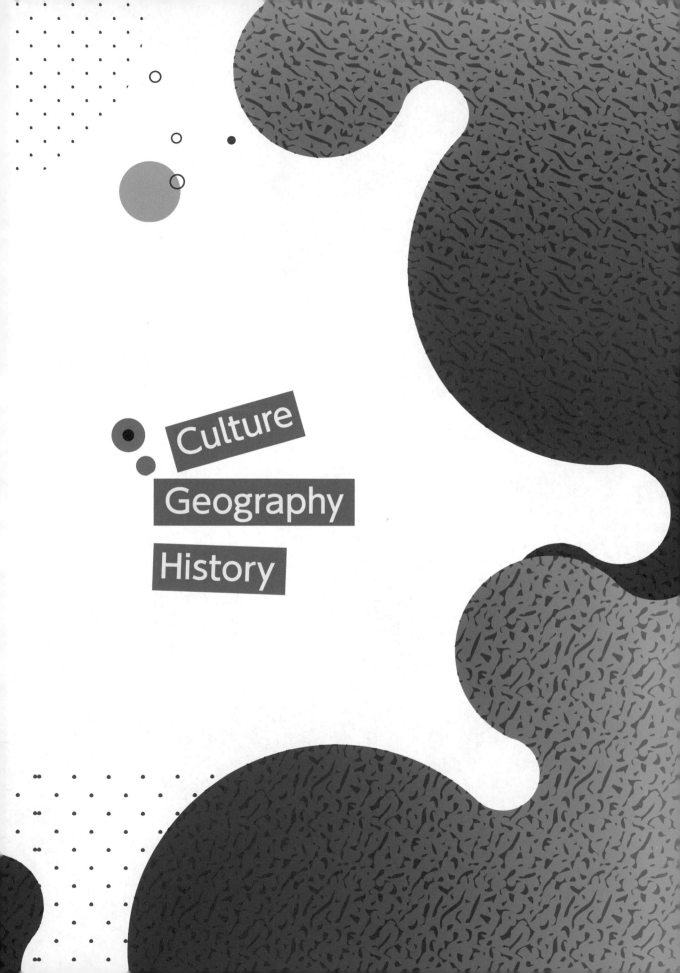

Culture

Geography

History

Culture

Culture & Economics

The American Government System

01 Good Neighbors

Your neighbors are the people who live near you. In our community, people help each other and care about one another. If you want to have a good neighbor, you have to be a good neighbor first. There are many ways to do this.

First, you can be nice to your neighbors. Always greet them and say, "Hello." Get to know them. Become friends with them. Also, don't be noisy at your home. And respect your neighbors' privacy. If they have any problems, help them out. They will help you too in the future. If you do all of these things, you can be a good neighbor.

Places Around Your Neighborhood

▲ city hall

▲ post office

▲ fire station

1 **What is the passage mainly about?**
   a. Why we need neighbors.
   b. How we should treat our neighbors.
   c. Where your neighbors live.

2 **Fill in the blanks.**
   a. _____ are people who live near you.
   b. Try to respect your neighbors' _____.
   c. Good neighbors often _____ their neighbors _____.

▲ subway

3 **Write the correct word and the meaning in Chinese.**

neighbor	help out	get to know	greet	community

   a. _____: to do a part of someone's work
   b. _____: a place where people live together
   c. _____: to meet someone with friendly words and actions

02 A Day at School

John and Sally go to elementary school. Their first class starts at 8 a.m. They go to their homeroom. They stand up, face the flag, and say the Pledge of Allegiance before their class begins. Then their teacher, Mrs. Smith, starts their lessons. They study math, social studies, English, and art, and then they go

▲ the Pledge of Allegiance

to the cafeteria for lunch. After lunch, they have recess, so all the students go outside and play for a while. Then they learn science, history, and music. Finally, it's 3 o'clock. It's time for them to go home!

Good Behavior at School

▲ Raise your hand to talk.

▲ Do not run in the hallways.

▲ Do not yell and scream.

1 When do John and Sally have recess?

　a. Before social studies.　　**b.** After lunch.　　**c.** At three o'clock.

2 What is true? Write T (true) or F (false).

　a. John and Sally's homeroom teacher is Mrs. Smith.　＿＿＿＿

　b. John and Sally study math and art before lunch.　＿＿＿＿

　c. John and Sally study science and social studies after lunch.　＿＿＿＿

3 Write the correct word and the meaning in Chinese.

recess	cafeteria	face	allegiance	homeroom

　a. ＿＿＿＿＿＿＿＿＿＿ : a classroom where students go at the beginning of each school day

　b. ＿＿＿＿＿＿＿＿＿＿ : a place where people get food at a counter and carry it to a table for eating

　c. ＿＿＿＿＿＿＿＿＿＿ : a time of rest

Christian Holidays

03

Christians are people who believe in Christianity. They believe that Jesus Christ is the Son of God. In Christianity, there are two very important holidays. They are Christmas and Easter.

Christmas is on December 25. Christians celebrate the birth of Jesus on this day. Christmas is a time of happiness and celebration.

Easter is in late March or early April every year. It is the most important Christian holiday. It is the day when Jesus Christ came back from the dead. Most Christians go to church on this day.

▲ **American Holidays**

▲ Christmas

▲ Thanksgiving Day

▲ Independence Day

▲ the birth of Jesus

◄ the coming back to life of Jesus

① **What is the passage mainly about?**
  a. The dates of Christmas and Easter.
  b. The reason that people celebrate Easter.
  c. Two important Christian holidays.

② **What is NOT true?**
  a. Christians believe that Jesus Christ is the Son of God.
  b. Easter is on December 25.
  c. Jesus was born on Christmas Day.

③ **Write the correct word and the meaning in Chinese.**

dead	Christianity	believe in	Easter	celebrate

  a. _____ : to be certain that something exists
  b. _____ : to rejoice; to observe with ceremonies
  c. _____ : no longer living

04 Different Kinds of Jobs

04

After people finish school, they often look for jobs. There are many kinds of jobs people do. But there are three main categories of jobs. They are service jobs, manufacturing jobs, and professional jobs.

People with service jobs provide services for others. They might deliver the mail or food. They often work in restaurants. And they work in stores as salespeople and cashiers.

People with manufacturing jobs make things. They make TVs, computers, cars, and other objects.

People with professional jobs often have special training. They are doctors and engineers. They are lawyers and teachers. They might need to attend school to learn their skills.

● **Different Kinds of Jobs**

——— Service Jobs ———   ——— Professional Jobs ———

▲ cook ▲ salesperson ▲ deliveryman ▲ doctor ▲ lawyer ▲ engineer

1 **Where might a person with a service job work?**
   a. At a factory.   **b.** In a school.   **c.** At a restaurant.

2 **Answer the questions.**
   a. When do people often look for jobs? _____
   b. What are the three main categories of jobs? _____
   _____
   c. What are some professional jobs? _____

3 **Write the correct word and the meaning in Chinese.**

look for	training	manufacturing	service job	deliver

   a. _____ : the process of making something
   b. _____: the process of learning the skills you need to do a
                                particular job
   c. _____: a job people do to provide service to others

Nowadays, we live in an advanced world. We use many new inventions that people long ago never imagined.

In the past, people could not regularly communicate with others. It took days, weeks, or even months just to send a letter. There were no telephones. So people had to talk face to face. Nowadays, we use cell phones to call anyone anywhere in the world. And we send email to people instantly thanks to the Internet.

In the past, traveling short distances took a long time. People either walked or rode on a horse. Now, most people own cars. They can drive long distances in short periods of time. And people can even fly around the world on airplanes now.

In the past, people often died because of poor medical treatment. Even a toothache could sometimes kill a person! Now, vaccines protect people from diseases. And doctors are making more and more discoveries every day.

Technology

▲ invention

▲ vaccine

▲ wireless communication

1 **What do cell phones let people do?**
   a. Travel short distances.
   b. Call people anywhere in the world.
   c. Send letters to people.

2 **Fill in the blanks.**
   a. We live in an _____ world today.
   b. People nowadays send email instantly thanks to the _____.
   c. In the past, people often died because of poor _____ _____.

3 **Write the correct word and the meaning in Chinese.**

| advanced | invention | face to face | medical treatment | vaccine |

   a. _____: a substance used to protect against a particular disease
   b. _____: modern and well developed
   c. _____: something that is newly invented

The president is the leader of the American government. He is elected by the people and serves for four years. He lives in the White House.

There are other government officials, too. Many serve in Congress. Congress is divided into two parts. They are the Senate and the House of Representatives. Every state has two senators. And every state has a different number of representatives in the House. Some have many. But some have just one or two. The members of Congress make all the laws for the country. They work from the Capitol in Washington, D.C.

American Symbols

▲ the White House

▲ the Capitol Building

▲ the American flag

▲ the bald eagle

▶ the Statue of Liberty

❶ What do the members of Congress do?
  a. They make American laws.
  b. They lead the government.
  c. They work at the White House.

❷ Answer the questions.
  a. Who leads the American government? _____
  b. How many senators does each state have? _____
  c. Where do the members of Congress work? _____

❸ Write the correct word and the meaning in Chinese.

bald eagle	Washington, D.C.	senator	representative

  a. _____ : a member of the Senate
  b. _____ : It is the capital of the U.S.
  c. _____ : It is a symbol of the U.S.

State and Local Governments

07

The federal government in the U.S. is very important. It is the central government of the U.S. But every state has its own government, too. And cities have governments also.

Every state has a governor. A governor is like the president. The governor is the most powerful person in the state. And every state has a legislature. There are many members in these legislatures. They represent small sections of their states. They pass the bills that become laws in the states.

Cities have governments, too. Most cities have mayors. Some have city managers though. A city manager is like a mayor. And the city council is like a legislature. But it usually has just a few members.

Some State Capitols in the U.S.

▲ Florida State Capitol

▲ New Jersey State House

▲ New York State Capitol

1 **What is the central government of the United States called?**
 a. The state government. b. The local government.
 c. The federal government.

2 **Answer the questions.**
 a. Who is the most powerful person in a state? _____
 b. Who passes the state's bills? _____
 c. What are the leaders of most cities called? _____

3 **Write the correct word and the meaning in Chinese.**

governor	legislature	represent	mayor	state capitol

 a. _____: the elected leader of a state
 b. _____: to act or speak officially for someone or something
 c. _____: the main government building in each state

08 The Jury System

Most criminal cases in the United States are done in a trial by jury. Jury trials are an important part of the justice system. A jury is made up of regular citizens. There are two kinds of juries: a grand jury and a petit jury.

A grand jury has between 12 and 23 members. The prosecutor presents his or her evidence to the grand jury. Then, the grand jury decides if there is enough evidence to have a trial. If the jury says yes, then there will be a trial. If the jury says no, there will be no trial.

A petit jury is also called a trial jury. This jury usually has 12 members. The members listen to actual court cases. They hear all of the evidence. Then, at the end of the trial, they must make a decision. They decide if the defendant is innocent or guilty.

Jury Trials

judge · criminal/defendant · police officer · lawyer · prosecutor · jury · witness

1 **What does a grand jury decide on?**
a. Whether or not a person is guilty.
b. Whether or not there should be a trial.
c. Whether or not a person is innocent.

2 **Answer the questions.**
a. How many kinds of juries are there? _____
b. What is another name for a trial jury? _____
c. What does a trial jury do? _____

3 **Write the correct word and the meaning in Chinese.**

evidence	jury	prosecutor	criminal	innocent

a. _____: a lawyer who tries to prove a defendant is guilty
b. _____: something which shows that something else exists or is true
c. _____: a person who has committed a crime

Geography

Geography Skills

American Geography

There are seven continents on Earth. Asia is the biggest of all of them. Europe has many countries located in it. Africa has both deserts and jungles in it. Asia, Europe, and Africa are often called "the Old World." Australia is the largest island on Earth. People call North and South America "the New World."

There are five oceans on Earth. The Pacific Ocean is the biggest. The Atlantic Ocean lies between the Old World and the New World. The Indian Ocean is the only ocean named for a country. The Arctic and Antarctic oceans are both very cold.

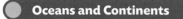

Oceans and Continents

Arctic Ocean

North America

Europe

Asia

Atlantic Ocean

Africa

Pacific Ocean

South America

Pacific Ocean

Indian Ocean

Australia

Antarctic Ocean

Antarctica

▲ island

▲ peninsula

Gulf of Mexico

▲ gulf

❶ **What is the New World?**
a. Europe and Asia.
b. North and South America.
c. Australia and Antarctica.

❷ **What is NOT true?**
a. Asia is part of the Old World.
b. The earth has seven oceans on it.
c. The Pacific Ocean is bigger than the Arctic Ocean.

❸ **Write the correct word and the meaning in Chinese.**

New World	continent	island	located	named for

a. _____: North, Central, and South America
b. _____: a piece of land surrounded by water
c. _____: a large landmass, such as Asia or Africa

10 What Is a Map

M aps are drawings of different places. They show what an area looks like. Some maps show very large areas, like countries. Other maps show small areas, like cities or neighborhoods.

Maps can show many things. On big maps, they show the land and water. These maps have countries, seas, oceans, and even continents on them. People use these maps to find countries and cities. Small maps might show one city or area. They have many details. They have individual buildings and streets on them. People use these maps to find their way somewhere.

Places on Maps

country border
lake
mountain
Great Plains
plain
Colorado Plateau
desert
river
ocean
gulf
ATLANTIC OCEAN

❶ **What is the passage mainly about?**
   a. How to make maps.
   b. Who uses maps.
   c. What maps show.

▲ political map

❷ **Fill in the blanks.**
   a. _____ show what an area looks like.
   b. Maps can show small areas, like _____ or neighborhoods.
   c. Big maps have countries, _____, oceans, and continents.

▲ physical map

❸ **Write the correct word and the meaning in Chinese.**

neighborhood	detail	individual	border	land

   a. _____: a feature; a single fact or piece of information
   b. _____: the solid part of the surface of the earth
   c. _____: a line separating one country or state from another

National Parks

The United States has many national parks. These are protected areas. So people cannot develop or damage them. The first national park was Yellowstone National Park. It is an area with stunning scenery and many wild animals. The Grand Canyon is also a national park. It is one of the largest canyons in the world.

Every year, millions of people visit these parks. They tour the parks and go hiking. Some even camp in the parks. They learn about the land and how to preserve it, too.

Some National Parks in the U.S.

▲ Yellowstone National Park

▲ Grand Canyon National Park

▲ Yosemite National Park

1 **What is special about the Grand Canyon?**
 a. Many wild animals live there.
 b. It was the first national park.
 c. It is a very large canyon.

2 **Answer the questions.**
 a. What was the first national park? _____
 b. What is one of the world's largest canyons? _____
 c. What do people do at national parks? _____
 _____

3 **Write the correct word and the meaning in Chinese.**

canyon	damage	stunning	go hiking	preserve

 a. _____ : a deep valley with steep rock sides and often a stream or river flowing through it
 b. _____ : to go for long walks in the countryside
 c. _____ : to save; to conserve

Endangered Animals

There are many animals on the earth. Some species have many animals. But there are just a few animals in other species. These animals are endangered. If we are not careful, they could all die and become extinct.

In China, the panda is endangered. In the oceans, the blue whale is endangered. In Africa, lions, tigers, and elephants are all endangered. There are many other endangered animals, too.

What can people do? People can stop hunting them. And people can set aside land for the animals to live on. Then, maybe one day, they will not be endangered anymore.

Some Endangered Animals

green sea turtle

elephant

panda

lion

blue whale

tiger

1 **What is an endangered animal in China?**
 a. The lion.
 b. The panda.
 c. The tiger.

2 **What is true? Write T (true) or F (false).**
 a. All animals are endangered. _____
 b. Some animals could all die and become extinct. _____
 c. People should stop hunting endangered animals. _____

3 **Write the correct word and the meaning in Chinese.**

endangered	set aside	become extinct	hunt

 a. _____: to chase and kill (wild animals) for food or pleasure
 b. _____: to save something for a particular purpose
 c. _____: rare; in danger of dying out completely

T he United States is a huge country with 50 states. Each region in the U.S. has different geographical features.

The Northeast is the New England area. It includes Massachusetts and Connecticut. The land there is hilly. The Southeast is another region. It includes Alabama, Tennessee, and Florida. It has some low mountains. There are many rivers and lakes, too. The Midwest is a very flat land. There are miles and miles of farms. Iowa and Illinois are located there. The Southwest is hot. It has some deserts. The Grand Canyon is located there. The Rocky Mountains are also there. The West includes California and Washington. It has both mountains and big forests.

▲ There are miles and miles of farms in the Midwest.

Sonoran Desert

▲ The Southwest has some deserts.

West
Southwest
Southeast
Northeast
Midwest

1 **What is the passage mainly about?**
   a. All of the states in the United States.
   b. The different regions in the United States.
   c. The mountains and deserts in the United States.

◄ Alaska is the 49th state in the U.S. It has very cold weather.

2 **Fill in the blanks.**
   a. Massachusetts is in the _____ area.
   b. Iowa and Illinois are in the _____.
   c. The _____ Mountains are in the Southwest.

◄ Hawaii is the 50th state in the U.S. It has very hot weather

3 **Write the correct word and the meaning in Chinese.**

region	geographical	feature	hilly	flat land

   a. _____ : land that has few or no hills or mountains
   b. _____ : having many hills
   c. _____ : a typical quality or an important part of something

The Southwest Region of the United States

The American Southwest covers a very large area. But it only has a few states. It includes the states Arizona, New Mexico, Texas, and Oklahoma.

Most of the land in these states is very dry. In fact, there are many deserts in these areas. Because of that, the people must practice water conservation all the time. But not all of the land there is desert. The Colorado River flows through Arizona. And the Rio Grande River flows through Texas. Also, the Rocky Mountains go through parts of Arizona and New Mexico.

Arizona itself has a very diverse geography. Much of its land is desert. But the Grand Canyon is in the northern part of the state. Much of the northern part of the state has mountains. Also, there are many forests in this area.

Texas is also a part of the Southwest. Much of the land is very dry. But many parts of Texas are rich with oil. The oil industry is a huge business in Texas. It's one of the biggest oil-producing states in the entire country.

Geographical Features

▲ Colorado River

▲ Colorado Plateau

▲ Painted Desert

1 **What is the passage mainly about?**
   a. The geography of the Southwest.
   b. The products made in the Southwest.
   c. The states located in the Southwest.

2 **What is NOT true?**
   a. There are many deserts in the Southwest.
   b. The Grand Canyon is in Oklahoma.
   c. Texas has a lot of oil.

3 **Write the correct word and the meaning in Chinese.**

plateau	conservation	rich with	diverse	oil industry

   a. _____: varied; different
   b. _____: a large flat area of land that is higher than other areas of land that surround it
   c. _____: having a lot of something

For many years, people in the South owned black African slaves. In the 1860s, the United States fought the Civil War because of slavery.

During the war, all of the slaves were freed. But there were still many problems between blacks and whites. There was a lot of discrimination against blacks. This means they were not treated fairly. Also, blacks and whites in the South were segregated. So they ate at separate restaurants. They went to separate schools. And they even sat in separate places on buses.

But in the 1950s, the Civil Rights Movement began in the South. Blacks began demanding equal treatment. The most famous leader of the movement was Martin Luther King, Jr. Blacks often organized boycotts of different places. They had sit-ins at restaurants where they were not allowed to eat. King tried to use nonviolence. But the police and others often used violence against blacks. Still, in 1964, the Civil Rights Act was passed. It guaranteed equal rights for people of all colors.

The Civil Rights Movement

▲ segregation

▲ Martin Luther King, Jr.

▲ the Civil Rights Movement

1 **What happened in 1964?**
   a. The Civil War ended.
   b. The Civil Rights Act was passed.
   c. The Civil Rights Movement began.

2 **Fill in the blanks.**
   a. The _____ _____ was fought because of slavery.
   b. In the South, blacks and whites went to _____ schools.
   c. _____ _____ _____ ___ was a famous leader of the Civil Rights Movement.

3 **Write the correct word and the meaning in Chinese.**

discrimination	slavery	guarantee	segregated	boycott

   a. _____: treating one person or group differently from another in an unfair way
   b. _____: separated; divided
   c. _____: to promise that something will happen or exist

Short Stories From the Northeast

Many of the first settlers from Europe went to the Northeast part of the United States. Most of them were English. They lived in New York and Pennsylvania. A lot of them lived in the Hudson River Valley area in New York. Some great American literature comes from this area.

▲ Washington Irving

The writer Washington Irving wrote many stories about this area. One of the most famous was *Rip van Winkle*. It takes place in the Catskill Mountains in New York. In the story, Rip goes off in the mountains by himself. After meeting some ghosts, he sleeps for twenty years. Then he wakes up, returns to his village, and sees how life has changed.

Another famous story by Irving was *The Legend of Sleepy Hollow*. It was also set in upstate New York. It involved the Headless Horseman, who was the ghost of a man with no head. Instead, he had a jack-o'-lantern for a head.

▲ *The Return of Rip Van Winkle*, by John Quidor

▲ *The Headless Horseman Pursuing Ichabod Crane*, by John Quidor

These stories and others by Irving became important in American culture. They depicted early life in the Northeast. And millions of children and adults have read them ever since.

1 **Where is the Hudson River Valley?**
   a. In Pennsylvania.   b. In England.   c. In New York.

2 **What is NOT true?**
   a. Many English lived in the upstate New York area.
   b. Washington Irving lived in the Catskill Mountains.
   c. *Rip van Winkle* was a story about early American life.

3 **Write the correct word and the meaning in Chinese.**

literature	go off	take place	jack-o'-lantern	upstate

   a. _____: towards or of the northern parts of a state in the U.S.
   b. _____: to leave a place and go somewhere else
   c. _____: to occur; to happen

History

The first people to America came from Asia. They crossed a land bridge, a narrow strip of land that connected Russia and Alaska. It was just ice that connected the continents across the sea. Then, they traveled down into the land from North to South America. They became Native Americans.

In the area that became the United States, there were a large number of tribes. Some were very powerful. Others were not. All of the tribes lived off the land. Some were nomads. They followed herds of buffalo all year long. Others lived in small groups or villages. They knew how to farm. They grew various crops. And they also hunted and fished.

Native Americans lived off the land.

▲ Some tribes were nomads.

◄ Some tribes fished.

▲ Native Americans hunted buffalo for their meat.

① **Where was the land bridge that people crossed to enter the Americas?**
   a. Between North and South America.   b. Between Russia and Alaska.
   c. Between Europe and the United States.

② **What is NOT true?**
   a. People first went to Asia from America.
   b. Asia and America were once connected.
   c. Some Native Americans were nomads.

③ **Write the correct word and the meaning in Chinese.**

herd	Native American	live off the land	tribe	nomad

   a. _____: to get food by farming, hunting, etc.
   b. _____: a member of a people or tribe that has no permanent home but travels from place to place
   c. _____: a group of animals that live or are kept together

Three Great American Empires

The first Americans from Asia settled in North and South America. As they learned to farm and made their homes, they built towns and cities. Some of these people made great empires. The three great American empires were the Maya, Aztec, and Inca.

▲ the Maya Empire

The first were the Mayans. They lived in Central America. They lived in the jungle. But they had a great empire. They were very advanced. The Mayans knew how to write by drawing pictures. They were also good at math. They built many amazing temples and other buildings.

▲ the Aztec Empire

The Aztecs lived in North America. Their capital was in modern-day Mexico. They were very warlike. They fought many battles. And they often defeated their enemies.

Machu Picchu

▲ the Inca Empire

The Incas lived in South America. They ruled much land there. And they built cities high in the Andes Mountains.

---

1 **What is the passage mainly about?**
   a. Where the Incas and Mayans lived.   b. How the Aztecs lived their lives.
   c. Three early empires in the Americas.

2 **Answer the questions.**
   a. Where did the first Americans come from? _____
   b. Where in Central America did the Mayans live? _____
   c. Where did the Aztecs live? _____

3 **Write the correct word and the meaning in Chinese.**

settle in	temple	defeat	capital	warlike

   a. _____: a place built to worship gods
   b. _____: to win a victory over someone in a war
   c. _____: a city that is the center of government of a country

The Anasazi

▲ homes built into cliffs

Today, there are many Native American tribes in North America. In the past, there were many more. However, some of them, like the Mayans and Aztecs, disappeared. This happened to another tribe of Native Americans many centuries ago. They were the Anasazi.

The Anasazi lived in the area that is the Southwest today. They lived in that area more than a thousand years ago. They had an impressive culture. They made their own unique pottery. And some of them even lived in homes built into cliffs.

However, around 1200, they suddenly disappeared. No one is sure what happened. Some people believe another tribe defeated the Anasazi in war. Others believe that a disease killed them. But most archaeologists think there was a drought. The area in the Southwest where they lived gets very little rain. The Anasazi had a lot of people in their tribes. If it did not rain for a while, they would have quickly run out of water. Perhaps a drought caused them to move to another area. Today, only artifacts and the ruins of Anasazi buildings remain. No one knows where the people went, though.

▲ Anasazi cave paintings

▲ Anasazi pottery shards

❶ Where did some of the Anasazi live?
   a. In homes beside lakes.
   b. In homes on top of mountains.
   c. In homes built into cliffs.

❷ Answer the questions.
   a. What happened to some Native American tribes? _____
   b. When did the Anasazi disappear? _____
   c. Why did the Anasazi disappear? _____

❸ Write the correct word and the meaning in Chinese.

drought	pottery	artifact	archaeologist	cliff

   a. _____ : a long period when there is little or no rain
   b. _____ : a high area of rock with a very steep side
   c. _____ : an object that was made by humans long ago

20 — The Fall of the Aztec and Inca Empires

Christopher Columbus discovered the New World in 1492. After him, many Europeans began to explore the land. Most of the early explorers came from Spain. The arrival of the Spanish in the Americas changed the Native American empires forever.

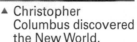

European Explorers

▲ Christopher Columbus discovered the New World.

▲ Hernando Cortés destroyed the Aztec Empire.

The Spanish wanted to get rich. So they looked for gold, silver, and other treasures in the Americas. Both the Aztecs and the Incas had a lot of gold and silver that the Spanish wanted. The Spanish made war on them. In 1521, Spanish soldiers led by Hernando Cortés defeated the Aztec Empire. In 1532, another Spanish conquistador, Francisco Pizarro, conquered the Inca Empire. The Spanish were very cruel to the natives. After their conquests, the Spanish enslaved the natives and took their treasures back to Spain.

▲ Francisco Pizarro conquered the Inca Empire.

1 **What is the passage mainly about?**
   a. What the Spanish did in the New World.
   b. How the Aztecs and Incas were defeated.
   c. How Christopher Columbus discovered the New World.

2 **Answer the questions.**
   a. What did the Spanish explorers look for? _____
   b. What Native Americans did the Spanish defeat? _____
   c. What did the Spanish do after their conquests of the Native Americans?

   _____

3 **Write the correct word and the meaning in Chinese.**

conquistador	enslave	treasure	conquest	cruel

   a. _____ : something valuable that is kept in a safe place
   b. _____ : a name for the Spanish conquerors who first came to the Americas in the 1500s
   c. _____ : extremely unkind and causing pain to people

In the 1400s, European explorers were only interested in finding a water route to Asia to become wealthy. They did not know how large the world was. But after Columbus's voyages to the Americas, many Europeans set sail for the Americas.

Spanish explorers went to present-day Florida. They went to Mexico and other places in Central America. And they went to South America, too.

The Portuguese mostly went to South America. They founded colonies in Brazil.

The French soon followed. They landed in present-day Canada. The French claimed very large areas of land in Canada and settled in there.

The English went to present-day Virginia and Massachusetts.

Reasons to Visit the New World

▲ gold   ▲ silver   ▲ spices   ▲ slaves

▲ to spread Christianity

1 **What is the main idea of the passage?**
   a. The Spanish explorers landed in Central and South America.
   b. European explorers wanted to find a water route to Asia.
   c. Many Europeans explored the Americas.

2 **What is NOT true?**
   a. The English settled in parts of Virginia.
   b. The French mostly claimed land in Canada.
   c. The Portuguese founded colonies in North America.

3 **Write the correct word and the meaning in Chinese.**

voyage	water route	wealthy	set sail	colony

   a. _____: a country or area that is ruled by another country
   b. _____: a long journey, especially by ship
   c. _____: having a lot of money and possessions

The English in America

The Spanish came to the New World for gold. But the English had another reason to go there. They wanted colonies. The English settled in North America. They started many colonies. Two were Virginia and Massachusetts.

The first English colony was Jamestown. It was in Virginia. Life was very hard for the colonists. Many died of hunger and disease. But more and more people came from England. Many of them wanted new lives in America. They came for religious freedom. That was why the Pilgrims and Puritans came. They founded colonies near Boston. They lived in Massachusetts.

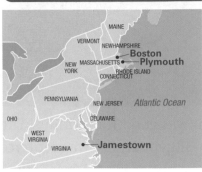

Early English Settlements

▲ Jamestown: the first English colony

▲ Plymouth: the colony where the Pilgrims settled

▲ Boston: the colony where the Puritans settled

▲ The Pilgrims came to America for religious freedom.

▲ The Pilgrims and native Americans shared a meal on the first Thanksgiving.

1 **How were the colonists' lives at Jamestown?**
    a. They were quite simple.   **b.** They were boring.
    c. They were very difficult.

2 **Fill in the blanks.**
    a. The English started colonies in _____ and Massachusetts.
    b. The first English colony was _____.
    c. The Puritans were looking for religious _____ in America.

3 **Write the correct word and the meaning in Chinese.**

colonist	disease	the Pilgrims	Jamestown	religious

    a. _____: the first town built by English people in North America
    b. _____: a group of people who went to North America on the *Mayflower* in search of religious freedom
    c. _____: an illness that affects a person, animal, or plant

Ancient Egyptian Civilization

pyramid

the Sphinx

pharaoh

Over 5,000 years ago, Egyptian civilization began. It was centered on the Nile River. Every year, the Nile flooded. The water from the floods made the land around the Nile very rich. So it was good for farming. This let a civilization start in Egypt.

Egyptian life was centered on the pharaohs. They were god-kings who ruled the entire land. Most Egyptians were slaves. They lived their lives to serve the pharaohs. The pharaohs were very wealthy. They built huge monuments. They also constructed the pyramids and the Sphinx. There are many pyramids all through Egypt.

Egypt also had its own form of writing. It was called hieroglyphics. It was a kind of picture writing. It didn't use letters. Instead, it used pictures. They represented different sounds and words.

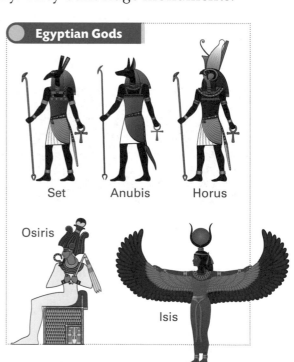

Egyptian Gods

Set   Anubis   Horus

Osiris

Isis

1 **Why was the soil around the Nile River very rich?**
a. Because Egyptian life was centered on the Nile River.
b. Because it was good for farming.
c. Because the river flooded every year.

2 **What is true? Write T (true) or F (false).**
a. Egyptian civilization began 500 years ago. _____
b. The Egyptians built the pyramids and the Sphinx. _____
c. Hieroglyphics was a form of picture writing. _____

3 **Write the correct word and the meaning in Chinese.**

civilization	monument	pharaoh	the Sphinx	hieroglyphics

a. _____: a large stone statue with a lion's body and a person's head
b. _____: a form of picture writing in ancient Egypt
c. _____: a ruler of ancient Egypt

Early Indus Civilization

I n the Indus Valley, which is in modern-day India and Pakistan, an early civilization formed long ago. It lasted from around 2500 B.C. to 1500 B.C. It is also known as the Harappan civilization.

▲ the Indus Valley civilization

The people in the Indus Valley civilization mostly farmed the land. So they knew the secret of agriculture. This let them stop living as nomads. But they were not just farmers. They also built many cities. Archaeologists have found several settlements where there were cities. They built palaces, temples, baths, and other buildings. They also planned their cities on a grid pattern. So they were laid out in squares.

The people of the Indus Valley were advanced in other ways, too. They made pottery. They made objects from both copper and bronze. And they even had their own writing system. It was based on pictographs. But it has not yet been translated. The Indus Valley was one of the world's first civilized areas. Little is known about it. But researchers are learning more and more every year.

ruins of an Indus city

▲ Indus script

1 **About how long did the Indus civilization last?**
a. 1,000 years.　　b. 1,500 years.　　c. 2,500 years.

2 **Answer the questions.**
a. What is the name of the civilization in the Indus Valley?
_____
b. What did the people of the Indus Valley use to make objects from?
_____
c. What kind of writing system did the people of the Indus Valley use?
_____

3 **Write the correct word and the meaning in Chinese.**

Harappan civilization　　lay out　　agriculture　　pictograph

a. _____ : a writing system that uses pictures
b. _____ : farming
c. _____ : another name for the Indus Valley civilization

Ancient Greece: Athens and Sparta

▲ The Acropolis was the center of ancient Greece.

There were many city-states in ancient Greece. They controlled the land around them. Two of the most famous were Athens and Sparta. These two city-states were very different from each other.

First, Athens was the birthplace of democracy. It let regular people vote and help run the city. Athens had a very open society. There were slaves in Athens, but many people were still free. Sparta was a lot different. It was a very warlike city-state. The men there trained to be soldiers from a young age. And the Spartans owned many slaves, too. Sparta and Athens sometimes fought wars against each other.

Athens is also known for its many accomplishments. There were many great thinkers in Athens. Socrates and Plato were two of the world's greatest philosophers. Plato recorded many of his and Socrates's thoughts. People still read his works today.

Greek Philosophers

▲ Socrates   ▲ Plato

1 **What was Spartan society like?**
- **a.** It was an open society.
- **b.** It was a warlike society.
- **c.** It had many great thinkers.

2 **Fill in the blanks.**
- **a.** Athens and _____ were the two most famous city-states.
- **b.** The birthplace of democracy was _____.
- **c.** Sparta was a very _____ city-state.

3 **Write the correct word and the meaning in Chinese.**

accomplishment   city-state   democracy   philosopher

- **a.** _____: a person who studies ideas about knowledge, truth, the nature and meaning of life, etc.
- **b.** _____: a great independent city in the ancient world, such as Athens or Sparta
- **c.** _____: something achieved

All Roads Lead to Rome

When it ruled the most land, the Roman Empire was enormous. It covered much of the known world. To the north, it stretched as far as England. To the west, it ruled land in Spain and western Africa. To the south, it covered much land in Africa. And to the east, it stretched far into the Middle East. However, the most important city in the empire was always Rome.

▲ the Roman Empire

There was an important saying: All roads lead to Rome. At that time, the emperors were trying to be connected to their provinces far from the capital. So they built many roads. And all of them led back to the capital. When

● **Famous Romans**

▲ Augustus Caesar

▲ Julius Caesar

▲ Nero

Rome was powerful, the empire was powerful, too. When Rome was weak, the empire was weak. In later years, Rome was defeated by invaders from Germany. How did the invaders get to Rome? They went there on one of the Roman roads!

1 **What is the main idea of the passage?**
   a. The Roman Empire built many roads.
   b. German invaders defeated the Roman Empire.
   c. The Roman Empire was enormous and connected by roads.

2 **What is NOT true?**
   a. Rome used to rule land in Germany.
   b. All of the Roman roads led to the capital.
   c. The invaders who conquered Rome traveled on the Roman roads.

3 **Write the correct word and the meaning in Chinese.**

stretch	province	enormous	invader	emperor

   a. _____: an army or country that uses force to enter another country
   b. _____: a man who rules an empire
   c. _____: very great in size or amount

The Spanish Conquer the New World

When Christopher Columbus discovered America in 1492, there were already millions of people living in the Americas. Some of them had formed great empires. Two of these were the Aztecs and the Incas. However, after a few years, the Spanish defeated both of them.

The Aztec Empire was in the area of modern-day Mexico. The Aztecs were very warlike. They had conquered many of their neighbors. But they did not have modern weapons like guns and cannons. In 1519, Hernando Cortés invaded the Aztec Empire. He only had about 500 soldiers. But many neighboring tribes allied with him. They disliked the Aztecs very much. There were several battles as Cortés and his men marched to Tenochtitlan, the Aztec capital. In 1521, Cortés captured the city and conquered the empire.

The Inca Empire was in South America in the Andes Mountains. In 1531, Francisco Pizarro arrived there with 182 soldiers. At that time, the Inca Empire was already weak. There had just been a civil war in the empire. By 1532, Pizarro and his men had captured the Incan emperor. The next year, they put their own emperor on the throne. They had succeeded in defeating the Incas.

ruins of Tenochtitlan

1 **What is the passage mainly about?**
   a. How the Spanish defeated two American empires.
   b. When the Aztecs and Incas were defeated by the Spanish.
   c. Who Hernando Cortés and Francisco Pissarro were.

2 **Fill in the blanks.**
   a. Two great empires in the Americas were the _____ and Inca empires.
   b. The Aztecs did not have modern _____ like cannons.
   c. The capital of the Aztec Empire was _____.

3 **Write the correct word and the meaning in Chinese.**

empire	ally	weapon	the throne	civil war

   a. _____: to help and support other people or countries
   b. _____: the position of king or queen
   c. _____: a tool that a person uses to fight with

28 The Reformation

28

F or centuries, the Catholic Church dominated life in Europe. But many priests in the Church were corrupt. They were more interested in money and living a good life than in religion. Some people were upset about that. One of them was Martin Luther. In 1517, he posted his 95 theses on a church door in Wittenberg, Germany. They were a list of his complaints about the Church. This was the beginning of the Protestant Reformation.

Luther did not intend to form a new church. He only wanted to reform the Roman Catholic Church. But the Church called him a heretic and excommunicated him. This caused a split in Germany. Many of the German people disliked the Church. But they wanted to remain Christians. The Reformation soon turned violent. In Germany, Catholics and Protestants fought against each other. This happened until 1555. That year, the Peace of Augsburg allowed every German prince to choose to be Catholic or Protestant.

At the same time as the problems in Germany, the Reformation quickly moved across Europe. Men like Jean Calvin and Ulrich Zwingli led their own protests against the Church. Soon, new Protestant sects were founded. There was the Lutheran sect. There were Presbyterians and Baptists. There were also Calvinists. And, in England, the Anglican Church was founded when Henry VIII broke away from the Roman Catholic Church.

▲ Martin Luther started the Reformation. ▲ Jean Calvin led the Reformation in France.

1 **What ended the religious violence in Germany?**
   a. The Protestant Reformation.
   b. The Peace of Augsburg.
   c. The founding of the Anglican Church.

2 **What is NOT true?**
   a. Martin Luther started the Protestant Reformation.
   b. Martin Luther remained a Catholic for his entire life.
   c. Jean Calvin was another leader of the Protestant Reformation.

3 **Write the correct word and the meaning in Chinese.**

reformation	thesis	corrupt	excommunicate	heretic

   a. _____ : to not allow (someone) to continue being a member of the Roman Catholic Church
   b. _____ : the main idea, opinion, or theory of a person, group
   c. _____ : an act or process of changing and improving something

The French Revolution

In France in the eighteenth century, life was difficult for most people. The ruler of France was the king. He ruled by divine right. This was the idea that God had chosen the king to be the ruler. This meant that the king could do anything he wanted. There were also nobles with great power in France. The clergy mostly lived good lives, too. But the rest of the people had difficult lives.

In the 1780s, the world was changing. The Americans had won their revolution with England and become free. The French people wanted the same thing. King Louis XVI and his wife, Marie Antoinette, were oppressive rulers. They taxed the people too much. But the people became tired of their poor lives. So, on July 14, 1789, they rebelled. They stormed the Bastille on that day. It was a prison in Paris. They freed the prisoners and took the weapons that were there. The French Revolution had begun.

The French Revolution was very violent. Louis XVI was beheaded during the revolution. More nobles and clergy were killed, too. Thousands of people died during the revolution. In the end, the monarchy was destroyed. But France did not become a democracy like the people had hoped. Instead, Napoleon Bonaparte, a general, became the emperor of France. He would then lead France to war with many European nations until he was finally defeated in 1815.

▲ Parisians storming the Bastille

❶ **What is the passage mainly about?**
   a. How the French Revolution proceeded.
   b. When the French Revolution took place.
   c. Why Napoleon Bonaparte became the emperor of France.

❷ **Answer the questions.**
   a. What two groups of people in France had good lives? _____
   b. Who ruled France when the French Revolution began? _____
   c. Who ruled France after the French Revolution ended? _____

❸ **Write the correct word and the meaning in Chinese.**

divine right	oppressive	revolution	clergy	monarchy

   a. _____: very cruel or unfair
   b. _____: the concept that a king was chosen by God
   c. _____: people who are the leaders of a religion

The Great War

For centuries, European countries had fought each other. But, from 1914 to 1918, there was a different kind of war. It was a world war. At that time, people called it the Great War. Later, it was called World War I (WWI). At first, people thought it would just be another war. By the time it ended, millions were dead. And many people were horrified by the carnage of war.

Before WWI began, many European countries had alliances with each other. They promised to defend other countries if they were in trouble. On June 28, 1914, Archduke Francis Ferdinand of Austria-Hungary was assassinated in Sarajevo. The Austrians quickly declared war on Serbia. However, because of the different alliances, what should have been a small war became an enormous one. The Central Powers led by Germany, Austria-Hungary, and the Ottoman Empire were on one side. The

▲ trench warfare

Allied Powers led by England, France, and Russia were on the other side. The Germans swiftly attacked France. However, the German advance was stopped. Neither side could move against the other. Thus trench warfare began. For four years, each side succeeded in killing many of the other's soldiers. Tanks and airplanes were used in war for the first time. So were chemical weapons.

Finally, the war ended. But it didn't end war. Around two decades later, World War II began. It was an even worse war than WWI had been.

① **What happened right after Archduke Francis Ferdinand was assassinated?**
a. The Germans attacked France.
b. The Central Powers formed.
c. Austria-Hungary declared war on Serbia.

② **What is true? Write T (true) or F (false).**
a. Archduke Francis Ferdinand was from Germany. _____
b. England was a member of the Allied Powers. _____
c. The first tanks were used in World War I. _____

③ **Write the correct word and the meaning in Chinese.**

trench	be horrified	carnage	alliance	assassinate

a. _____: to kill someone famous or important
b. _____: a treaty or association between nations or individuals
c. _____: a deep, narrow hole in the ground that is used as
                              protection for soldiers

Chapter

2

Science

Life Science

Earth Science

Physical Science

Life Science

A World of Living Things

Ecosystems

Exploring the Human Body

How Plants Grow

Let's grow some plants in a garden. First, we need some seeds. We have to plant the seeds in the soil, and then we should give them water. After a few days or weeks, the plants will start growing above the ground. First, they will be tiny, but they will become taller every day.

Now, the plants need plenty of sunlight, water, and nutrients in order to get bigger. Slowly, the stems will grow higher, and the plants will get branches and leaves. Some of them will start to blossom. These blossoms will turn into fruit we can eat later. A part of these blossoms makes seeds. They help plants make new plants.

Parts of a Plant

flower · seed · fruit · stem · leaf · branch · trunk

1 **How long does it take for a seed to grow above the ground?**
   a. One or two days.   b. A few days or weeks.   c. Several months.

2 **What is true? Write T (true) or F (false).**
   a. Plants grow from seeds.   _____
   b. Seeds do not need water.   _____
   c. Blossoms often become fruit later. _____

3 **Write the correct word and the meaning in Chinese.**

soil	seed	nutrient	branch	blossom

   a. _____: the top layer of earth in which plants grow
   b. _____: a part of a tree that grows out from the trunk
   c. _____: substance that provides energy to plants and animals

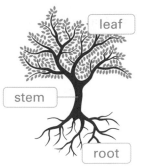

leaf

stem

root

Plants are made up of many parts. Three of the most important are their roots, stems, and leaves. All three of them have various functions.

The roots are found at the bottom of the plant. Roots grow underground. They help anchor the plant to the ground. This keeps the plant from being washed away by rain or blown away by the wind. Also, a plant's roots help it extract nutrients from the ground. These nutrients include water and various minerals.

The stems have several important responsibilities. First, they move water and nutrients from the roots to the leaves. They also store some nutrients and water if the plant has too much of them. And they transport food, such as sap, down from the leaves to the roots. Finally, they provide support for the leaves.

The leaves have a very important role. They contain chloroplasts. These let photosynthesis take place. Because of this, plants can create sugar, which they use for food. And they also take carbon dioxide and turn it into oxygen. This lets all of the other animals on Earth breathe.

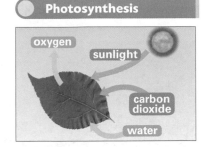

Photosynthesis

oxygen
sunlight
carbon dioxide
water

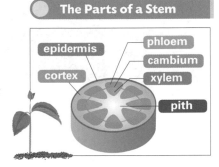

The Parts of a Stem

epidermis
cortex
phloem
cambium
xylem
pith

① **Which part of the plant is responsible for photosynthesis?**
  a. The stem.   b. The leaves.   c. The roots.

② **Fill in the blanks.**
  a. The three most important parts of plants are the roots, _____, and leaves.
  b. Roots help extract water and _____ from the ground.
  c. _____ are what allow photosynthesis to take place.

③ **Write the correct word and the meaning in Chinese.**

function	transport	anchor	sap	photosynthesis

  a. _____: a watery juice inside a plant that carries the plant's food
  b. _____: to keep something from moving; to hold
  c. _____: to move things from one place to another

Places to Live

An animal's habitat is very important. It has everything an animal needs to survive. Most animals can't live in other habitats. Fish live in the water. They can't survive in the desert. Deer live in the forest. They can't survive in the jungle.

What makes a habitat unique? There are many things. Two of them are more important than the others. They are weather and temperature. These two help certain plants grow. Many animals use these plants for food and shelter. Without them, the animals could not live in those habitats.

Types of Habitats

▲ ocean/water   ▲ forest   ▲ desert

▲ grassland   ▲ tundra

1 What is the main idea of the passage?

a. Habitats often have unique weather and temperatures.

b. Deer and other animals live in forest habitats.

c. Habitats provide places for animals to live.

2 What is true? Write T (true) or F (false).

a. Deer can live in the jungle.   _____

b. A habitat's weather is very important.   _____

c. Animals use plants to make shelter.   _____

3 Write the correct word and the meaning in Chinese.

habitat	temperature	unique	shelter	survive

a. _____: a place where living things live

b. _____: to remain alive; to continue to live

c. _____: the measured amount of heat in a place

Living Things vs. Nonliving Things

Everything on Earth is either living or nonliving. A living thing is alive. A nonliving thing is not alive. Both animals and plants are living things. Rocks, air, and water are nonliving things.

There are many kinds of animals and plants. But they are similar in some ways. All of them need oxygen to survive. They also need food and water. When they eat and drink, they get nutrients. Nutrients provide energy for them. Most plants and animals need sunlight, too. Living things can also make new living things like themselves.

Nonliving things are not alive. They cannot move. They cannot breathe. They cannot make new things like themselves.

Differences Between Living Things and Nonliving Things

▲ Living things need food, water, and oxygen.

▲ Living things need shelter.

▲ Nonliving things do not need food, water, oxygen, and shelter.

① **What provides energy for living things?**
    a. Oxygen.   **b.** Nutrients.   **c.** Sunlight.

② **Fill in the blanks.**
    a. Everything on Earth is either _____ or nonliving.
    b. Living things need oxygen, food, and _____ to survive.
    c. Nonliving things cannot _____ new things like themselves.

③ **Write the correct word and the meaning in Chinese.**

shelter	living	similar	nonliving	breathe

    a. _____: not alive
    b. _____: a safe place to live
    c. _____: almost the same as someone or something else

How Are Animals Different

There are five types of animals. They are mammals, birds, reptiles, amphibians, and fish. They are all different from each other.

Mammals are animals like dogs, cats, cows, lions, tigers, and humans. They give birth to live young. And they feed their young with milk from their mothers.

Birds have feathers, and most of them can fly. Penguins, hawks, and sparrows are birds.

Reptiles and amphibians are similar. Both of them lay eggs. Snakes are reptiles, and frogs and toads are amphibians. Amphibians live on land and in the water.

Fish live in the water. They lay eggs. They use gills to take in oxygen from the water. Sharks, bass, and catfish are all fish.

Kinds of Animals

Mammals
dolphin
lion
cow

Birds
penguin
sparrow
hawk

Reptiles
snake
turtle
lizard

Amphibians
toad
frog
salamander

Fish
bass
shark
catfish

1 Which animals give birth to live young?

  a. Reptiles.
  b. Birds.
  c. Mammals.

2 What is NOT true?
  a. There are five types of animals.
  b. Mammals are animals like snakes and lizards.
  c. Fish use gills to breathe.

3 Write the correct word and the meaning in Chinese.

feed	mammal	lay eggs	reptile	amphibian

  a. _____: to give food to
  b. _____: an animal that is capable of living on land and in the water
  c. _____: to produce eggs outside of the body

Warm-Blooded vs. Cold-Blooded Animals

All animals are either warm-blooded or cold-blooded. This refers to how the animals maintain their body temperature.

Warm-blooded animals can regulate their body temperature. So, even if it is very cold outside, their bodies will stay warm. But warm-blooded animals have to eat a lot of food. They use the food to produce energy. That helps keep their bodies warm. Mammals are warm-blooded, and so are birds.

Cold-blooded animals rely upon the sun for heat. So their internal temperatures can change all the time. These animals often rest in the sun for hours. This lets their bodies soak up heat and become warm. Most cold-blooded animals don't live in cold places. They prefer hot places instead. Reptiles, amphibians, and fish are all cold-blooded.

Vertebrates and Invertebrates

Vertebrates

fish

amphibians

birds

reptiles

mammals

Invertebrates

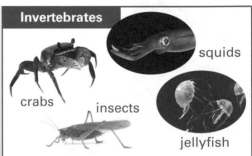

squids

crabs

insects

jellyfish

1 **How do warm-blooded animals produce energy?**
   a. By eating food.
   b. By resting in the sun.
   c. By regulating their body temperatures.

2 **Fill in the blanks.**
   a. _____ animals can control their body temperature.
   b. _____ and birds are both warm-blooded.
   c. Reptiles, _____, and fish are cold-blooded animals.

3 **Write the correct word and the meaning in Chinese.**

soak up	internal	cold-blooded animal	regulate

   a. _____: existing or located on the inside of something
   b. _____: to control
   c. _____: to take in

37 An Insect's Body

There are many kinds of insects. They include ants, bees, butterflies, grasshoppers, and crickets. They look different from each other. But they have the same body parts in common.

All insects have three main body parts. They are the head, thorax, and abdomen. The head has the insect's mouth, eyes, and antennae. An insect uses its antennae to feel and taste things. The thorax is the middle body part. It has three pairs of legs. Adult insects have six legs. Some insects have wings on their bodies. The abdomen is the third and final part of the insect.

The Three Parts of Insects

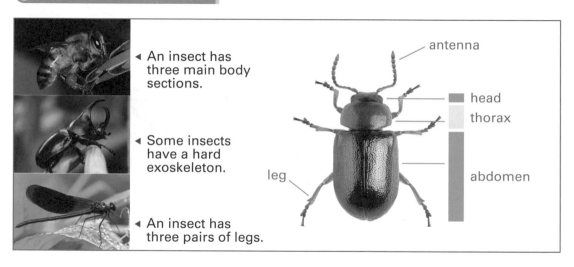

◄ An insect has three main body sections.

◄ Some insects have a hard exoskeleton.

◄ An insect has three pairs of legs.

antenna

head
thorax

leg

abdomen

1 **Where are an insect's legs located?**
   a. On its head.　　　　b. On its thorax.　　　　c. On its abdomen.

2 **What is NOT true?**
   a. All insects have a head, thorax, and abdomen.
   b. An insect's antennae are on its thorax.
   c. Adult insects have six legs.

3 **Write the correct word and the meaning in Chinese.**

antenna	insect	thorax	abdomen	exoskeleton

   a. _____: the middle part of an insect's body
   b. _____: a hard outer layer that covers the body of an insect
   c. _____: a thin sensitive organ on the head of an insect that is
      used mainly to feel and touch things

The Life Cycles of Cats and Frogs

Every animal has a life cycle. This is the period from birth to death.

Cats are mammals, so they are born alive. Baby cats are called kittens. A mother cat takes care of her kittens for many weeks. The mother cat feeds her kittens with milk from her body. As the kittens get bigger, they become more independent. After about one year, they become adult cats, and they can take care of themselves.

Frogs have different life cycles. Frogs are born in eggs. When they hatch, they are called tadpoles. Tadpoles have long tails and no legs. They use gills to breathe in the water. Soon, they grow legs and start to use lungs to breathe. Later, they can leave the water. When this happens, they become adult frogs.

A Frog's Life Cycle

tadpole

adult frog

egg

A Cat's Life Cycle

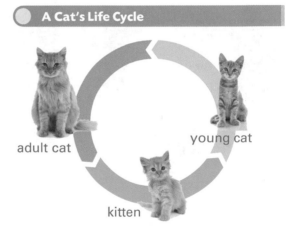

adult cat

young cat

kitten

1 **What is the main idea of the passage?**

a. Animals all go through life cycles.   b. Frogs have unique life cycles.

c. Cats are born alive and frogs are born in eggs.

2 **Answer the questions.**

a. What is a baby cat called? _____

b. How long does it take for kittens to become adults? _____

c. How are frogs born? _____

3 **Write the correct word and the meaning in Chinese.**

life cycle   hatch   gill   kitten   tadpole

a. _____: a baby frog

b. _____: to come out of an egg

c. _____: the organ through which water creatures breathe

The Life Cycle of a Pine Tree

Every plant, like pine trees, has its own life cycle. A pine tree's life cycle begins with a seed. Adult pine trees have pine cones. Inside the pine cones are tiny seeds. Every year, many pine cones fall to the ground. Some of them stay near the pine tree, but other times, animals pick them up and move them. The wind and rain might move them, too. Sometimes, the seeds fall out of the pine cones and get buried in the ground. They often start to sprout. These are called seedlings. These seedlings get bigger and bigger. After many years, they become adult pine trees. Then they too have pine cones with seeds. So a new life cycle begins again.

A Pine Tree's Life Cycle

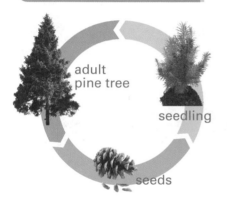

adult pine tree

seedling

seeds

Some Kinds of Trees

▲ spruce tree   ▲ birch

▲ maple tree

▲ oak tree

▲ cedar

1 **What is the passage mainly about?**
   a. Where pine trees are usually found.
   b. How pine trees grow and reproduce.
   c. What pine cones and seedlings are.

2 **Fill in the blanks.**
   a. Pine trees have pine _____.
   b. Pine cones fall to the _____ every year.
   c. When a buried seed sprouts, it is called a _____.

3 **Write the correct word and the meaning in Chinese.**

get buried	cactus	pine cone	sprout	seedling

   a. _____ : a young plant
   b. _____ : the brown seed container of a pine tree
   c. _____ : to produce new leaves, buds, etc.

Photosynthesis

Every living creature needs food and water to survive. Without food and water, a creature would die. Plants are also living creatures. So they need to have these things, too. Plants can create their own food. They do this in a process called photosynthesis.

Plants need sunlight in order to make energy. First, when the sun shines, chlorophyll in the plants captures the sunlight. Sunlight is just energy. So the chlorophyll is capturing energy. Then a plant needs two more things: water and carbon dioxide. That is when photosynthesis can take place. In photosynthesis, a plant undergoes a chemical reaction. Thanks to the chlorophyll, it creates sugar. The plant feeds on the sugar. The reaction also produces oxygen. The plant releases oxygen into the air, and people breathe it. So, without photosynthesis, people could not survive either.

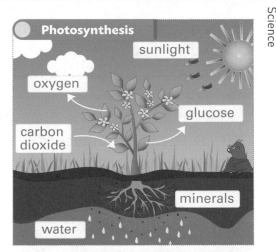

Photosynthesis

sunlight · oxygen · glucose · carbon dioxide · minerals · water

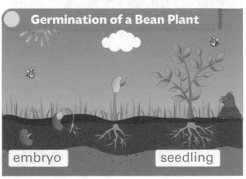

Germination of a Bean Plant

embryo · seedling

❶ **What does photosynthesis produce?**
  a. Sugar and oxygen.　　**b.** Water and carbon dioxide.　　**c.** Water and sugar.

❷ **What is true? Write T (true) or F (false).**
  a. Plants can make their own water.　　_____
  b. Chlorophyll helps plants go through photosynthesis.　　_____
  c. Plants breathe oxygen.　　_____

❸ **Write the correct word and the meaning in Chinese.**

capture	creature	photosynthesis	release	chlorophyll

  a. _____: the food-making process in plants that uses sunlight
  b. _____: to get and hold
  c. _____: to allow (a substance) to enter the air, water, soil, etc.

What Is a Food Chain

All animals must eat to survive. Some eat plants. Some eat animals. And others eat both plants and animals. A food chain shows the relationship of each animal to the others.

At the bottom of a food chain are the plant eaters. They are often prey animals. They are usually small animals like squirrels and rabbits. Sometimes they are bigger animals like deer. Animals higher on the food chain eat these animals. They might be owls, snakes, and raccoons. Then, bigger animals like bears and wolves eat these animals. Finally, we reach the top of the food chain. The most dangerous animal of all is here: man.

Food Chain

hawk

snake

frog

grasshopper

grass

▲ plant eater

▲ meat eater

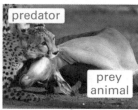
predator

prey animal

1 **What is an example of a big prey animal?**
- a. A bear.
- b. A deer.
- c. A squirrel.

2 **Fill in the blanks.**
- a. Some animals eat both _____ and animals.
- b. Plant eaters are at the _____ of a food chain.
- c. Squirrels and rabbits are _____ animals.

3 **Write the correct word and the meaning in Chinese.**

| food chain | plant eater | prey animal | relationship | bottom |

- a. _____ : the lowest part or level of something
- b. _____ : an animal that gets hunted by other animals
- c. _____ : the way in which two or more things are connected

Fishing and Overfishing

The ocean has many different habitats for many plants and animals. It helps the earth stay healthy. So we have to be careful not to hurt the ocean.

Many people around the world enjoy eating seafood. Fishermen catch food in the ocean for us to eat. This includes shellfish as well as fish. Shellfish are animals like shrimp, clams, crabs, and lobsters. Because people eat so much seafood, there are many fishermen.

Unfortunately, the fishermen are catching too many fish these days. So the number of fish in the oceans is decreasing. Many fishing grounds are getting smaller and smaller. Fishermen need to stop catching so many fish. They must give the fish time to increase their numbers.

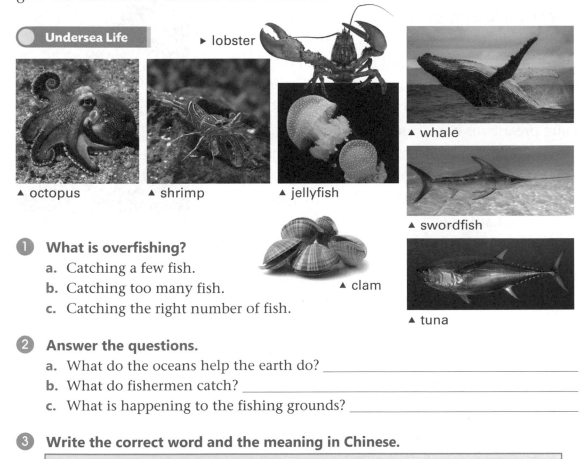

Undersea Life

▶ lobster

▲ octopus   ▲ shrimp   ▲ jellyfish

▲ whale

▲ swordfish

▲ clam

▲ tuna

1 **What is overfishing?**
   a. Catching a few fish.
   b. Catching too many fish.
   c. Catching the right number of fish.

2 **Answer the questions.**
   a. What do the oceans help the earth do? _____
   b. What do fishermen catch? _____
   c. What is happening to the fishing grounds? _____

3 **Write the correct word and the meaning in Chinese.**

seafood	overfish	fisherman	fishing ground	shellfish

   a. _____ : a sea creature that has a shell
   b. _____ : an area of water where fishes gather and fishing is good
   c. _____ : to catch too many fish so that there are not enough left

How Animals Become Extinct

There has been life on Earth for billions of years. These organisms are always changing. In fact, many organisms no longer live on Earth. They all died. So people say that they are extinct. Many animals are extinct. The dinosaurs are extinct. The dodo bird is extinct. The woolly mammoth is also no longer alive.

▲ Humans often destroy animals' environments.

Why do animals become extinct? There are many reasons. Natural disasters such as fires, floods, droughts, and earthquakes can destroy habitats. People can destroy habitats, too. Pollution can also harm organisms. Some animals are hunted by people. All these things are harmful to plants and animals, and they can cause the changes to ecosystems.

▲ Animals compete against each other in the wild.

When a large change occurs in an ecosystem, some organisms have trouble surviving. Then they can be endangered and may become extinct. So, it is important to protect our natural environment and ecosystems. What do you think we can do for endangered animals?

mimicry

▲ An animal that cannot adapt will die.

① **Which of the following is an example of a natural disaster?**
   a. Pollution. **b.** Hunting. **c.** A drought.

② **What is NOT true?**
   a. The dinosaurs are extinct.
   b. Only natural disasters make animals become extinct.
   c. Changes in an ecosystem can make animals go extinct.

③ **Write the correct word and the meaning in Chinese.**

natural disaster	pollution	woolly mammoth	ecosystem

   a. _____: a type of large, hairy elephant that lived in ancient times
   b. _____: all the plants and animals in an environment and their interactions with each other
   c. _____: the action or process of making land, water, air, etc. dirty and not safe or suitable to use

Staying Healthy

A person's body is like a machine. It has many parts that help keep it running. If these parts are running well, a person will be healthy. But sometimes a person's body breaks down. Then that person gets sick.

Many times, germs make a person sick. When germs attack a body, it needs to fight back. Sometimes, the person's body alone can defeat the germs. Other times, the person might need medicine from a doctor to get better. Fortunately, many medicines can kill germs and help bodies become healthy again.

The Systems of the Body

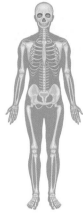  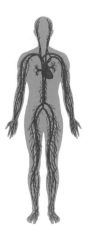 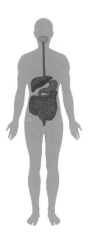 

▲ skeletal system   ▲ muscular system   ▲ circulatory system   ▲ digestive system   ▲ nervous system

1 **What happens when a person's body breaks down?**
- **a.** The person becomes sick.
- **b.** The person gets healthy.
- **c.** The person defeats germs.

2 **Fill in the blanks.**
- **a.** _____ sometimes make people sick.
- **b.** When germs attack a body, sometimes the person's body can _____ the germs.
- **c.** Doctors give people _____ to make them get better.

3 **Write the correct word and the meaning in Chinese.**

break down	get sick	fight back	germ	medicine

- **a.** _____: to stop working properly
- **b.** _____: to attack someone who is attacking you
- **c.** _____: a very small organism that causes disease

Caring for the Five Senses

Everyone has five senses. The five senses are sight, hearing, smell, taste, and touch. We use different body parts for different senses. We need to take care of the parts of our bodies that let us use our senses.

For example, you use your eyes for seeing. You should protect your eyes and have a doctor regularly check your eyesight. Don't sit too close to the TV or computer monitor, and don't read in the dark or in dim light. Never look directly at the sun or at very bright lights.

Your ears let you hear the things around you. You should clean your ears all the time. Don't listen to loud music, and try to avoid places that are really loud. Protect your ears when you play sports.

Your nose cleans the air you breathe and lets you smell things. Avoid things that have very strong smells.

Your tongue help you taste things you eat and drink. Your skin protects your body from germs and gives you your sense of touch. Always wash your hands after blowing your nose, playing outside, or using the restroom. Protect your skin from sunburns. Use sunscreen to protect your skin from the sun.

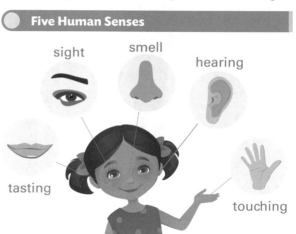

Five Human Senses: sight, smell, hearing, tasting, touching

---

1 **What body part allows a person to have a sense of smell?**
a. The skin.　　　b. The ears.　　　c. The nose.

2 **What is true? Write T (true) or F (false).**
a. Everyone has five senses. _____
b. It is okay to sit very close to the TV. _____
c. Putting sunscreen on your skin prevents sunburns. _____

3 **Write the correct word and the meaning in Chinese.**

taste	eyesight	blow your nose	sunburn	sunscreen

a. _____ : the reddening of the skin due to exposure to the sun
b. _____ : to force air from your lungs and through your nose to clear it
c. _____ : to sense the flavor of

The Organs of the Human Body

Organs are very important parts of the human body. They help do certain body functions. There are many different organs.

One important organ is the heart. It pumps blood all throughout the body. Without a heart, a person cannot live. The brain runs the body's nervous system. It controls both mental and physical activities. People can breathe thanks to their lungs. A person has two lungs. The stomach helps digest food. It breaks food down into nutrients so that the rest of the body can use it. The liver also helps with digestion. One of the most important organs is the biggest. It's the skin. It covers a person's entire body!

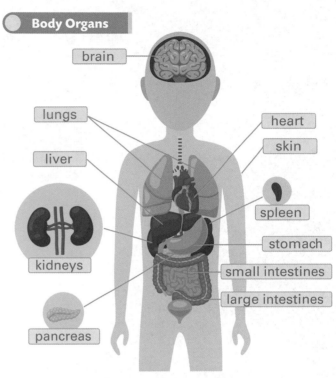

Body Organs

brain
lungs
liver
kidneys
pancreas
heart
skin
spleen
stomach
small intestines
large intestines

1 **What does the liver do?**
 a. It lets the body breathe air.
 b. It controls the body's nervous system.
 c. It helps with digestion.

2 **Fill in the blanks.**
 a. The brain runs the body's _____ _____.
 b. The _____ pumps blood throughout the body.
 c. The biggest organ is the _____.

3 **Write the correct word and the meaning in Chinese.**

organ	pump blood	nervous system	digest	stomach

 a. _____: to move blood through your body by beating
 b. _____: to change food in your stomach into substances that your body can use
 c. _____: a part of the body that has a particular function, such as the heart and lungs

Earth Science

Weather and Space

Earth's Surface

The Universe

There are four seasons in a year. They are spring, summer, fall, and winter. Sometimes people say "autumn" instead of fall.

Each season has different kinds of weather. In spring, the air gets warmer, and the weather is often rainy. Everything comes back to life. Flowers start to bloom, and leaves start growing on trees. In summer, the weather is usually very hot and sunny. In fall, the temperature starts to decrease. The weather gets cooler. The leaves on trees start changing colors. Winter is the coldest season. It usually snows during the winter.

Types of Weather

▲ sunny

▲ rainy

▲ cloudy

▲ foggy

▲ snowy

▲ windy

1 What happens in fall?
- a. Flowers start to bloom.
- b. The temperature goes down.
- c. It often snows.

2 What is true? Write T (true) or F (false).
- a. Another word for fall is "autumn." _____
- b. The flowers begin blooming in summer. _____
- c. It might snow during the winter. _____

3 Write the correct word and the meaning in Chinese.

bloom	season	weather	temperature	foggy

- a. _____ : to produce flowers
- b. _____ : a time of year that has a certain kind of weather
- c. _____ : having or filled with fog

How Can Water Change

Water has three forms. It can be a solid, a liquid, or a gas. Why does it change? It changes because of the temperature. Water's normal state is liquid. But water sometimes becomes a solid. Why? It gets too cold. Water freezes when heat is taken away from it. Water in its solid form is called ice. Also, sometimes water becomes a gas. Why? It gets too hot. Water boils when its temperature gets high enough. Then it turns into steam. This steam is a gas. When water is a gas, it is called water vapor.

Three Forms of Matter

Solids — ice, gold, book

Liquids — water, juice, milk

Gases — steam, air, oxygen

1 **What form is water vapor?**
   a. Solid.   b. Liquid.   c. Gas.

2 **Fill in the blanks.**
   a. Water can be a solid, a _____, or a gas.
   b. Water's normal _____ is liquid.
   c. Water in its solid form is called _____.

3 **Write the correct word and the meaning in Chinese.**

solid	freeze	liquid	boil	water vapor

   a. _____: to become so hot that bubbles are formed in a liquid and rise to the top
   b. _____: something that is hard
   c. _____: to become a hard substance because of cold

The earth is a huge planet. But it is divided into three parts. They are the crust, mantle, and core. Each section is different from the others.

The crust is the outermost part of the earth. That's the surface of the earth. Everything on top of the earth—the oceans, seas, rivers, mountains, deserts, and forests—is part of the crust. Beneath the crust, there is a thick layer of hot, melted rock. It's called the mantle. The mantle is the biggest section. The mantle is extremely hot. The innermost part of the earth is the core. Part of it is solid, and part is liquid.

Earth's Layers

surface
crust
mantle
outer core
inner core

Kinds of Rocks

▲ granite

▲ marble

▲ sandstone

▲ limestone

▲ slate

▲ quartz

❶ What is the main idea of the passage?
  a. The core is at the earth's center.
  b. The earth has three separate sections.
  c. The surface of the earth has three layers.

❷ Answer the questions.
  a. How many parts is the earth divided into? _____
  b. What is the top part of the earth called? _____
  c. What is the biggest section of the earth? _____

❸ Write the correct word and the meaning in Chinese.

crust	mantle	layer	surface	core

  a. _____ : the innermost part of the earth
  b. _____ : the outside of something
  c. _____ : a covering piece of material or a part that lies over or under another

How to Conserve Our Resources

Earth has many natural resources. But many of them are resources that cannot be reused or replaced easily. Once nonrenewable resources are used up, they are gone forever. That means we should conserve our resources as much as possible. Everyone can help do this in many ways.

Water is a valuable resource. So we shouldn't waste it. When you're brushing your teeth, turn the water off. Don't take really long showers either. We should also be careful about using electricity. Don't turn on any lights if you aren't going to use them. Don't leave your computer on all night long. Recycling is another way to save natural resources. Try to reuse things like papers and boxes. Reducing the amount of energy you use is also a good way to conserve our resources.

Some Types of Pollutants

 ▲ smoke

 ▲ sewage

 ▲ oil spills

1. **How can people save electricity?**
   a. By leaving their computers on all night.
   b. By taking long showers.
   c. By turning off unneeded lights.

 ▲ garbage

2. **Answer the questions.**
   a. What kind of resources cannot be replaced easily? _____
   b. What should people do while brushing their teeth? _____
   c. What can recycling do? _____

3. **Write the correct word and the meaning in Chinese.**

oil spill	conserve	natural resource	waste	recycling

   a. _____ : the act of reusing something to make new things
   b. _____ : a release of oil into the environment
   c. _____ : to use carefully in order to prevent loss or waste

51 **What Changes the Earth's Surface**

The surface of the earth is constantly changing. Mountains and hills break down. Rocks and soil move from one place to another. Some changes are very slow. Weathering and erosion can cause these changes.

Weathering occurs when wind and water break down rocks into pieces. Erosion occurs when weathered rocks or sand are carried away. There are many types of erosion. The most powerful is water. Water can break down mountains and form canyons. Water erosion made the Grand Canyon over millions of years. Water also moves dirt and soil to oceans and seas. The wind can move sand in deserts from place to place. And it can erode valuable topsoil and make deserts that way.

Earthquakes, volcanoes, and violent storms can change the earth's surface quickly. Earthquakes can make huge cracks in the land. Volcanoes can cover entire cities in ash and lava. And storms can drop huge amounts of water and causes floods.

Changes on Earth's Surface

▲ erosion

▲ earthquake

▲ volcano

▲ violent storm

1 **What can water erosion do?**
   a. Make deserts.   b. Create canyons.   c. Make cracks in the land.

2 **What is NOT true?**
   a. All changes on the earth's surface are slow.
   b. The Grand Canyon was made by water erosion.
   c. Volcanoes can change the earth's surface quickly.

3 **Write the correct word and the meaning in Chinese.**

break down	weathering	erosion	topsoil	lava

   a. _____: the breaking down of rocks into small pieces by the wind and water
   b. _____: the top layer of ground in which plants grow
   c. _____: to become separated or to separate (something) into simpler substances

Sometimes people go to the museum. They see many bones of dinosaurs or other animals. There are even some plant fossils! But, what exactly are fossils? And how do fossils form?

Fossils are the imprints or remains of dead animals or plants. They can form in many ways. The most common way is like this: a long time ago, an animal died. Then it got buried in the ground. Over time, the skin and muscles rotted away. But the bones remained. Then, minerals entered the animal's bones. The bones then became as hard as rock. This might have taken thousands or millions of years to occur.

Scientists like to study fossils. They can learn a lot about the animals and plants that lived a long time ago. Scientists can learn how big they are. Scientists can even learn what kind of food they ate. Thanks to fossils, scientists today know a lot about dinosaurs and other animals.

▲ remains

▲ imprints

1 **What is the passage mainly about?**
   a. How scientists study fossils.
   b. How fossils get formed.
   c. Which animals become fossils.

2 **Fill in the blanks.**
   a. Fossils are the imprints or _____ of dead animals or plants.
   b. _____ enter bones to make fossils.
   c. It takes thousands or millions of years for _____ to form.

3 **Write the correct word and the meaning in Chinese.**

imprint	fossil	remains	get buried	rot away

   a. _____: a mark created by pressing against a surface
   b. _____: to decay; to decompose; to break up
   c. _____: to be covered with something

The solar system is the sun and the planets going around the sun. There are eight planets in it. In order of distance from the sun, they are: Mercury, Venus, Earth, Mars, Jupiter, Saturn, Uranus, and Neptune. Scientists used to consider Pluto the ninth planet in the solar system. But they do not think that way now. Instead, they consider Pluto to be a minor planet. There are many objects like Pluto in the outer solar system. And scientists don't think they are planets. So they don't consider Pluto a planet anymore.

The Solar System

1. **What is the farthest planet from the sun?**
   a. Neptune.   b. Pluto.   b. Uranus.

2. **What is true? Write T (true) or F (false).**
   a. There are nine planets in the solar system.   _____
   b. Saturn is the fifth planet from the sun.   _____
   c. Pluto is considered the ninth planet in the solar system.   _____

3. **Write the correct word and the meaning in Chinese.**

solar system	distance	planet	object	minor planet

   a. _____: the sun and all of the objects that orbit the sun
   b. _____: the amount of space between two people or things
   c. _____: a thing that you can see and touch and that is not alive

The moon takes about 29 days to orbit the earth. During this time, the moon seems to change shapes. We call these looks "phases." The phases change as the moon moves around the earth.

The first phase is the new moon. The moon is invisible now. However, it starts to get brighter. It looks like a crescent. This next phase is called waxing crescent. Waxing means it is getting bigger. Soon, it is at the first quarter phase. Half the moon is visible. Then it becomes a full moon. The entire moon is visible. Now, the moon starts to wane. It is beginning to disappear. It goes to the last quarter stage. Then it is a waning crescent. Finally, it becomes a new moon again.

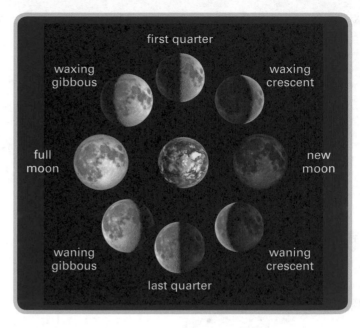

1 **What is the moon called when it begins to disappear?**
   a. A full moon.
   b. A waning crescent moon.
   c. A waxing crescent moon.

2 **What is NOT true?**
   a. The moon orbits the earth in 19 days.
   b. The moon has different phases.
   c. The moon is not visible during the new moon phase.

3 **Write the correct word and the meaning in Chinese.**

crescent	orbit	wane	phase	waxing

   a. _____ : the shape of the part of the moon that is visible at different times during a month
   b. _____ : the shape of the visible part of the moon when it is less than half full
   c. _____ : to appear to become thinner or less full

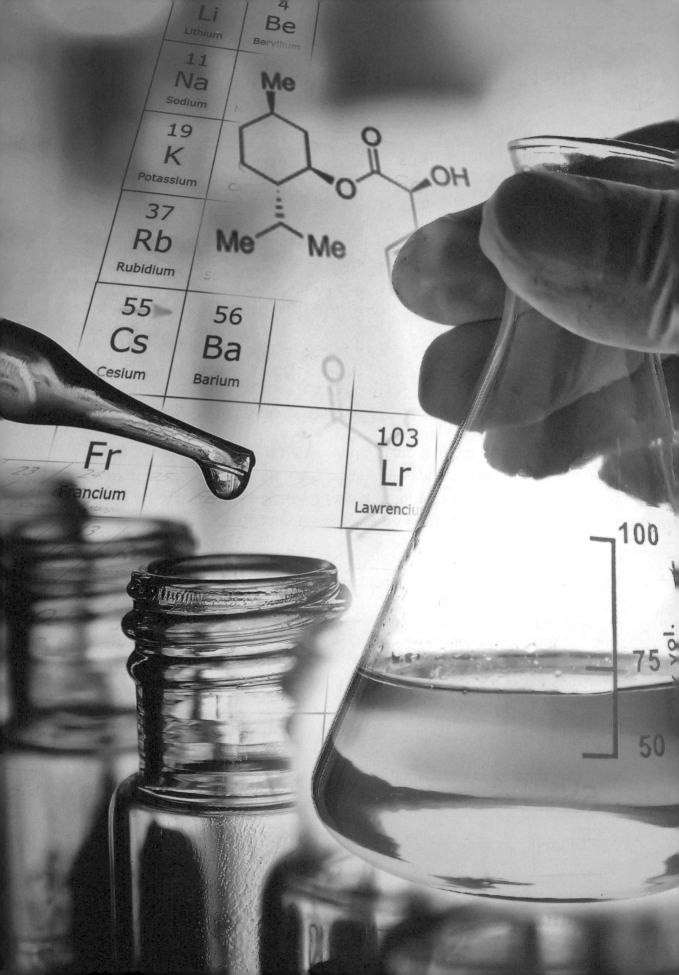

Physical Science

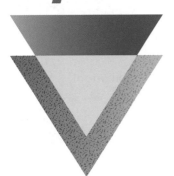

Matter and Energy

It's time to make some cookies. We have all the ingredients. Now, we need to measure everything before we start cooking.

First, we need 1 cup of butter. After that, we need $\frac{3}{4}$ cup of white sugar, the same amount of brown sugar, and $2\frac{1}{4}$ cups of flour. We also need $1\frac{1}{2}$ teaspoons of vanilla extract, 1 teaspoon of baking soda, and $\frac{1}{2}$ teaspoon of salt. We have to measure $1\frac{1}{2}$ cups of chocolate chips, too. Finally, we need 2 eggs. Now we have measured all of our ingredients. Let's start cooking.

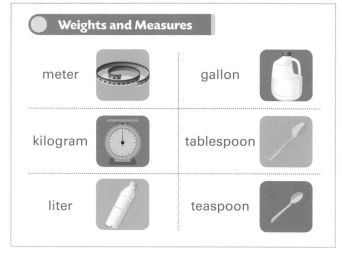

Weights and Measures

meter		gallon	
kilogram		tablespoon	
liter		teaspoon	

1 **What is the passage mainly about?**

a. Measuring ingredients to make cookies.

b. The ingredients needed to bake cookies.

c. The types of ingredients in a kitchen.

2 **Answer the questions.**

a. What is the person making? _____

b. How much brown sugar is needed? _____

c. How many chocolate chips are needed? _____

3 **Write the correct word and the meaning in Chinese.**

| ingredient | teaspoon | measure | gallon | extract |

a. _____ : a unit of liquid measurement equal to 3.785 liters

b. _____ : a thing that is used to make something, especially in cooking

c. _____ : a spoon that is used for measuring dry and liquid ingredients and that holds an amount equal to $1/3$ tablespoon

Benjamin Franklin

Benjamin Franklin was a great American scientist. He lived more than 200 years ago. He was very curious about lightning. He thought that it was electricity. But he wasn't sure. So he decided to do an experiment.

Franklin tied a metal key to a kite. Then he waited for a storm to begin. He flew the kite in the storm. Lightning was striking in the area. Electric charges from the lightning got on the key. When Franklin touched the key, he got shocked. He had just proved that lightning was a form of electricity!

Electric vs Electrical

─── Electric ─── | ─── Electrical ───

▲ electric current ▲ electric light ▲ electrical appliance

▲ electrical outlet

1 **How did Benjamin Franklin prove that lightning was electricity?**

   a. He did an experiment.   **b.** He watched lightning during a storm.

   c. He read many books about it.

2 **Fill in the blanks.**

   a. Franklin believed that lightning was _____.

   b. Franklin flew a _____ in a storm.

   c. When Franklin touched the _____, he got shocked.

3 **Write the correct word and the meaning in Chinese.**

curious	lightning	electric charge	kite	get shocked

   a. _____: to get an electric shock

   b. _____: a very bright flash of light often seen during a thunderstorm

   c. _____: the amount of electricity that a substance carries

Some objects are attracted to each other. And some objects repel each other. A magnet is an object that can attract or repel other objects. Magnets can move things like iron or steel without touching them. How does a magnet work?

A magnet is a piece of magnetized metal like iron or nickel. It has two separate poles. It has a north-seeking pole, or N pole, and a south-seeking pole, or S pole. This creates a magnetic field. So it can attract or repel different metals. If the north pole of a magnet is near the south pole of another one, the two will be attracted. But if two north poles of two magnets are near each other, they will repel each other.

Types of Magnets

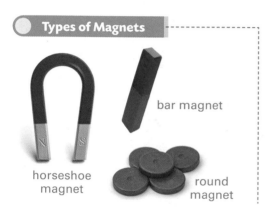

bar magnet

horseshoe magnet

round magnet

Magnetic Poles and Field

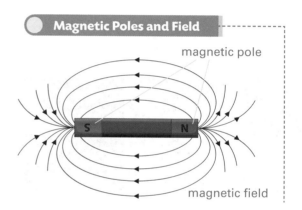

magnetic pole

magnetic field

1 What can a magnet do?
   a. Only attract objects.   **b.** Only repel objects.
   c. Both attract and repel objects.

2 Answer the questions.
   a. What is a magnet made of? _____
   b. What are a magnet's two poles? _____
   c. If two north poles of two magnets are near, what will happen?

   _____

3 Write the correct word and the meaning in Chinese.

attract	magnetic pole	magnetic field	repel	magnet

   a. _____ : either one of the two ends of a magnet
   b. _____ : to push away
   c. _____ : an area that the power of a magnet affects

The Invention of the Telephone

▲ Alexander Graham Bell (1847–1922)

A long time ago, there were no telephones. But people knew that sound travels by vibrations. So many people tried to invent the telephone.

Alexander Graham Bell was one of these people. He wanted to use electricity to transmit sound. He thought he could turn sound into electric pulses. Then it could move through wires. He worked very hard on his project. One day in 1876, he had an accident in his office. He needed his assistant Watson. He said, "Watson, come here. I want you." Watson was in another part of the house. But he heard Bell over the telephone. Finally, Bell was successful. He had invented the telephone!

What does sound travel through?

▲ gases, such as air

▲ liquids, such as water

▲ solids, such as wood

1 **What is the main idea of the passage?**
   a. Many people tried to invent the telephone.
   b. Alexander Graham Bell invented the telephone.
   c. Alexander Graham Bell had an accident when he was working on the telephone.

2 **Fill in the blanks.**
   a. Alexander Graham Bell wanted to invent the _____.
   b. Bell wanted to use _____ to transmit sound.
   c. In _____, Bell made the first telephone.

3 **Write the correct word and the meaning in Chinese.**

vibration	pulse	electricity	transmit	accident

   a. _____: a shaking motion
   b. _____: to send out an electronic signal such as a radio signal
   c. _____: an amount of physical energy that something produces for a short time

Physical and Chemical Changes

Matter often undergoes many changes. There are two main types of changes. They are physical and chemical changes.

There are a lot of physical changes. In a physical change, matter changes in size, shape, or state. But it does not change a substance into a new one. For instance, melting ice to get water is a physical change. And boiling water to get water vapor is another one. The states are changed, but ice, water, and steam are all different forms of the same thing. So a new substance is not made. It is also possible to make physical changes in other ways. For instance, put some sugar in water and then stir it. The sugar dissolves. That is a physical change. Or, simply tear up a piece of paper. That is another physical change.

Chemical changes are different. Chemical changes involve the forming of a new substance or compound. A chemical change is also called a chemical reaction. For instance, if sodium and chlorine come together, they undergo a chemical reaction. The result is the creation of salt. Photosynthesis is another chemical reaction. Water and carbon dioxide change into sugar and oxygen.

Physical Changes

Chemical Changes

Photosynthesis
Sunlight
Oxygen
Carbon Dioxide
Water
Minerals

---

1 **What happens during a chemical change?**
   a. A gas or liquid is created.   **b.** A substance changes into a solid.
   c. A new compound gets formed.

2 **What is NOT true?**
   a. Matter can undergo physical or chemical changes.
   b. Ice melting to become water is a chemical change.
   c. Sugar dissolving in water is a physical change.

3 **Write the correct word and the meaning in Chinese.**

matter	chemical change	compound	dissolve

   a. _____ : a chemical that combines two or more elements
   b. _____ : physical substance in the universe
   c. _____ : to melt

Heat is a form of energy. It can move from place to place. There are three ways it can move: conduction, convection, and radiation.

When heat touches matter, it makes the particles in that matter move. These particles then touch other nearby ones. They start moving, too. This is conduction, and it is the reason why the pot handle gets hot. Conduction usually occurs in solids and between objects that are touching.

Convection is the second way that heat moves. Convection happens because of temperature differences in different parts of the liquids or gases. In convection, warm liquid or gas is forced up by cooler liquid or gas. Then, the cooler liquid or gas is heated and is forced up. This happens over and over in a circular flow. Ovens work by convection. Coils in the oven heat the air. The air rises, where it cooks the food. The air then cools, so it goes down. Then, the coils heat it again, so it rises once more.

Radiation is the third way that heat moves. This occurs when heat moves as waves, so it does not require matter at all. The sun heats the earth by radiation. The sun sends out heat in the form of waves. The waves reach the earth, where they provide heat.

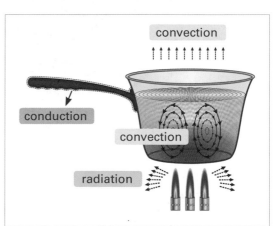

1 **What kind of heat moves as waves?**
   a. Radiation.   b. Convection.   c. Conduction.

2 **Fill in the blanks.**
   a. _____ explains why pot handles get hot.
   b. Most ovens cook food because of _____.
   c. The earth is heated by the sun through _____.

3 **Write the correct word and the meaning in Chinese.**

conduction	convection	force	particle	radiation

   a. _____: the movement of heat through a heated liquid or gas
   b. _____: an extremely small piece of something
   c. _____: to move something by physical effort

Chapter

3

Mathematics

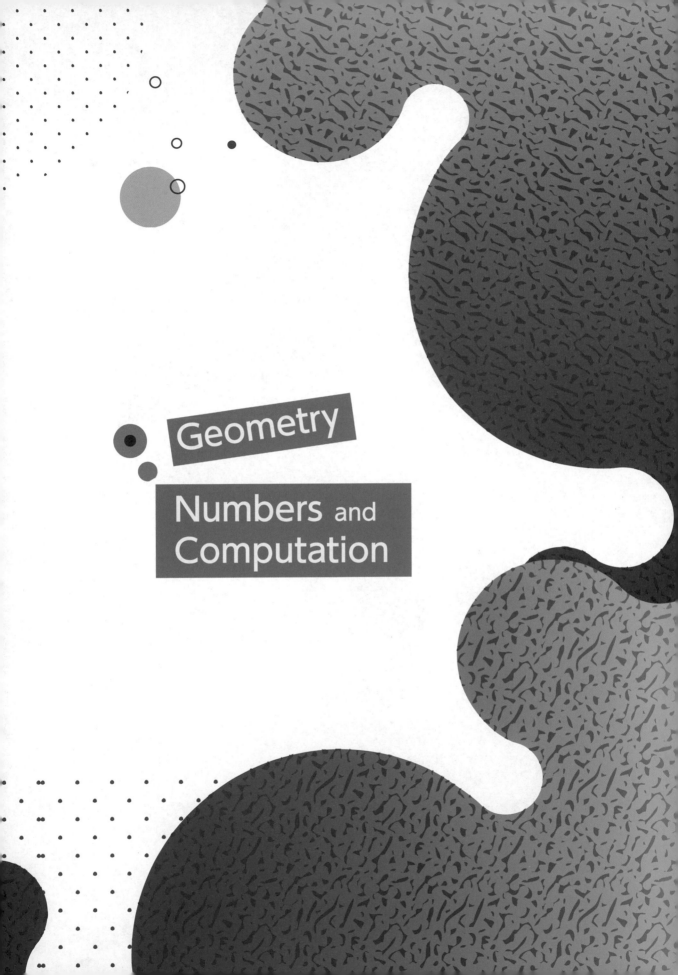

Geometry

Numbers and
Computation

Geometry

Five Simple Shapes

There are five basic shapes: the square, rectangle, triangle, circle, and oval. There are many other shapes, but they all resemble these five basic ones.

Every object has a certain shape. For example, a box may look like a square or rectangle. A piece of pizza might resemble a triangle. A soccer ball and a baseball are both circles. And eggs are oval-shaped.

There are also other more complicated shapes. A mountain might resemble a pyramid. A funnel looks like a cone.

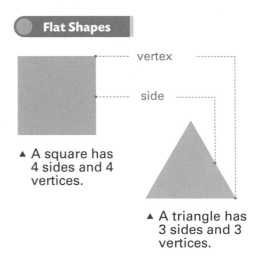

Solid Shapes

vertex
edge
face

▲ A cube has 6 faces, 12 edges, and 8 vertices.

▲ A pyramid has 5 faces, 8 edges, and 5 vertices.

Flat Shapes

vertex
side

▲ A square has 4 sides and 4 vertices.

▲ A triangle has 3 sides and 3 vertices.

1 **Which object has the shape of a cone?**
   a. A baseball.   b. A funnel.   c. A pyramid.

2 **What is true? Write T (true) or F (false).**
   a. A pyramid is one of the five basic shapes.   _____
   b. An egg is shaped like an oval.   _____
   c. Some mountains resemble pyramids.   _____

3 **Write the correct word and the meaning in Chinese.**

resemble	pyramid	oval	complicated	cone

   a. _____ : a solid shape with a polygonal base and triangular sides that form a point at the top
   b. _____ : a shape like an egg; egg-shaped
   c. _____ : a shape with a flat, round or oval base and a top that becomes narrower until it forms a point

Plane Figures and Solid Figures

Geometry is the study of regular shapes. We can divide these shapes into two kinds: plane figures and solid figures.

There are many kinds of plane figures. Squares, rectangles, triangles, and circles are all plane figures. Plane figures have both length and width. They are flat surfaces, so you can draw them on a piece of paper.

Solid figures are different from plane figures. They have length, width, and height. A box is a solid figure. We call that a cube in geometry. A globe is a solid figure. That's a sphere. Also, a pyramid and a cone are two more solid figures.

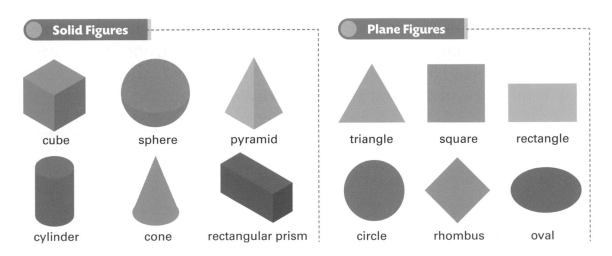

Solid Figures

cube   sphere   pyramid

cylinder   cone   rectangular prism

Plane Figures

triangle   square   rectangle

circle   rhombus   oval

① **What is a solid figure?**
a. A figure with length.   b. A figure with length and width.
c. A figure with length, width, and height.

② **What is NOT true?**
a. There are two kinds of shapes.
b. A square is a plane figure.
c. A circle is a solid figure.

③ **Write the correct word and the meaning in Chinese.**

sphere   geometry   plane figure   rhombus   solid figure

a. _____: an object shaped like a ball
b. _____: a figure with length, width, and height
c. _____: a shape with four sides that are equal in length and with four angles that are not always right angles

There are many different types of polygons. There are two requirements for an object to be a polygon. It must be made of three or more line segments. And it must be a closed figure. That means that all of the lines in the polygon meet each other.

A three-sided polygon is a triangle. Some four-sided polygons are squares, rectangles, or rhombuses. A five-sided one is a pentagon. An octagon has eight sides. A polygon can have any number of sides. It could have 10, 100, or even 1,000 sides! But circles are not polygons.

Sometimes two polygons are congruent figures. This means they have the same shape and size. For example, two squares have sides that are three inches long. They are identical. So they are congruent figures. But if one square's sides are two inches long while the other's sides are three inches long, they are not congruent. Also, a triangle and a square can never be congruent.

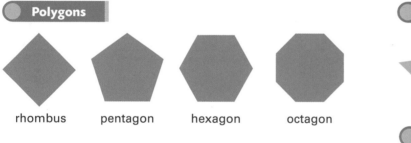

Polygons

rhombus   pentagon   hexagon   octagon

Congruent Figures

Symmetric Figures

① What is a polygon?
    a. A closed figure with three or more line segments.
    b. An object that has the same size and shape as another.
    c. A closed figure with any number of sides.

② Answer the questions.
    a. At least how many line segments can make a polygon? _____
    b. What are some four-sided polygons? _____
    c. What does it mean when two figures are congruent?

    _____

③ Write the correct word and the meaning in Chinese.

symmetric figures	line segment	polygon	congruent figures

    a. _____: figures that have sides or halves that are the same
    b. _____: a flat shape with three or more sides and angles
    c. _____: two figures that are the same shape and size

Numbers and Computation

64 Addition and Subtraction

Addition is adding two or more numbers together. When you add numbers together, the answer you get is called the *sum*. For example, the sum of 5+2 is 7.

Subtraction is taking a number away from another. Imagine you have 5 apples. You take away 2 apples and give them to your brother. How many are left? There were 5 apples, but you took away 2, so now you have 3 apples. 5–2=3. The number you have left is called the difference. So, the difference of 5–2 is 3.

▲ plus sign

▲ equal sign

▲ minus sign

Addition

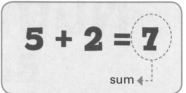

▲ 5 plus 2 is/equals/makes 7.

Subtraction

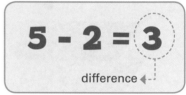

▲ 5 minus 2 is/equals 3.

① What is the answer in an addition problem called?
  a. The sum.   **b.** The difference.   **c.** The product.

② What is NOT true?
  a. The sum of 5 plus 2 is 7.
  b. The difference of 5–2 is 3.
  c. Putting two numbers together is subtraction.

③ Write the correct word and the meaning in Chinese.

addition	sum	take away	minus sign	difference

  a. _____ : a symbol used for showing that one number is to be taken from another
  b. _____ : the answer to a subtraction problem
  c. _____ : the process of adding two or more numbers together

Making Change

People use money to buy many different goods and services. Money can be both paper bills and coins. All bills and coins have different values.

Learn to recognize the coins so that you can know how much they are worth. You might buy some candy at a store. It costs seventy-five cents, so you give the clerk a dollar. One dollar is worth 100 cents. How much change will you get back? Twenty-five cents. You'll receive one quarter. But maybe you don't want a quarter. Tell the clerk, "I'd like two dimes and a nickel, please." That is how you make change.

American Bills

one-dollar bill

two-dollar bill

fifty-dollar bill

one-hundred-dollar bill

American Coins

penny   nickel   dime   quarter   half dollar   dollar

1 **What is a bill?**

   a. A coin.   b. A check.   c. Paper money.

2 **Answer the questions.**

   a. What do people buy with money? _____

   b. How much is one quarter worth? _____

   c. What coins are worth the same as a quarter? _____

3 **Write the correct word and the meaning in Chinese.**

dime   bill   coin   nickel   value

   a. _____ : the amount that something is worth, measured especially in money

   b. _____ : a U.S. coin that is worth 10 cents

   c. _____ : paper money

66 Greater and Less Than

All numbers have a certain value. So some numbers are greater than others. And some numbers are less than others.

A number that comes after another number is greater than it. For example, 6 comes after 5. So we can say, "6 is greater than 5." In math terms, we write it like this: 6 > 5.

A number that comes before another number is less than it. For example, 2 comes before 3. So we can say, "2 is less than 3." In math terms, we write it like this: 2 < 3.

▲ 10 is greater than 6.

▲ 5 is less than 6.

▲ 3 is equal to 3.

1 **What is the passage mainly about?**
   a. The values of numbers.
   b. How some numbers are greater than others.
   c. How to use the symbols > and <.

2 **Fill in the blanks.**
   a. 6 comes _____ 5.
   b. 5 is _____ than 4.
   c. 2 is _____ than 3.

3 **Write the correct word and the meaning in Chinese.**

value	less than	come after	equal	math term

   a. _____: a mathematical expression
   b. _____: the same in amount, number, or size
   c. _____: having a smaller number or amount than

Number Sentences

People use sentences when they speak, but they can also use sentences when they do math. How can they do this? It's easy. They use number sentences.

Let's think of a math problem. You have four apples, but then you add two more. That gives you a total of six apples. Now, let's make that a number sentence. It would look like this: 4+2=6. You can make number sentences for addition, and you can make them for subtraction, too. Your friend has ten pieces of candy, but he eats five pieces. Now he has five pieces left. Let's make a number sentence for that. Here it is: 10−5=5.

How to add?

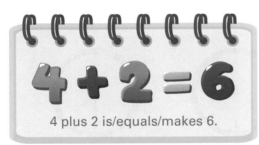

4 plus 2 is/equals/makes 6.

▲ Use a number sentence.

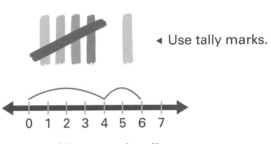

◄ Use tally marks.

▲ Use a number line.

1 **What is the passage mainly about?**
   a. How to solve addition and subtraction problems.
   b. How to use addition to solve problems.
   c. How to make and solve number sentences.

2 **Fill in the blanks.**
   a. People use _____ _____ when they do math.
   b. One _____ three is five.
   c. You can make number sentences for _____ and subtraction.

3 **Write the correct word and the meaning in Chinese.**

number sentence	number line	addition	tally	subtraction

   a. _____: a record or count of a number of things
   b. _____: a drawing that represents all the numbers that exist
   c. _____: a mathematical equation

John wakes up in the morning at seven A.M. School starts at eight o'clock, so he has one hour to get there. When he arrives at school, it's seven forty-five. School will begin in fifteen minutes. School runs from eight until three o'clock. That's a total of seven hours.

In the morning, John has class from eight until noon, so he has a total of four hours of class. Then he has lunch from twelve o'clock until a quarter to one. After that, from twelve forty-five until three P.M., he has more classes. That's a total of two hours and fifteen minutes. Finally, at three, school finishes, and John can go home.

Telling Time

▲ It is one o'clock.

▲ It is one ten.
▲ It is ten minutes after one.

▲ It is two fifteen.
▲ It is fifteen minutes after two.
▲ It is a quarter after two.

▲ It is four thirty.
▲ It is thirty minutes after four.
▲ It is half past four.

1 **What time does lunch finish?**

   a. 1:15 P.M.   **b.** 12:45 P.M.   **c.** 12:00 P.M.

2 **Answer the questions.**

   a. What time does John arrive at school? _____

   b. How many hours of class does John have in the morning?

   _____

   c. What time does John's school finish? _____

3 **Complete the sentences with the words below.**

until	half past	in	run from	a quarter

   a. `6:45` It is ____ _____ to seven.

   b. Jane has dinner from six o'clock _____ six thirty.

   c. It is eight thirty. It is _____ _____ 8.

Why Do We Multiply

Sometimes, you might want to add many groups of things together. For example, you might have five groups of apples. Each group has two apples. You could add 2 five times like this: 2+2+2+2+2=10. But that's too long. Instead, use multiplication. You can write that as a multiplication problem like this: 2×5=10. When you multiply, you add equal groups of numbers many times.

Multiplication is useful because it makes math easier. However, remember a couple of things about it. First, when you multiply any number by 1, the product is always the same as that number: 5×1=5. 100×1=100. Also, when you multiply any number by 0, the product is always 0: 2×0=0. 100×0=0.

Multiplication

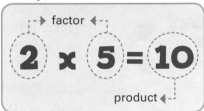

▲ 2 times 5 equals 10.

1 **Why do we multiply?**
   a. Because it adds many groups of things together.
   b. Because it multiplies equal groups of numbers many times.
   c. Because it makes math easier.

2 **Fill in the blanks.**
   a. When you multiply, you add _____ _____ of numbers many times.
   b. Any number times _____ is the same as that number.
   c. Any number times 0 is _____.

3 **Write the correct word and the meaning in Chinese.**

multiplication	factor	product	multiply	equal groups

   a. _____: a number that evenly divides a larger number
   b. _____: to add a number to itself a certain number of times
   c. _____: the answer to a multiplication problem

Solve the Problems (1)

1 Mrs. White is a teacher. She is giving a test to the students. Each test has 3 sheets of paper. She has 10 students in her class. How many sheets of paper does she need?
→ The answer is 30 because 3 × 10 = 30.

2 Some families are going to go on a picnic together. Each family has a mother, father, and two children. There are 8 families. How many people are going on the picnic?
→ The answer is 32 because 4 × 8 = 32.

3 Jenny has 24 pieces of candy. She wants to share all of the candy with her friends. There are 5 people plus Jenny. How many pieces of candy should each person get?
→ The answer is 4 because 24 ÷ 6 = 4.

4 5 students find some coins in a jar. They want to share the coins with each other. They count the coins and see that there are 25 coins. How many coins does each student get?
→ The answer is 5 because 25 ÷ 5 = 5.

1 **What is the passage mainly about?**
a. Some problems students solve at school.
b. How multiplication is easier than division.
c. Multiplication and division word problems.

2 **What is true? Write T (true) or F (false).**
a. Thirty-two people go on the picnic together. _____
b. Jenny gives six pieces of candy to each friend. _____
c. Six students find twenty-five coins in the jar. _____

3 **Complete the sentences with the words below.**

plus	give a test	go on a picnic	share	count

a. Joe has to _____ the apples on the table to see if there are enough apples for everyone.
b. You should _____ that pie with everyone.
c. The two girls _____ Amy are going to spend their vacation in Sydney.

Solve the Problems (2)

Mathematics

1 Mary is baking a cake. She needs to use flour to make the cake. She needs 2 pints of flour. But her measuring cup can only fill 1 cup at a time. How many cups of flour does she need?

➡ She needs 4 cups. 2 cups is 1 pint. So 4 cups is 2 pints.

2 Chris likes to run. Today, he ran 2,500 meters. How many kilometers did he run?

➡ He ran 2.5 kilometers. There are 1,000 meters in 1 kilometer.

3 Peter gets a ruler and measures himself. He is 60 inches tall. How many feet tall is he?

➡ He is 5 feet tall. There are 12 inches in one foot. So $60 \div 12 = 5$.

4 Lucy steps on a scale. She sees that she weighs 38 kilograms. How many grams does she weigh?

➡ She weighs 38,000 grams.
There are 1,000 grams in one kilogram.
So $1,000 \times 38 = 38,000$.

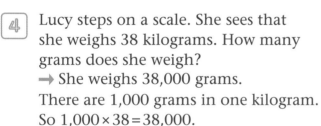

1 **How many cups are in one pint?**

   a. 1 cup.   **b.** 2 cups.   **c.** 4 cups.

2 **Fill in the blanks.**

   a. Chris ran 2.5 _____ today.

   b. Peter is five feet _____.

   c. There are 1,000 grams in one _____.

3 **Write the correct word and the meaning in Chinese.**

bake	at a time	weigh	ruler	scale

   a. _____: to have a heaviness of a stated amount

   b. _____: an instrument that measures weight

   c. _____: at the same time

Y ou can write both fractions and decimals as numbers and words. There are many ways to do this.

For example, write the fraction two-thirds as $\frac{2}{3}$. However, there are other ways to say fractions. You can say that $\frac{1}{6}$ is one-sixth or one out of six. And the fraction $\frac{5}{8}$ could be five divided by eight.

As for decimals, usually just say the individual numbers to the right of the decimal point. For example, 1.1 is one point one. 2.45 is two point four five. However, for some decimals, you can say them as fractions. 0.1 is zero point one or one-tenth. 0.7 is zero point seven or seven tenths.

Sometimes, you can write a fraction in easier terms. This is called its simplest form. For instance, think about the fraction $\frac{4}{8}$. In its simplest form, it is $\frac{1}{2}$. And the simplest form of $\frac{3}{9}$ is $\frac{1}{3}$. Finally, you can sometimes write fractions as decimals. The fraction $\frac{2}{10}$ can be 0.2. The fraction $\frac{9}{10}$ can be 0.9. This is why you can read the decimal 0.1 as one-tenth.

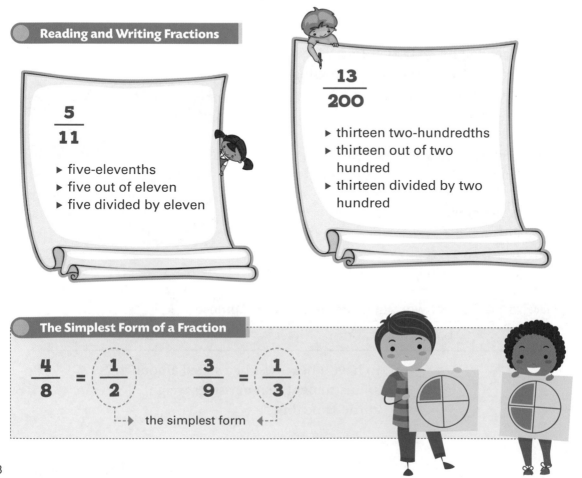

Reading and Writing Fractions

$$\frac{5}{11}$$

▸ five-elevenths
▸ five out of eleven
▸ five divided by eleven

$$\frac{13}{200}$$

▸ thirteen two-hundredths
▸ thirteen out of two hundred
▸ thirteen divided by two hundred

The Simplest Form of a Fraction

$$\frac{4}{8} = \frac{1}{2} \qquad \frac{3}{9} = \frac{1}{3}$$

the simplest form

Reading and Writing Decimals

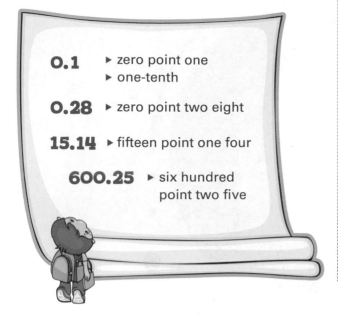

0.1 ▸ zero point one
▸ one-tenth

0.28 ▸ zero point two eight

15.14 ▸ fifteen point one four

600.25 ▸ six hundred point two five

Fractions and Decimals

Fraction	Decimal	Read
$\frac{1}{10}$	0.1	one-tenth
$\frac{1}{100}$	0.01	one-hundredth
$\frac{1}{1000}$	0.001	one-thousandth

1. **What is the easiest way to write a fraction?**
   a. In its word form.
   b. In its simplest form.
   c. In its decimal form.

2. **Answer the questions.**
   a. How do you write one-sixth? _____
   b. How can you read 2.45? _____
   c. What is the simplest form of $\frac{4}{8}$? _____

3. **Write the correct word and the meaning in Chinese.**

| fraction   decimal   decimal point   the simplest form |

   a. _____: a part of something; a portion of a whole
   b. _____: a number with one or more digits to the right of the decimal point
   c. _____: used to call a fraction when its top number and bottom number cannot be made any smaller

Chapter 4

Language •
Visual Arts •
Music

Language and Literature

Visual Arts

Music

Language and Literature

Aesop's Fables

▲ Aesop

▲ *Aesop's Fables* always had a moral at the end.

Aesop was a slave who lived in ancient Greece. He lived more than 2,000 years ago. He is famous because of the collection of stories he told. Today, we call them *Aesop's Fables*.

Aesop's Fables are short stories. Often, animals are the main characters. Through the stories about animals, Aesop teaches us how we should act as people. At the end of the fable, Aesop always tells us a lesson. The lesson is called the moral of the story. Many of his stories are still famous today. *The Tortoise and the Hare* is very popular. So is *The Ant and the Grasshopper*. *The Lion and the Mouse* and *The Fox and the Grapes* are also well-known.

The Ant and the Grasshopper

▲ Animals talk and act like people in many of *Aesop's Fables*.

The Tortoise and the Hare

▲ *The Tortoise and the Hare* has an important lesson in it.

① **What is the main idea of the passage?**
   a. Animals are the main characters in *Aesop's Fables*.
   b. *The Tortoise and the Hare* is a popular fable.
   c. *Aesop's Fables* are short stories with morals.

② **What is true? Write T (true) or F (false).**
   a. *Aesop's Fables* are very long stories. _____
   b. The characters in *Aesop's Fables* are often animals. _____
   c. *The Ant and the Mouse* is a famous story from *Aesop's Fables*. _____

③ **Write the correct word and the meaning in Chinese.**

character	lesson	ancient	*Aesop's Fables*	moral

   a. _____: an experience that teaches you how to behave better
   b. _____: the message that you understand from a story about how you should or should not behave
   c. _____: a person in a book or story

The Greek Gods and Goddesses

Myths are stories that have been around for thousands of years or more. Myths tell about brave heroes, great battles, monsters, and gods and goddesses. Some wonderful myths come to us from ancient Greece. These tales are a part of Greek mythology. Now, let's meet some of the main Greek gods and goddesses.

Greek Gods and Goddesses

▲ Zeus   ▲ Hera

▲ Poseidon   ▲ Apollo

The Greeks believed that the gods lived on Mount Olympus, a mountain in Greece. At Mount Olympus, Zeus was the most powerful god. He was the king of the gods. He controlled the heavens and decided arguments among the gods. Poseidon was the god of the sea, and Hades was the god of the underworld. They were the three strongest gods. Hera was Zeus's wife. She was the goddess of marriage. Athena was Zeus's daughter. She was the goddess of wisdom. Apollo and Artemis were twins. Apollo was the god of light, and Artemis was the goddess of the hunt. Ares was the god of war. And Aphrodite was the goddess of love. There were some other gods. But they were the most powerful of all.

1 **Who was Apollo?**
   a. The god of the underworld.   **b.** The god of war.   **c.** The god of light.

2 **Fill in the blanks.**
   a. The Greek gods lived on Mount _____.
   b. _____ was Zeus's wife.
   c. The god of war was _____.

3 **Write the correct word and the meaning in Chinese.**

monster	hero	mythology	powerful	underworld

   a. _____: having the ability to control or influence people or things
   b. _____: a legend; traditional stories about gods and heroes from the past
   c. _____: a person who is admired for great or brave acts

August 31, 2012

Dear John,

My name is Sara.

I live in Seoul, Korea.
Where do you live?

I go to Central Elementary School.
I like to ride my bike. Please
write me back and tell me about
yourself.

Sincerely,

Sara

Date: Begin with the date at the top. Use a capital letter for the name of the month.

Greeting: Start your greeting with "Dear." Use a capital D.

Capitalization: Use capital letters to begin a sentence.

Question: Use question marks at the end of questions.

Names: Capitalize the names of people, places, and things.

Closing: End the letter with a closing and your name.

Use a capital letter to begin the closing and put a comma after the closing.

Don't forget that your name should start with a capital letter, too.

small letter / lowercase letter

capital letter / uppercase letter

① **How should the first word in a sentence begin?**
   a. With a capital letter.
   b. With the greeting "Dear."
   c. With a comma.

② **Fill in the blanks.**
   a. A letter should have the _____ at the top.
   b. Use question marks at the end of _____.
   c. Use a _____ letter for the names of people, places, or things.

③ **Write the correct word and the meaning in Chinese.**

capital letter	capitalization	greeting	closing

   a. _____: an ending of a letter or speech
   b. _____: an uppercase letter, such as A, B, or C
   c. _____: a word of salutation

Parts of Speech

There are many words in the English language. We use words to make sentences. But there are also many types of words. We call these "parts of speech," and we make sentences with them. Nouns, verbs, adjectives, and prepositions are all parts of speech.

Every sentence needs a subject and a verb. The subject is often a noun. Nouns are words that name a person, place, or thing. Look around your room. Think of the names of everything you see. All those words are nouns. Verbs describe actions. Think of some activities you do. The names of those activities are verbs.

Sometimes we also use other parts of speech. Adjectives describe other words like nouns and pronouns. *Hot*, *cold*, *white*, *black*, *windy*, *rainy*, and *sunny* are all adjectives.

▲ **Run**, **eat**, and **sleep** are action verbs.

mug

mugs

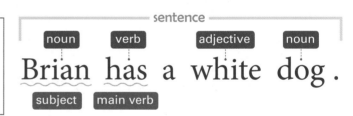

▲ A **singular noun** refers to just one thing. ▲ A **plural noun** refers to more than one.

1 What part of speech is the name of a place?

   a. A noun.   **b.** A verb.   **c.** An adjective.

2 Answer the questions.

   a. What does every sentence need? _____

   b. What do verbs do? _____

   c. What do adjectives do? _____

3 Write the correct word and the meaning in Chinese.

part of speech	action verb	subject	describe	adjective

   a. _____: a part of a sentence which tells what the sentence is about

   b. _____: a word that describes nouns and pronouns

   c. _____: a verb that expresses action

Different Types of Sentences

There are four types of sentences in English. They are declarative, interrogative, exclamatory, and imperative sentences.

Declarative sentences are the most common. They are just statements. Use them to state facts. You always end these sentences with a period. All of the sentences in this paragraph are declarative ones.

An interrogative is a question. Use this kind of sentence to ask other people about something. They always end with a question mark. You know what that is, don't you?

Sometimes, you might be really excited about something. Or perhaps you are happy. Or maybe you have a strong emotion. Then you use an exclamatory sentence. You end these with an exclamation point!

Finally, you might want to give a person an order. Use an imperative sentence to do this. In these sentences, the subject is "you." But don't say that word. Instead, just give the order.

Four Kinds of Sentences
➡ declarative sentence = statement
➡ interrogative sentence = question
➡ exclamatory sentence = exclamation
➡ imperative sentence = command

Punctuation Marks

•	,	?	!	:	;
period	comma	question mark	exclamation point	colon	semicolon
—	-	" "	'	/	•••
dash	hyphen	quotes	apostrophe	slash	ellipsis

1 **How do people use interrogative statements?**
   a. To make exclamations.   b. To state facts.   c. To ask questions.

2 **Answer the questions.**
   a. What is the most common kind of sentence? _____
   b. What is an interrogative? _____
   c. How do you end an exclamatory sentence? _____

3 **Write the correct word and the meaning in Chinese.**

declarative sentence   exclamation point   imperative sentence   emotion

   a. _____: a feeling that you experience
   b. _____: the kind of sentence that makes a statement
   c. _____: an order

118

Common Mistakes in English

Writing in English is not easy. There are many grammar rules. So you have to be very careful. Two common mistakes are sentence fragments and comma splices.

A sentence fragment is an incomplete sentence. A sentence must always have a subject and a verb. Look at the following sentence fragments:

    attends the school   My father, who is a doctor

Neither of these is complete. The first fragment needs a subject. The second fragment needs a verb. Make them complete sentences like this: "Jane attends the school." "My father, who is a doctor, is home now."

Comma splices are also common mistakes. These are sentences that use a comma to connect two independent clauses. Look at the following comma splices:

    My brother studies hard, he's a good student.
    I'm sorry, it was an accident.

Neither of these is correct. The first sentence either needs a period or the word because: "My brother studies hard because he's a good student." The second sentence needs a period, not a comma: "I'm sorry. It was an accident."

① **Why is a comma splice incorrect English?**
   a. It contains two sentence fragments.
   b. It fails to have either a subject or a verb.
   c. It joins two independent clauses with a comma.

② **What is true? Write T (true) or F (false).**
   a. A sentence fragment is a complete sentence.   _____
   b. A comma splice is good grammar.   _____
   c. A comma splice often needs a period instead of a comma.   _____

③ **Write the correct word and the meaning in Chinese.**

period	independent clause	sentence fragment	comma splice

   a. _____: an incomplete sentence
   b. _____: an improper use of a comma to join two complete sentences
   c. _____: a clause that could be used by itself as a simple sentence
                           but that is part of a larger sentence

Some Common Sayings

Every language has common sayings. People use them in various situations. They are hard to translate into other languages. But they make sense in their own language.

English has many common sayings. One is "Better late than never." This means it is better to do something late than never to do it. Another is "Two heads are better than one." This means a second person can often help one person doing something. And "An apple a day keeps the doctor away" is a common saying. It means that eating apples every day helps keep you healthy. So the person will not get sick and won't have to see a doctor.

Common Sayings

▲ An apple a day keeps the doctor away.

▲ Practice makes perfect.

▲ Where there's a will, there's a way.

① **What is the main idea of the passage?**
   a. Most people know what "Two heads are better than one" means.
   b. There are many common sayings in every language.
   c. Some sayings are hard to translate into foreign languages.

② **What is true? Write T (true) or F (false).**
   a. Common sayings are easy to translate into other languages. _____
   b. "Better late than never" is a common saying. _____
   c. "An apple a day keeps the teacher away" is a common saying. _____

③ **Write the correct word and the meaning in Chinese.**

saying	will	translate into	keep away	make sense

   a. _____ : be reasonable or logical
   b. _____ : an expression; a proverb
   c. _____ : determination

Visual Arts

Primary and Secondary Colors

There are three basic colors. They are red, yellow, and blue. We call these three primary colors. You can make other colors when you mix these colors together. For example, mix red and yellow to create orange. Combine yellow and blue to make green. And you get purple or violet when you mix red and blue together. We call these secondary colors.

Of course, there are many other colors. You can make black by mixing red, yellow, and blue all together. You can also mix primary and secondary colors to get other colors.

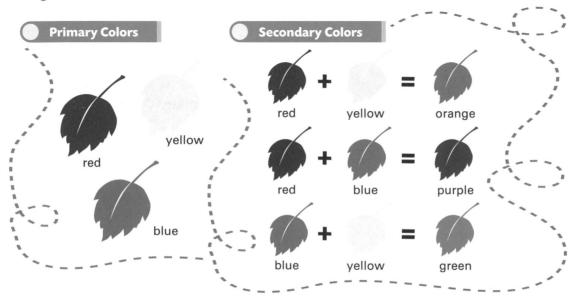

Primary Colors

red
yellow
blue

Secondary Colors

red + yellow = orange
red + blue = purple
blue + yellow = green

1 **How can a person create a secondary color?**

a. By mixing together two secondary colors.

b. By mixing together two primary colors.

c. By mixing together all three primary colors.

2 **Fill in the blanks.**

a. Red, _____, and blue are three primary colors.

b. Green, orange, and purple are _____ colors.

c. _____ is a combination of red, yellow, and blue.

3 **Write the correct word and the meaning in Chinese.**

primary color	combine	violet	secondary color	basic

a. _____ : red, yellow, or blue

b. _____ : green, purple, or orange

c. _____ : to join (two or more things) to make a single thing

Famous Painters

Michelangelo 1475–1564 | *The Creation of Adam*

Rembrandt 1606–1669 | *Anatomy Lesson of Dr. Nicolaes Tulp*

Art galleries display the works of lots of painters. There have been many painters. Some of them are very famous. Artists make many different kinds of paintings. But they are all beautiful in their own way.

Picasso was a famous modern painter. Manet, Monet, Cézanne, and van Gogh painted more than 100 years ago. Leonardo da Vinci was very famous also. He painted the most famous portrait in the world: the *Mona Lisa*. Rembrandt was a painter from a long time ago. So was Michelangelo. He painted around 500 years ago.

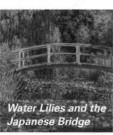

Monet 1840–1926 | *Water Lilies and the Japanese Bridge*

Leonardo da Vinci 1452–1519 | *Mona Lisa*

Cézanne 1839–1906 | *The Card Players*

1 What kind of painting is the *Mona Lisa*?

a. A modern painting.　　b. A portrait.　　c. A landscape.

2 Answer the questions.

a. Where can you see the works of painters? _____

b. Who painted the *Mona Lisa*? _____

c. How long ago did Michelangelo paint? _____

3 Write the correct word and the meaning in Chinese.

gallery	display	artist	painter	portrait

a. _____: someone who paints, draws, or makes sculptures

b. _____: a picture of a person

c. _____: a public building where you can look at paintings and other works of art

Realistic Art and Abstract Art

There are two main kinds of art. They are realistic art and abstract art. Some artists like realistic art, but others prefer abstract art.

Realistic art shows objects as they look in reality. For example, a realistic artist paints a picture of an apple. The picture will look exactly like an apple. Most art in the past was realistic art.

Abstract art looks different than realistic art. Abstract art does not always look exactly like the real thing. For example, an abstract artist paints a picture of an apple. It will not look like an apple. It might just be a red ball. That is abstract art. Nowadays, much art is abstract.

Realistic Art and Abstract Art

Realistic Painting

▲ *The Gleaners*
by Jean-François Millet

Abstract Painting

▲ *Composition VI*
by Wassily Kandinsky

Other Kinds of Art

Landscape

▲ *The Oxbow*
by Thomas Cole

Still Life

▲ *Still Life With Melon and Peaches*
by Édouard Manet

① **What was most art in the past?**
   a. Abstract art.   b. Realistic art.   c. Impressionist art.

② **Fill in the blanks.**
   a. _____ art shows objects that look real.
   b. _____ art does not always look real.
   c. In abstract art, an apple might look like a _____ ball.

③ **Write the correct word and the meaning in Chinese.**

| realistic art | still life | abstract art | landscape | exactly |

   a. _____: a type of painting of objects that do not move, such as flowers, fruit, bowls, etc.
   b. _____: a painting which shows a scene in the countryside
   c. _____: art that does not look like real things

What Do Architects Do

Architects have very important jobs. They design buildings. Some design tall buildings like skyscrapers. Others design restaurants, hotels, or banks. And others just design houses.

Architects need to have many skills. They must be engineers. They must be good at math. They must be able to draw. They must have a good imagination. And they must work well with the builders, too.

Architects draw blueprints for their buildings. Blueprints show how the building will look. They are very detailed. When the blueprints are done, the builders can start working.

Types of Buildings

▲ stadium

▲ skyscraper

▲ shopping mall

▲ hotel

1 **What does an architect need?**
a. A good imagination.
b. A lot of money.
c. An ability to sing.

2 **What is NOT true?**
a. Architects design buildings.
b. Skyscrapers are very tall buildings.
c. Architects buy blueprints.

▲ apartment

▲ house

3 **Write the correct word and the meaning in Chinese.**

architect	detailed	imagination	blueprint	skyscraper

a. _____ : a person who designs buildings
b. _____ : including many small facts or aspects
c. _____ : a very tall building

Elements of Painting

People often visit art galleries and museums to look at paintings. There are many famous paintings in places around the world. People call the greatest paintings "masterworks." What makes a painting great? There are many different elements.

First, the lines and shapes that an artist uses are important. Realistic artists make their lines and shapes imitate reality. Abstract artists do not. The way of using lines and shapes is the main difference between realistic and abstract art.

Also, the colors in the painting are important. The colors should go well with each other. Light and shadows are important elements of paintings, too. Light can affect the way you feel. The way that artists use light in their paintings can affect your emotions as well. So some artists may use a sharp contrast between dark and light.

An artist should also have a good sense of space. This means that the painting should not be too crowded or too empty. The painter should always try to find balance in a painting. That makes great art.

Elements of Painting

▲ contrast

▲ light and shadow

▲ shapes and lines

▲ a sense of space

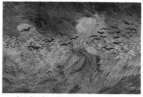
▲ bright colors and dark colors

1 **What is the passage mainly about?**
   a. Why lines and colors are important in paintings.
   b. How to make contrasts between dark and light.
   c. What artists use to create their works.

2 **What is NOT true?**
   a. Great paintings are called masterworks.
   b. Realistic artists and abstract artists make different kinds of art.
   c. Light and shadows are not important in art.

3 **Write the correct word and the meaning in Chinese.**

masterwork	museum	balance	affect	contrast

   a. _____ : an extremely good painting
   b. _____ : a difference; a distinction
   c. _____ : a state where things are of equal weight or force

Most people think that art is just painting or drawing. But there are many other kinds of unique art.

For example, some artists love cold weather. The reason they like the cold is that they make ice sculptures. They take huge blocks of ice and use saws, hammers, and chisels to create sculptures. Of course, when the weather gets warmer, their artwork disappears.

Most people don't think of bed covers as art, but others do. Many people make quilts. These are bed covers. But the quilt makers put many designs on their quilts. The designs can be simple, or they can be very complicated. But no two quilts are ever alike. Quilt making is a popular form of folk art in some places.

In America, Native Americans have many unique forms of art. Some of them paint rocks. Others make tiny sculptures from rocks, wood, or bone. And some Native Americans even use sand to make art! This is called sand painting. It can produce many beautiful pieces of art.

▲ Native American sand painting

Kinds of Unique Art

▲ ice sculpture

▲ quilt

▲ collage

▲ mosaic

1 **What do some Native Americans make art from?**
   a. Ice.   b. Quilts.   c. Wood.

2 **Answer the questions.**
   a. What do artists use to make ice sculptures? _____
   b. What is another name for a bed cover? _____
   c. Who does sand painting? _____

3 **Write the correct word and the meaning in Chinese.**

ice sculpture	chisel	artwork	quilt	folk art

   a. _____ : a decorative cover for a bed
   b. _____ : a tool with a flat metal blade used for cutting wood or stone
   c. _____ : traditional art

Music

Musicians and Their Musical Instruments

▲ jazz musician

There are so many kinds of musical instruments. They make many different sounds. So there are also many kinds of music. Rock musicians often use the guitar and drums. Jazz music needs a piano and saxophone. And classical music uses many various kinds of instruments.

People often play two or more instruments together. They do this in a band or an orchestra. But the musicians must all play at the same time. Many of them read sheet music. This tells them what notes to play. If they play well together, they create a harmonious sound.

▶ violinist

Musicians

▲ pianist

▲ flutist

▲ guitarist

▲ drummer

① **How can musicians make different sounds?**
   a. By reading sheet music.
   b. By using different musical instruments.
   c. By creating harmonious sounds.

▶ trumpeter

② **What is true? Write T (true) or F (false).**
   a. Jazz musicians often play the piano. _____
   b. The drums are common in rock music. _____
   c. Musicians read music to learn what
      instrument to play. _____

③ **Write the correct word and the meaning in Chinese.**

musical instrument	note	sheet music	orchestra	harmonious

   a. _____ : melodious; tuneful
   b. _____ : a large group of musicians playing a variety of different
                            instruments together
   c. _____ : an individual sound in music

Popular Children's Songs

What makes a song popular? There are many factors involved. Often, the simplest songs are the most popular with people. The words to the song might be easy, so people can remember them easily. Or the melody is easy to play or remember, so people often hum or whistle the music.

Some songs are well-liked by young people. *Bingo* is one of these songs. *Old MacDonald* is another, and so are *Twinkle, Twinkle, Little Star* and *La Cucaracha*. Why do people like them? The words often repeat, the words rhyme, and the tunes are catchy.

1 **What is the passage mainly about?**
   a. The titles of some popular children's songs.
   b. Why some songs become popular.
   c. How to hum the music of a song.

2 **Fill in the blanks.**
   a. Many times, _____ songs are popular.
   b. Some people like to _____ or whistle music.
   c. Popular songs often have _____ tunes.

3 **Write the correct word and the meaning in Chinese.**

rhyme	popular	hum	melody	catchy

   a. _____ : to sing with one's lips closed
   b. _____ : to have or end with a sound that corresponds to another
   c. _____ : a tune or song, especially a simple one

Different Kinds of Music

People have different tastes in music. Some like slow music. Others like fast music. Some like to hear singing. Others like to hear musical instruments. So there are many different kinds of music.

Classical music relies upon musical instruments. It has very little singing in it. On the other hand, folk music and traditional music use both instruments and singing. Every country has its own kind of folk music. It's usually fun to listen to.

There are also many kinds of modern music. Rock music is one popular genre. So is jazz. Some people prefer rap or R&B. Overall, there is some kind of music for everyone.

Modern Music

▲ dance music

▲ R&B

Types of Songs

▲ folk song

▲ hymn

▲ vocals

▲ rock music

▲ rap music

1 **What is the main idea of the passage?**
   a. Not everyone likes listening to the same music.
   b. Some music needs instruments and singing.
   c. There are many types of modern music.

2 **What is true? Write T (true) or F (false).**
   a. People like different kinds of music.   _____
   b. Classical music has a lot of singing in it.   _____
   c. Folk music uses no instruments.   _____

3 **Write the correct word and the meaning in Chinese.**

taste	folk music	R&B	rap	genre

   a. _____: rhythm and blues
   b. _____: a type of popular music in which the words are spoken,
                              not sung
   c. _____: traditional music

Different Kinds of Musical Instruments

Language • Visual Arts • Music

Some instruments look alike or have common characteristics. We can put many of these instruments into families. There are some different families of musical instruments.

keyboard instruments

Keyboard instruments have keys to press. The piano, organ, and keyboard are in the keyboard family. The violin, viola, and cello have strings. So they are called string instruments. There are two kinds of wind instruments: brass and woodwinds. Brass instruments include the trumpet, trombone, and tuba. Woodwinds are the clarinet, flute, oboe, and saxophone. Percussion instruments are fun to play. You hit or shake them with your hands or with a stick.

There are many other kinds of instruments. Apart, they make lots of sounds. Together, they combine to make beautiful music.

string instruments	brass instruments	woodwind instruments	percussion instruments

1. **Which of the following is a string instrument?**
   a. The tuba.　　　　　b. The viola.　　　　　c. The organ.

2. **Fill in the blanks.**
   a. The piano, organ, and keyboard are in the _____ family.
   b. Brass and _____ are wind instruments.
   c. You _____ or shake percussion instruments with your hands.

3. **Write the correct word and the meaning in Chinese.**

woodwind	tuba	characteristic	percussion instrument

   a. _____: an instrument like a drum that one beats
   b. _____: any wind instrument other than the brass instruments
   c. _____: a typical or noticeable quality of someone or something

The Nutcracker

Every Christmas season, people all around the world go to the ballet. And many of them see *The Nutcracker*. It is one of the most famous and popular ballets in the world. It was composed by Peter Tchaikovsky.

In the story, it is Christmas Eve. Clara receives a nutcracker as a present. She falls asleep in a room with the nutcracker. Suddenly, the nutcracker and the toys grow big, and they come to life. Then, they battle an army of mice and defeat them. The nutcracker becomes a prince, and he and Clara go to his castle. They watch many dances there. Then, Clara wakes up and learns it was only a dream.

The music and dances in *The Nutcracker* are very famous. The music is beautiful, and the dances require great skill. Along with the story, they have made *The Nutcracker* an important part of Christmas for many people.

Famous Ballets

▲ The Nutcracker   ▲ Swan Lake   ▲ Giselle   ▲ The Sleeping Beauty

1 What do the nutcracker and his soldiers fight?

   a. An army of mice.   **b.** An army of spiders.   **c.** An army of ants.

2 Fill in the blanks.

   a. *The Nutcracker* was composed by Peter _____.

   b. The events in *The Nutcracker* take place on _____ Eve.

   c. The nutcracker turns into a _____.

3 Write the correct word and the meaning in Chinese.

ballet	come to life	composed by	nutcracker	battle

   a. _____ : to become lively or animated

   b. _____ : to fight

   c. _____ : written by

Michael A. Putlack

專攻歷史與英文，擁有美國麻州 Tufts University 碩士學位

e-Creative Contents

一群專門為非母語英語課程及非母語英語教學學生開發英語學習產品的創意小組

國家圖書館出版品預行編目 (CIP) 資料

超級英語閱讀訓練 . 1, FUN 學美國英語課本精選 (寂天雲隨
身聽 APP 版) / Michael A. Putlack, e-Creative Contents 著
; Cosmos Language Workshop 譯 . -- 二版 . -- [臺北市] :
寂天文化 , 2021.10
　面；　公分

ISBN 978-626-300-042-1 (第 1 冊 : 16K 平裝)

1. 英語　2. 讀本

805.18　　　　　　　　　　　　　　　110011975

超級英語閱讀訓練 1

作　　　　者	Michael A. Putlack, e-Creative Contents
譯　　　　者	Cosmos Language Workshop
特 約 編 輯	丁宥榆
校　　　　對	黃詩韻
主　　　　編	丁宥暄
內 文 排 版	丁宥榆／林書玉
封 面 設 計	林書玉
圖　　　　片	Shutterstock
製 程 管 理	洪巧玲
出　版　者	寂天文化事業股份有限公司
電　　　　話	+886-(0)2-2365-9739
傳　　　　真	+886-(0)2-2365-9835
網　　　　址	www.icosmos.com.tw
讀 者 服 務	onlineservice@icosmos.com.tw
出 版 日 期	2024 年 5 月 二版再刷（寂天雲隨身聽 APP 版）（0202）

郵 撥 帳 號	1998620-0　寂天文化事業股份有限公司
	訂書金額未滿 1000 元，請外加運費 100 元。
	〔若有破損，請寄回更換，謝謝。〕

超級 SUPER READING TRAINING BOOK 1
英語閱讀訓練

FUN學美國英語課本精選 二版

Michael A. Putlack &
e-Creative Contents_著
Cosmos Language Workshop_譯

1

TRAINing BOOK

MP3

寂天雲 APP

如何下載 MP3 音檔

❶ 寂天雲 APP 聆聽：掃描書上 QR Code 下載
「寂天雲－英日語學習隨身聽」APP。加入會員
後，用 APP 內建掃描器再次掃描書上 QR
Code，即可使用 APP 聆聽音檔。

❷ 官網下載音檔：請上「寂天閱讀網」
（www.icosmos.com.tw），註冊會員／登入後，
搜尋本書，進入本書頁面，點選「MP3 下載」
下載音檔，存於電腦等其他播放器聆聽使用。

Table of Contents

Chapter

1

Social Studies

Culture

Geography

History

Your neighbors / are the people / who live near you. In our **community**, / people help **each other** / and **care about one another**. If you want / to have a good neighbor, / you **have to** / be a good neighbor / first. There are / many ways / to do this.

First, / you can be nice / to your neighbors. Always **greet** them / and say, "Hello." **Get to know** them. **Become friends / with them.** Also, don't be noisy / at your home. And **respect** / your neighbors' **privacy**. If they have / any **problems**, / **help** them **out**. They will help you / too / **in the future**. If you do / all of these things, / you can be / a good neighbor.

單字提示
• 藉由文中重點單字畫記，理解字彙如何運用

課文斷句
• 透過分離基本句型，迅速讀懂英文
• 反覆聽音檔，練習把課文大聲唸出來

你的鄰居 neighbor 就是住在你家附近的人。在我們的社區 community 裡，人們會互相幫忙 help each other、彼此關心 care about one another。若是想要有個好鄰居，你必須先成為一個好鄰居 be a good neighbor。要做到這點有很多方法 many ways。

首先 first，你可以對鄰居表示友好 be nice。要經常和他們打招呼 greet，並且說「你好」。去認識他們 get to know them，和他們成為朋友 become friends。還有，不要在家裡製造噪音 don't be noisy，並且要尊重鄰居的隱私 respect privacy。他們若是遇到問題 problems，你可以幫助他們 help them out，將來 in the future 他們也會幫助你的。如果這些你都做到了，你就是個好鄰居 good neighbor。

中文翻譯與重要字彙片語中英對照

Words to Know

• **community** 社區	• **each other** 互相（兩者之間）	• **care about** 關懷
• **one another** 互相（三者以上）	• **have to** 必須	• **greet** 打招呼
• **get to know** 認識	• **become friends with sb.** 與某人做朋友	
• **respect** 尊重	• **privacy** 隱私	• **problem** 問題 • **help out** 幫助擺脫困難
• **in the future** 日後；未來		

單字學習

02 A Day at School 學校裡的一天

John and Sally / go to **elementary school**. Their first class / starts at 8 a.m. They go to their **homeroom**. They stand up, / face the flag, / and say the **Pledge of Allegiance** / before their class begins. Then their teacher, / Mrs. Smith, / starts their lessons. They study **math**, / **social studies**, / English, / and art, / and then / they go to the **cafeteria** / for lunch. After lunch, / they have **recess**, / so all the students / **go outside** / and play / **for a while**. Then / they learn **science, history**, / and **music**. Finally, / it's 3 o'clock. **It's time** / **for them** / **to go home**!

約翰和莎莉在上小學 elementary school。他們的第一堂課 first class 從早上 8 點開始 start at 8 a.m.。他們到大教室去 go to homeroom。在開始上課之前,他們會起立 stand up、面向國旗,並且說出「忠誠宣誓」say the Pledge of Allegiance,之後他們的老師史密斯太太才會開始上課 start lessons。他們上了數學課 math、社會課 social studies、英文課 English 和美術課 art,然後到自助餐廳 go to the cafeteria 吃午餐。中餐過後 after lunch 是他們的休息時間 recess,所以全體學生都會到戶外玩一陣子。接下來 Then,他們還上了自然課 science、歷史課 history 和音樂課 music。最後到了三點鐘,就是他們該回家 go home 的時候了!

Words to Know

- **elementary school** 小學　　• **homeroom** 同年級學生定期集會,接受導師指導的教室
- **Pledge of Allegiance** 美國的「效忠誓詞」　• **math** 數學　• **social studies** 社會學科
- **cafeteria** 自助餐廳　• **recess** 休息　• **go outside** 去戶外　• **for a while** 一陣子
- **science** 科學　• **history** 歷史　• **music** 音樂
- **It's time for sb. to do sth.** 是某人做某事的時候了

Christians are people / who **believe in Christianity**. They believe / that **Jesus Christ** is / the Son of **God**. In Christianity, / there are / two very important holidays. They are / Christmas and **Easter**.

Christmas is / on December 25. Christians **celebrate** / the birth of Jesus / on this day. Christmas is a time / of happiness and **celebration**.

Easter is / in late March / or early April / every year. It is / the most important / Christian holiday. It is / the day / when Jesus Christ **came back** / **from the dead**. Most Christians / go to church / on this day.

基督教徒 Christians 就是信仰 believe in 基督教的人。他們相信耶穌基督 Jesus Christ 是上帝的兒子 the Son of God。基督教有兩個非常重要的節日 important holidays，那就是聖誕節 Christmas 和復活節 Easter。

聖誕節是在 12 月 25 日 on December 25，基督徒會在這天慶祝耶穌的誕生 the birth of Jesus。聖誕節是一段充滿歡樂和慶祝的時光。

復活節是在每年的三月底或四月初 in late March or early April，它是基督教最重要的節日。這一天是耶穌基督死而復活 come back from the dead 的日子。大部分的基督徒這天都會上教堂 go to church。

Words to Know

- **Christian** 基督教的；基督徒 　• **believe in** 信仰 　• **Christianity** 基督教
- **Jesus Christ** 耶穌基督 　• **God** 上帝 　• **Easter** 復活節 　• **celebrate** 慶祝
- **celebration** 慶祝活動 　• **come back from the dead** 死而復活

Different Kinds of Jobs 不同類型的工作

After people finish school, / they often **look for** jobs. There are / many kinds of jobs / people do. But there are / three **main categories** of jobs. They are / service jobs, / **manufacturing** jobs, / and **professional** jobs.

People with service jobs / **provide** services / for others. They **might deliver** / the mail or food. They often work / in restaurants. And they work / in stores / as salespeople and **cashiers**.

People with manufacturing jobs / make things. They make TVs, / computers, / cars, / and other **objects**.

People with professional jobs / often have special **training**. They are / doctors and **engineers**. They are / **lawyers** and teachers. They might need to / **attend** school / to learn their **skills**.

人們在畢業後 finish school，通常會開始找工作 look for jobs。人們從事各種不同的工作，但工作的主要種類型有三 main categories of jobs：服務業 service job、製造業 manufacturing job，以及專業工作 professional job。

從事服務業者，提供服務 provide services 給他人，他們有可能會送信或是外送食物 deliver the mail or food。服務業者通常在餐廳工作 work in restaurants，也會在商店裡擔任銷售員 salespeople 與收銀員 cashier。

從事製造業者專門生產東西 make things，像是電視、電腦、汽車，與其他物品。

從事專業工作者通常受過特別訓練 have special training，他們會擔任醫師 doctor 與工程師 engineer、律師 lawyer 與教師 teacher 的工作。這些人也許需要去學校上課 attend school 習得技術。

Words to Know

- **look for** 尋找　　• **main** 主要的　　• **category** 種類；類型　　• **manufacturing** 製造業（的）
- **professional** 專業的　• **provide** 提供　• **might** 可能　• **deliver** 遞送　• **cashier** 收銀員
- **object** 物品　• **training** 訓練　• **engineer** 工程師　• **lawyer** 律師　• **attend** 上（學）
- **skill** 技能

Nowadays, / we live / in an **advanced** world. We use / many new **inventions** / that people long ago / never **imagined**.

In the past, / people could not / **regularly communicate** / with others. It took / days, weeks, or even months / just to send a letter. There were / no telephones. So people had to / talk **face to face**. Nowadays, / we use cell phones / to call anyone / anywhere / in the world. And we send email to people / **instantly** / thanks to the Internet.

In the past, / traveling **short distances** / took a long time. People **either** walked / **or** rode on a horse. Now, / most people own cars. They can drive long distances / **in short periods of time**. And people can even fly / around the world / on airplanes / now.

In the past, / people often died / **because of** poor **medical treatment**. Even a toothache could / sometimes / kill a person! Now, / **vaccines protect** people / from **diseases**. And doctors are making / more and more **discoveries** / every day.

現今，我們生活在一個先進的世界 advanced world，我們使用許多過去的人從未想像過的新發明 many new inventions。

從前，人們無法經常與彼此溝通 regularly communicate，光是送信就要耗時幾天、幾週甚至是幾個月。由於當時沒有電話 telephone，人們必須要面對面 face to face 才能講話。現在，用手機 cell phone 就能打電話給世界上任何角落的任何人 call anyone，由於有網路 thanks to the Internet，我們能立即傳送電子郵件給他人。

在過去，短程旅行也相當耗時 take a long time，人們不是走路就是騎馬。而今，大部分的人擁有自己的車 own cars，他們可以在短時間內開車到很遠的地方，人們現在甚至能搭乘飛機前往世界各地 fly around the world。

過去人們經常死於醫療的貧乏 poor medical treatment，甚至連牙痛 toothache 有時亦能致人於死！如今，疫苗 vaccines 讓人們免於疾病之苦 protect from diseases，而且，醫生 doctor 每天都有越來越多的醫療新發現 make discoveries。

Words to Know

- **technology** 科技　• **nowadays** 現今　• **advanced** 先進的　• **invention** 發明
- **imagine** 想像　• **regularly** 定期地；規律地　• **communicate** 溝通　• **face to face** 面對面
- **instantly** 立即；馬上　• **short distance** 近距離　• **either . . . or . . .** 不是……就是……
- **in short periods of time** 在短時間內　• **because of** 因為；由於
- **medical treatment** 醫藥治療　• **vaccine** 疫苗　• **protect** 保護　• **disease** 疾病
- **discovery** 發現；探索

06 The Leaders of the American Government
美國政府的領導者

The **president** is the leader / of the American **government**. He **is elected** / by the people / and **serves** / for four years. He lives / in **the White House**.

There are / other government **officials**, / too. Many serve / in **Congress**. Congress **is divided** / **into** two parts. They are / **the Senate** / and **the House of Representatives**. Every **state** has / two **senators**. And every state has / a different number of **representatives** / in the House. Some have many. But some have / just one or two. The members of Congress / make all the laws / for the country. They work from **the Capitol** / in Washington, D.C.

總統 president 是美國政府的領導人 the leader。他是由人民所選出來的 be elected by people，任期為四年 serve for four years，住在白宮 live in the White House。

還有其他政府官員 government officials，多數人都任職於國會 serve in Congress。國會分成兩個部分，也就是參議院 the Senate 和眾議院 the House of Representatives。每個州都有兩位參議員 senator，每州的眾議員 representative 數量則不一。有些州有好幾位，但有的只有一、兩位。國會議員 the member of Congress 制定了全國法律，他們工作的地點在華盛頓特區裡的國會大廈。

Words to Know

- **leader** 領導者　　• **president** 總統　　• **government** 政府　　• **be elected** 被選出
- **serve** 任（職）　• **the White House** 白宮　　• **official** 官員　　• **Congress** 美國國會
- **be divided into** 被分成　　• **the Senate** 參議院　　• **the House (of Representatives)** 眾議院
- **state** 州　　• **senator** 參議員　　• **representative** 眾議員　　• **the Capitol** 國會大廈

The **federal** government / in the U.S. / is very important. It is the **central** government / of the U.S. But every state has / its own government, / too. And cities have governments / also.

Every state has / a **governor**. A governor / is like the president. The governor / is the most powerful person / in the state. And every state has / a **legislature**. There are / many members / in these legislatures. They **represent** / small **sections** / of their states. They pass / the **bills** / that become laws in the states.

Cities have governments, / too. Most cities have / mayors. Some have / **city managers** / **though**. A city manager / is like a mayor. And the **city council** / is like a legislature. But it usually has / just a few members.

　　美國的聯邦政府 the federal government 十分重要，它是美國的中央政府 the central government。每一州 every state 同時也擁有自己的政府，各級都市亦是如此。

　　每州有一位州長 governor，州長就像是總統，是一州中權力最大的 the most powerful 人。每一州也設有立法機關 legislature，其中成員眾多 many members，各自代表每一州的各個小區域 represent small sections，負責通過法案 pass the bills，使其形成州立法律。

　　都市也有政府，而大多數的都市 most cities 都各自有一位市長 mayor，有些都市則還有市行政官 city manager。市行政官好比市長，而市議會 city council 就好比立法機關，不過通常只會有幾名成員而已。

Words to Know

- **local** 當地的；本地的　・**federal** 聯邦政府的　・**central** 中央的　・**governor** 州長
- **legislature** 立法機關；州議會　・**represent** 代表　・**section** 區域　・**bill** 議案；法案
- **city manager** 市行政官　・**though** 然而；還是　・**city council** 市議會

08 The <u>Jury</u> System 陪審團制度

Most **criminal** cases / in the United States / are done / in a **trial** / by jury. Jury trials / are an important part / of the **justice system**. A jury / **is made up of** / **regular citizens**. There are / two kinds of juries: / a **grand jury** / and a **petit jury**.

A grand jury has / between 12 and 23 members. The **prosecutor** presents / his or her **evidence** / to the grand jury. Then, / the grand jury decides / if there is enough evidence / to have a trial. If the jury says yes, / then there will be / a trial. If the jury says no, / there will be / no trial.

A petit jury / is also called / a trial jury. This jury usually / has 12 members. The members listen to / **actual court cases**. They hear / all of the evidence. Then, / at the end of the trial, / they must **make a decision**. They decide / if the **defendant** / is **innocent** or **guilty**.

美國大部分的刑事案件 criminal case 都需經過陪審團的審判 trial by jury，陪審團審理 jury trial 是司法制度 justice system 上很重要的一個部分。陪審團 jury 由普通公民組成，可分為大陪審團 grand jury 和小陪審團 petit jury 兩種。

大陪審團由 12 到 23 人組成，他們根據檢察官 prosecutor 提供的證據 present evidence 來決定罪證是否足夠進行審判 have a trial。若陪審團認為罪證足夠，則會進行接下來的審判；若陪審團否決 say no，則否。

小陪審團也可稱作 trial jury，通常由 12 名陪審員組成。陪審員會在場旁聽案件的審理 listen to actual court cases 並聽取所有的證據 hear all of the evidence，接著，在審判結束前，他們必須做出決定 make a decision，決定被告 defendant 的有罪與否 innocent or guilty。

Words to Know

- **jury** 陪審團　• **criminal** 犯法的　• **trial** 審問；審判　• **justice system** 司法系統
- **be made up of** 由……組成　• **regular citizen** 一般市民　• **grand jury** 大陪審團
- **petit jury** 小陪審團　• **prosecutor** 檢察官　• **evidence** 證據　• **actual** 實際的
- **court case** 法庭案例　• **make a decision** 做決定　• **defendant** 被告　• **innocent** 無辜的
- **guilty** 有罪的

There are seven continents / on Earth. **Asia** is the biggest / of all of them. Europe has many countries / **located in** it. **Africa** has / both **deserts** and **jungles** / in it. Asia, Europe, and Africa / are often called / "the Old World." **Australia** is the largest island / on Earth. People call / North and South America / "the New World."

There are five oceans / on Earth. **The Pacific Ocean** / is the biggest. **The Atlantic Ocean lies** / between the Old World / and the New World. **The Indian Ocean** / is the only ocean / named for a country. **The Arctic and Antarctic oceans** / are both very cold.

世界有七大洲 **seven continents**，其中亞洲 **Asia** 的面積最大 **the biggest**。許多國家都位於歐洲 **Europe**，而沙漠和叢林都在非洲 **Africa**。亞洲、歐洲和非洲一般稱為「舊大陸」**the Old World**。澳洲 **Australia** 則是全世界最大的島 **the largest island**。人們稱北美洲和南美洲 **North and South America** 為「新大陸」**the New World**。

世界有五大海洋 **five oceans**，其中以太平洋 **the Pacific Ocean** 的面積最大。大西洋 **the Atlantic Ocean** 位於舊大陸與新大陸之間。印度洋 **the Indian Ocean** 是唯一以國家名稱命名的海洋。北極海 **the Arctic Ocean** 和南極海 **the Antarctic Ocean** 都非常寒冷。

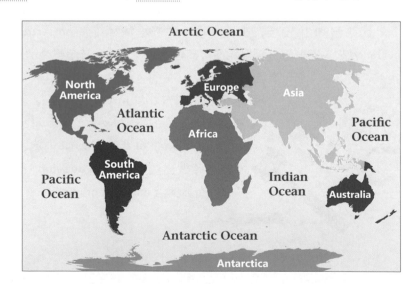

Words to Know

- **continent** 大陸 ・**Asia** 亞洲 ・**located in** 位於；座落 ・**Africa** 非洲 ・**desert** 沙漠
- **jungle** 叢林 ・**Australia** 澳洲 ・**the Pacific Ocean** 太平洋 ・**the Atlantic Ocean** 大西洋
- **lie** 位於 ・**the Indian Ocean** 印度洋 ・**the Arctic Ocean** 北冰洋
- **the Antarctic Ocean** 南冰洋

10 What Is a Map 何謂地圖

Maps are drawings / of different places. They show / what an area looks like. Some maps show / very large areas, / like countries. Other maps show / small areas, / like cities or **neighborhoods**.

Maps can show / many things. On big maps, / they show / the land and water. These maps have / countries, seas, oceans, / and even continents on them. People use these maps / to find countries and cities. Small maps might show / one city or area. They have many **details**. They have / **individual buildings** and streets / on them. People use these maps / to find their way somewhere.

地圖 map 是指不同地方的製圖,能夠呈現出一個地方的樣貌 what an area looks like。有些地圖涵蓋了廣大範圍 large areas,如整個國家。有些地圖則以小區域 small areas 呈現,像是城市或鄰近地區。

地圖可以呈現出許多事物 show many things。大地圖上有陸地和水域 land and water,這些地圖中有國家、海洋,甚至是大陸 countries, seas, oceans, and even continents。人們利用這些地圖尋找國家和城市。小地圖則可能呈現出一座城市或地區 one city or area,圖中有許多細節 many details,像是獨立的建築物和街道 individual buildings and streets。人們會利用這些地圖尋找方位 to find their way。

Words to Know

· **neighborhood** 鄰近地區　· **detail** 細節　· **individual** 個別的　· **building** 建築物

The United States has / many national parks. These are / **protected** areas. So people cannot / **develop** or **damage** them.

The first national park / was Yellowstone National Park. It is an area / with **stunning scenery** / and many wild animals. The Grand **Canyon** / is also a national park. It is / one of the largest canyons / in the world.

Every year, / millions of people / visit these parks. They **tour** the parks / and go hiking. Some even camp / in the parks. They learn about the land / and how to **preserve** it, / too.

美國有許多座國家公園 national parks，這些地方都是保育區 protected areas。因此，人們不可以開發或破壞 cannot develop or damage 它們。

第一座國家公園是黃石國家公園 Yellowstone National Park。它是一個風光明媚 stunning scenery 的地方，還有許多野生動物 many wild animals。大峽谷 the Grand Canyon 也是一座國家公園，它是全世界最廣大的峽谷之一 one of the largest canyons。

每年有上百萬人 millions of people 造訪這些公園。他們會參觀 tour 公園和健行 go hiking，有些人甚至會在公園裡露營 camp。他們也認識了關於這塊土地的故事，還有要如何保護 how to preserve 它。

12 <u>Endangered</u> Animals 瀕臨絕種的動物

There are / many animals / on the earth. Some **species** / have many animals. But there are / just a few animals / in other species. These animals / are endangered. If we are not careful, / they could all die / and become **extinct**.

In China, / the panda is endangered. In the oceans, / the **blue whale** is endangered. In Africa, / lions, tigers, and elephants / are all endangered. There are / many other endangered animals, / too.

What can people do? People can / stop hunting them. And people can / **set aside** land / for the animals / to live on. Then, / maybe one day, / they will not be endangered / anymore.

世界上有許多動物。有些種類 some species 的動物數量很多 many animals，而有些種類 other species 則為數不多 just a few animals。這些動物瀕臨絕種 be endangered，我們要是再不謹慎小心，牠們很可能會全數死亡，並且絕種 become extinct。

在中國 in China，熊貓 panda 就快要絕種。在海裡 in the oceans，藍鯨 blue whale 瀕臨絕種。在非洲 in Africa，獅子、老虎和大象 lions, tigers, and elephants 全都將要滅絕。還有許多其他瀕臨絕種的動物。

什麼是人類可以做的呢？人們可以停止獵殺 stop hunting 牠們，還可以把棲息地留給 set aside land 動物們。然後，也許有一天 maybe one day，牠們就不會絕種了。

Words to Know

• endangered 快要絕種的 • species 物種 • extinct 絕種的 • blue whale 藍鯨
• set aside 撥出；留出

The United States / is a huge country / with 50 states. Each region / in the U.S. / has different **geographical features**.

The Northeast / is the New England area. It includes / Massachusetts and Connecticut. The **land** / there / is **hilly**. The Southeast / is another region. It includes / Alabama, Tennessee, and Florida. It has / some low mountains. There are / many rivers and lakes, / too. The Midwest / is a very **flat** land. There are / miles and miles of farms. Iowa and Illinois / are located there. The Southwest is hot. It has some deserts. The Grand Canyon / is located there. The Rocky Mountains / are also there. The West includes / California and Washington. It has / both mountains and big **forests**.

美國是一個擁有 50 州 **50 states** 的大國 **a huge country**，每個區域有其不同的地理特徵 **geographical feature**。

東北部 **the Northeast** 是新英格蘭區 **the New England area**，包括麻薩諸塞州和康乃迪克州，地形多山丘 **hilly**；東南部 **the Southeast** 則是另一個區域，包括阿拉巴馬州、田納西州和佛羅里達州。這個區域擁有一些低矮山脈 **low mountains**，也孕有許多河流與湖泊 **many rivers and lakes**。中西部 **the Midwest** 是一片非常平坦的土地 **very flat land**，農場綿延了好幾英里 **miles and miles of farms**，愛荷華州和伊利諾州便座落於此。西南部 **the Southwest** 天氣炎熱，擁有好幾座沙漠 **some deserts**。大峽谷 **the Grand Canyon** 與落磯山脈 **the Rocky Mountains** 都位於此區。西部 **the West** 包括加州與華盛頓州，這裡擁有山脈與大型森林 **mountains and big forests**。

West
Southwest
Southeast
Northeast
Midwest

Words to Know

- **geographical** 地理的　• **feature** 特徵；特色　• **land** 土地；國土　• **hilly** 多山丘的
- **flat** 平坦的　• **forest** 森林

The Southwest Region of the United States

14 美國的西南部地區

The American Southwest / **covers** / a very large area. But it only has / a few states. It includes / the states Arizona, New Mexico, Texas, and Oklahoma.

Most of the land / in these states / is very dry. In fact, / there are many deserts / in these areas. Because of that, / the people must **practice** / water **conservation** / all the time. But not all of the land / there / is desert. The Colorado River / **flows through** Arizona. And the Rio Grande River / flows through Texas. Also, / the Rocky Mountains / go through / parts of Arizona and New Mexico.

Arizona itself has / a very **diverse** geography. Much of its land / is desert. But the Grand Canyon / is in the northern part / of the state. Much of the northern part of the state / has mountains. Also, / there are many forests / in this area.

Texas is also a part / of the Southwest. Much of the land / is very dry. But many parts of Texas / are **rich with** oil. The oil **industry** / is a huge business / in Texas. It's / one of the biggest **oil-producing** states / in the **entire** country.

美國西南部 the American Southwest 涵蓋非常廣大的區域 very large area，卻只有少數幾個州 a few states，包括亞利桑納州、新墨西哥州、德州以及奧克拉荷馬州。

其中大部分的土地都非常乾燥 very dry。事實上，這些區域有許多的沙漠 many deserts。正因如此，這裡的人時時刻刻都要節約用水。不過，這裡的土地也並非全是沙漠。科羅拉多河 the Colorado River 流經亞利桑納州；里約格蘭德河 the Rio Grande River 流經德州。此外，落磯山脈 the Rocky Mountains 貫穿部分的亞利桑納州和新墨西哥州。

亞利桑納州 Arizona 本身擁有多樣性的地理環境 diverse geography，它的土地大多是沙漠 desert。而大峽谷 the Grand Canyon 位於此州的北部，所以北部大部分的地區都有山脈 mountains。同時，此區也擁有許多森林 many forests。

德州 Texas 也位在美國西南部地區，它大部分的土地都非常乾燥。然而德州許多地方富含石油 rich with oil。石油工業 oil industry 為德州重大的產業，德州同時也是全美最大的產油州 oil-producing states 之一。

Words to Know

- **cover** 覆蓋；遮蓋　• **practice** 執行；實施　• **conservation**（對自然資源的）保護；管理
- **flow through** 流經　• **diverse** 不同的；多種多樣的　• **rich with** 富含
- **industry** 工業；產業　• **oil-producing** 產油的　• **entire** 全部的；整個的

For many years, / people in the South / owned black African slaves. In the 1860s, / the United States / **fought the Civil War** / because of **slavery**.

During the war, / all of the slaves / **were freed**. But there were / still many problems / between blacks and whites. There was / a lot of **discrimination** / against blacks. This means / they **were** not **treated** / **fairly**. Also, / blacks and whites / in the South / **were segregated**. So they ate / at separate restaurants. They went to separate schools. And they even sat / in separate places on buses.

But in the 1950s, / the Civil Rights Movement / began in the South. Blacks began **demanding** / equal treatment. The most famous leader / of the **movement** / was Martin Luther King, Jr. Blacks often **organized** / **boycotts** of different places. They had **sit-ins** / at restaurants / where they **were** not **allowed to** eat. King tried to use / **nonviolence**. But the police and others / often used violence / against blacks. Still, / in 1964, / **the Civil Rights Act** / was passed. It **guaranteed** / equal rights / for people of all colors.

多年以來 for many years，美國南部的 in the South 人擁有自己的非洲黑奴 black African slaves。在 1860 年代，美國因著奴問題 because of slavery 引發了南北戰爭 the Civil War。

戰爭期間，所有的奴隸都獲得自由 be freed。然而，黑人和白人之間仍存在許多問題。黑人依舊飽受歧視 a lot of discrimination against blacks，這意味著他們並沒有受到平等的待遇 not treated fairly。此外，南方的黑人與白人 blacks and whites 之間實行了種族隔離 be segregated，所以他們在不同的 separate 餐廳吃飯、上不同的學校，甚至在公車上都要坐不同的區域。

但是在 1950 年代，美國南方開始了民權運動 the Civil Rights Movement。黑人開始要求平等的對待 demand equal treatment。其中最有名的領導人士 the most famous leader 就是馬丁路德 · 金恩 Martin Luther King, Jr.。黑人常在不同的地方進行聯合抵制 organize boycotts，他們在禁止黑人飲食的餐廳靜坐抗議 have sit-ins。金恩博士試圖使用非暴力手段 use nonviolence，然而警方以及其他人卻經常使用暴力 use violence 來對待黑人。《民權法案》the Civil Rights Act 直到 1964 年才通過，保障 guarantee 了不論膚色，所有人 people of all colors 的平等權 equal rights。

Words to Know

- **the Civil Rights Movement** 民權運動　• **fight** 打（仗）　• **the Civil War** 內戰（南北戰爭）
- **slavery** 奴隸制度　• **be freed** 被釋放　• **discrimination** 歧視　• **be treated** 被對待
- **fairly** 公平地　• **be segregated** 被隔離　• **demand** 需求；要求
- **movement**（社會）運動；活動　• **organize** 組織；安排　• **boycott** 抵制　• **sit-in** 靜坐抗議
- **be allowed to** 被允許；能夠　• **nonviolence** 非暴力行為　• **the Civil Rights Act** 民權法案
- **guarantee** 保證；保障

Short Stories From the Northeast 東北部的短篇小説

Many of the first **settlers** / from Europe / went to the Northeast part / of the United States. Most of them / were English. They lived / in New York and Pennsylvania. A lot of them lived / in the Hudson River **Valley** area / in New York. Some great American **literature** / comes from this area.

The writer Washington Irving / wrote many stories / about this area. One of the most famous / was *Rip van Winkle*. It **takes place** / in the Catskill Mountains / in New York. In the story, / Rip goes off / in the mountains / by himself. After meeting some **ghosts**, / he sleeps / for twenty years. Then he wakes up, / returns to his **village**, / and sees how life has changed.

Another famous story / by Irving / was *The **Legend** of Sleepy Hollow*. It **was** also **set in** / **upstate** New York. It involved / the **Headless** Horseman, / who was the ghost of a man / with no head. Instead, / he had a **jack-o'-lantern** / for a head.

These stories and others / by Irving / became important / in American culture. They **depicted** / early life in the Northeast. And millions of children and adults / have read them / **ever since**.

許多來自歐州的首批移民者 **first settlers** 前往美國的東北部 **the Northeast part**。他們大部分都是英國人 **English**。這些人定居於紐約和賓夕法尼亞州。這當中有很多人住在紐約的哈德遜河谷區 **the Hudson River Valley area**。美國有些偉大的文學作品 **some great American literature** 就是來自此區。

作家華盛頓‧歐文 **Washington Irving** 寫了許多關於此區的小説 **write many stories**，其中最有名的就屬《李伯大夢》**Rip van Winkle**。這個故事發生在紐約的卡茨基爾山。在故事中，李伯 **Rip** 自行前往山上 **go off in the mountains**。在遇見一些鬼魂後，他沉睡了二十年 **sleep for twenty years**。當李伯醒來 **wake up** 後回到村莊，卻發現人事已非 **see how life has changed**。

歐文另一個著名的小説是《沉睡谷傳奇》**The Legend of Sleepy Hollow**，故事的背景仍設定在紐約州北部。這是一個關於無頭騎士 **the Headless Horseman** 的故事。這個男鬼魂沒有頭，長著一個南瓜頭 **jack-o'-lantern**。

歐文所著的上述小説以及其他故事，在美國文化中非常重要。它們刻畫了美國東北部的早期生活 **depict early life in the Northeast**。從那時起 **ever since**，它們就是無數大人和小孩必讀 **have read** 的作品。

Words to Know

- **settler** 移民者　- **valley** 河谷；山谷　- **literature** 文學　- **take place** 發生　- **ghost** 鬼魂
- **village** 村莊　- **legend** 傳説　- **be set in** 以……為背景　- **upstate New York** 紐約州北部
- **headless** 無頭的　- **jack-o'-lantern**（中空式）南瓜燈　- **depict** 描繪；描寫
- **ever since** 自此之後

The first people / to America / came from Asia. They crossed / a **land bridge**, / a **narrow strip** of land / that **connected** Russia and Alaska. It was / just ice / that connected the continents / across the sea. Then, / they **traveled down** / into the land / from North to South America. They became / **Native Americans**.

In the area / that became the United States, / there were / a large number of tribes. Some were / very powerful. Others were not. All of the tribes / lived off the land. Some were **nomads**. They followed / **herds** of buffalo / all year long. Others lived in small groups / or villages. They knew / how to farm. They grew / **various** crops. And they also hunted / and fished.

第一批來到美洲的人 the first people to America 來自亞洲 come from Asia。他們橫跨一座陸橋 cross a land bridge，也就是連接俄國與阿拉斯加的狹長土地 a narrow strip of land，而連接兩塊大陸的僅是海面上的冰層。接著，這批人順著陸路從北美洲走到 travel down 了南美洲，他們就是印地安人 become Native Americans。

在成為美國的這片國土上，住著為數眾多的印地安部落 a large number of tribes，其中一些部落十分強大，其他則不然。全數的部落都以土地為生 live off the land，其中有些是游牧民 nomad，終年逐水牛群而居 follow herds of buffalo，其他則是過著小團體生活或住在村落裡 live in small groups or villages。這些部落族人知道如何耕作 know how to farm，種植各式作物 grow various crops，此外他們還會狩獵與捕魚 hunt and fish。

- **land bridge** 陸橋　• **narrow** 狹窄的　• **strip** 條；帶　• **connect** 連接
- **travel down** 遷移；移動　• **Native American** 美洲原住民；印第安人　• **nomad** 遊牧者
- **herd** 畜群　• **various** 不同的；各式各樣的

18 Three Great American Empires 美洲三大帝國

The first Americans / from Asia / **settled** in North and South America. As they learned to farm / and made their homes, / they built towns and cities. Some of these people / made great empires. The three great American empires / were **the Maya, Aztec, and Inca**.

The first / were the Mayans. They lived in Central America. They lived in the jungle. But they had / a great empire. They were very advanced. The Mayans knew / how to write / by drawing pictures. They were also good at math. They built / many **amazing temples** / and other buildings.

The Aztecs / lived in North America. Their **capital** / was in **modern-day** Mexico. They were very **warlike**. They fought / many **battles**. And they often defeated / their enemies.

The Incas / lived in South America. They **ruled** / much land there. And they built cities / high in **the Andes Mountains**.

第一批來自亞洲的美洲人定居在北美洲和南美洲 in North and South America。就在他們學習農耕，建造自己的家園的同時，也興建城鎮與都市，其中有些人建立了偉大的帝國 great empires。這三個偉大的美洲帝國 the three great American empires，分別是馬雅帝國 the Maya (Empire)、阿茲提克帝國 the Aztec (Empire) 和印加帝國 the Inca (Empire)。

第一個帝國由馬雅人 the Mayans 創立。馬雅人定居中美洲 in Central America，生活在叢林中 in the jungle，不過他們的帝國仍然強大。馬雅人十分先進 very advanced，他們懂得運用繪畫 by drawing pictures 來書寫 to write，同時他們的數學能力很好 good at math，興建了壯觀的神殿與其他建築 build temples and other buildings。

阿茲提克人 the Aztecs 居於北美洲 in North America，帝國的首都就在今日的墨西哥。阿茲提克族非常好戰 very warlike，參與過許多戰役 fight many battles，而且通常都讓對手吃下敗仗。

印加人 the Incas 居住在南美洲 in South America，統治了南美大半土地 rule much land，甚至在高聳的安地斯山區 in the Andes Mountains 建立起城市。

Words to Know

- **empire** 帝國   • **settle** 移居；殖民   • **the Maya** 馬雅   • **the Aztec** 阿茲提克
- **the Inca** 印加   • **amazing** 令人驚異的   • **temple** 神殿；寺廟   • **capital** 首都
- **modern-day** 現代的；今日的   • **warlike** 好戰的   • **battle** 戰役   • **rule** 統治；管理
- **the Andes Mountain** 安地斯山

Today, / there are / many Native American tribes / in North America. In the past, / there were many more. However, / some of them, / like the Mayans and Aztecs, / disappeared. This happened / to another tribe of Native Americans / many centuries ago. They were the Anasazi.

The Anasazi lived in the area / that is the Southwest today. They lived in that area / more than a thousand years ago. They had / an **impressive** culture. They made / their own **unique pottery**. And some of them / even lived in homes / built into **cliffs**.

However, / around 1200, / they suddenly disappeared. No one is sure / what happened. Some people believe / another tribe defeated the Anasazi / in war. Others believe / that a **disease** killed them. But most **archaeologists** think / there was a drought. The area in the Southwest / where they lived / gets very little rain. The Anasazi had / a lot of people / in their tribes. If it did not rain / for a while, / they would have / quickly / **run out of** water. Perhaps / a drought caused them / to move to another area. Today, / only **artifacts** / and the **ruins** of Anasazi buildings / **remain**. No one knows / where the people went, / though.

現今北美洲有許多印地安部落 native American tribes，過去定居於此的部落更多，然而其中像是馬雅人 the Mayans 和阿茲提克人 the Aztecs 都已不復存在 disappear。這樣的情況在數個世紀以前 many centuries ago，也曾發生 happen 在另一個印地安部落身上，他們是阿納薩齊人 the Anasazi。

一千多年前，阿納薩齊人居住於現今的美國西南部地區。他們有個令人印象深刻的文化 impressive culture：獨特的手工陶器 unique pottery。部分族人甚至住在嵌入懸崖的房子 home built into cliffs 裡。

然而，在 1200 年左右，阿納薩齊人突然消失 suddenly disappear 了，沒有人確定發生了什麼事 no one is sure what happened。有人相信另一個部落在戰爭中擊敗 defeat 了阿納薩齊人，也有人認為他們是感染疾病而滅亡，多數考古學家 most archaeologists 則認為是旱災 drought 所致。當時阿納薩齊人居住的西南部地區雨水稀少 get very little rain，然而部落的人口眾多，只要一陣子不下雨，很快就會缺水 run out of water，也許是某次旱災使他們遷移到別處 move to another area。如今，僅存工藝品 artifacts 和阿納薩齊建築遺跡 ruins，至於他們到哪裡去了卻不得而知。

Words to Know

- **the Anasazi** 阿納薩齊人　• **impressive** 令人印象深刻的　• **unique** 獨特的　• **pottery** 陶器
- **cliff** 懸崖；峭壁　• **disease** 疾病　• **archaeologist** 考古學家　• **run out of** 用光
- **artifact** 手工藝品　• **ruins** 遺跡；廢墟　• **remain** 剩下；餘留

The Fall of the Aztec and Inca Empires

阿茲提克帝國和印加帝國的衰敗

Christopher Columbus **discovered** / the New World / in 1492. After him, / many Europeans / began to **explore** / the land. Most of the early explorers / came from **Spain**. The **arrival** of the Spanish / in the Americas / changed the Native American empires / forever.

The Spanish wanted to get rich. So they looked for / gold, silver, and other **treasures** / in the Americas. Both the Aztecs and the Incas / had / a lot of gold and silver / that the Spanish wanted. The Spanish **made war** / **on** them. In 1521, / Spanish **soldiers** / **led by** Hernando Cortés / defeated the Aztec Empire. In 1532, / another Spanish **conquistador**, / Francisco Pissarro, / **conquered** the Inca Empire. The Spanish were very **cruel** / to the natives. After their **conquests**, / the Spanish **enslaved** the natives / and took their treasures back to Spain.

克里斯多福・哥倫布 Christopher Columbus 在 1492 年發現了新大陸 discover the New World。自他以降，許多歐洲人 many Europeans 便開始探索這塊土地 explore the land。大部分早期的探險家 the early explorers 來自西班牙，他們抵達美洲，永久改變 change forever 了美洲原住民的帝國。

西班牙人 the Spanish 想要致富 want to get rich，因此在美洲尋找 look for 金銀財寶。阿茲提克人和印加人 the Aztecs and the Incas 擁有許多金礦銀礦 have a lot of gold and silver，令西班牙人覬覦。西班牙人對他們發動戰爭 make war。1521 年時，由赫南多・科特斯所帶領的西班牙軍隊擊敗了阿茲提克帝國 defeat the Aztec Empire。1532 年時，另一位西班牙征服者法蘭西斯克・皮澤洛征服了印加帝國 conquer the Inca Empire。西班牙人對待原住民非常殘忍 very cruel to the natives，他們征服這些帝國之後，便奴役這些原住民 enslave the natives，並將他們的財寶帶回西班牙。

Words to Know

- **discover** 發現　• **explore** 探險　• **Spain** 西班牙　• **arrival** 到達；抵達
- **treasure** 財富；貴重物品　• **make war on** 對……發動戰爭　• **soldier** 士兵；軍人
- **led by** 由……領導　• **conquistador** 征服者　• **conquer** 戰勝；攻取　• **cruel** 殘酷的
- **conquest** 征服；佔領　• **enslave** 奴役

In the 1400s, / European explorers / were only interested in / finding a **water route** / to Asia / to become **wealthy**. They did not know / how large the world was. But after Columbus's **voyages** / to the Americas, / many Europeans **set sail** / for the Americas.

Spanish explorers went to / **present-day** Florida. They went to Mexico / and other places in Central America. And they went to / South America, / too.

The **Portuguese** / mostly went to / South America. They founded **colonies** / in Brazil.

The French soon followed. They landed in / present-day / Canada. The French **claimed** / very large areas of land / in Canada / and settled in there.

The English went to / present-day Virginia and Massachusetts.

在 1400 年代，歐洲探險家 European explorers 只想找到通往亞洲的水路 find a water route to Asia，好讓自己致富 to become wealthy。他們不知道世界有多大。但是在哥倫布航向美洲之後 after Columbus's voyages to the Americas，許多歐洲人也向美洲啟航 set sail for the Americas。

西班牙探險家 Spanish explorers 到達了今日的 present-day 佛羅里達州，還抵達了墨西哥與中美洲的其他地區，他們也踏上南美洲的土地。

葡萄牙人 the Portuguese 主要前往南美洲，在巴西建立了殖民地 found colonies。

法國人 the French 隨後亦跟上腳步，他們於現今的加拿大登陸 land。法國人在加拿大奪下大塊土地 claim very large areas of land 並就此定居 settle in。

英國人 the English 則是來到了今日的維吉尼亞州和麻薩諸塞州。

Words to Know

- **water route** 水路　　· **wealthy** 富有的　　· **voyage** 航海；航行　　· **set sail** 開航
- **present-day** 現今的；今日的　　· **the Portuguese** 葡萄牙人　　· **colony** 殖民地；移居地
- **claim** 要求；索取

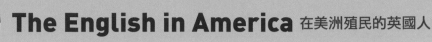

22 The English in America 在美洲殖民的英國人

The Spanish came to the New World / for gold. But the English had / another **reason** / to go there. They wanted **colonies**. The English settled / in North America. They started / many colonies. Two were / Virginia and Massachusetts.

The first English colony / was Jamestown. It was in Virginia. Life was very hard / for the colonists. Many **died of** / **hunger** and disease. But more and more people / came from England. Many of them / wanted new lives / in America. They came / for **religious freedom**. That was / why **the Pilgrims and Puritans** came. They founded colonies / near Boston. They lived in Massachusetts.

西班牙人為了黃金 for gold 來到了新大陸 the New World，但是英國人 the English 卻是為了別的理由踏上這裡：他們想要殖民地 want colonies。英國人在北美洲定居 settle in North America，建立了許多殖民地 start many colonies，其中兩個是維吉尼亞州與麻薩諸塞州 Virginia and Massachusetts。

第一個英國的殖民地 the first English colony 是詹姆士鎮 Jamestown，位於維吉尼亞州。殖民地開拓者的生活很困苦 life is very hard，許多人死於飢餓與疾病 die of hunger and disease，但仍然有越來越多人從英國來到這裡。許多移居者希望在美洲展開新生活 want new lives，他們為了宗教自由 for religious freedom 而來，這正是移民先輩 the Pilgrims 與英國清教徒 the Puritans 到美洲的原因。這些移居者在波士頓附近 near Boston 建立殖民地 found colonies，定居於麻薩諸塞州。

Words to Know

· **reason** 理由；原因　· **colony** 殖民地　· **die of** 死於……　· **hunger** 飢餓　· **religious** 宗教的
· **freedom** 自由　· **the Pilgrims** 1620 年搭五月花號到美洲的英國清教徒　· **the Puritans** 清教徒

Over 5,000 years ago, / Egyptian civilization began. It **was centered on** / **the Nile River**. Every year, / the Nile flooded. The water from the floods / made / the land around the Nile / very rich. So it was good for / **farming**. This let a civilization / start in Egypt.

Egyptian life was centered on / the **pharaohs**. They were / god-kings / who ruled the entire land. Most Egyptians were slaves. They lived their lives / to serve the pharaohs. The pharaohs were very wealthy. They built huge **monuments**. They also **constructed** / the **pyramids** and **the Sphinx**. There are / many pyramids / all through Egypt.

Egypt also had / its own form of writing. It was called / **hieroglyphics**. It was / a kind of picture writing. It didn't use letters. Instead, / it used pictures. They represented / different sounds and words.

埃及文明 Egyptian civilization 起源於五千多年前，以尼羅河為中心 be centered on the Nile River。尼羅河每年都會氾濫 flood，氾濫的河水 floods 為尼羅河兩岸帶來肥沃的 very rich 土地，故有利於農業 be good for farming，這也開啟了埃及文明的大門。

埃及人的生活以法老為中心 be centered on the pharaohs，法老是統治整個國家的神王 god-king。大部分的埃及人 most Egyptians 都是奴隸 slaves，他們為服侍法老 serve the pharaohs 而活。法老非常富有，他們建造了巨大的紀念碑 huge monuments，蓋了金字塔 the pyramids 以及獅身人面像 the Sphinx。埃及到處遍布著許多金字塔。

埃及有屬於自己的書寫方式 form of writing，稱作象形文字 hieroglyphics，它是一種圖畫書寫的形式 a kind of picture writing。象形文字不使用字母 don't use letters，而是 instead 運用圖畫來表達意義。這些圖畫各自代表著不同的聲音與詞彙。

Words to Know

- **Egyptian** 埃及人；埃及的　• **civilization** 文明　• **be centered on** 以……為中心
- **the Nile (River)** 尼羅河　• **farming** 農業　• **pharaoh** 法老（古埃及國王）　• **monument** 紀念碑
- **construct** 建造　• **pyramid** 金字塔　• **the Sphinx** 獅身人面像　• **hieroglyphics** 象形文字

24 Early Indus Civilization 早期的印度河文明

In the Indus Valley, / which is in modern-day India and Pakistan, / an early civilization **formed** / long ago. It lasted / from around 2500 B.C. / to 1500 B.C. It **is** also **known** / **as** the Harappan civilization.

The people / in the Indus Valley civilization / mostly farmed the land. So they knew / the **secret** of agriculture. This let them / stop living as nomads. But they were not / just farmers. They also built / many cities. Archaeologists have found / several settlements / where there were cities. They built / **palaces**, temples, baths, and other buildings. They also planned their cities / on a **grid pattern**. So they **were laid out** / in **squares**.

The people of the Indus Valley / were advanced / in other ways, / too. They made pottery. They made **objects** / from both **copper** and **bronze**. And they even had / their own writing system. It **was based on** / **pictographs**. But it has not yet **been translated**. The Indus Valley / was one of the world's first **civilized** areas. Little is known / about it. But **researchers** are learning / more and more / every year.

很久以前，早期的文明 an early civilization 在印度河流域 in the Indus Valley 一帶建立，即今日的印度與巴基斯坦，此文明又稱作哈拉帕文明 the Harappan civilization，大約從西元前 2500 年持續 last 到西元前 1500 年。

生活在印度河流域文明 the Indus Valley civilization 的人們大多耕種土地 farm the land，所以他們曉得農業上的訣竅，這使他們不再過游牧民族的生活 stop living as nomads。不過他們不只是農夫，他們還建造了多個城市 build many cities。考古學家發現多處曾是城市的遺跡 several settlements，他們造了宮殿、廟宇、浴場與其他建物。他們還將城市規劃成棋盤狀 on a grid pattern，以方格的形狀呈現 be laid out in squares。

印度河流域的人民在其他方面也相當進步，他們製陶、以銅與青銅製作物品 make object from copper and bronze，他們甚至還有自己的一套書寫系統 writing system。此系統是依據象形文字 be based on pictographs 而來，但目前尚未得以翻譯。

印度河流域是世界上最早出現文明的地方之一，有關此地的資訊甚少 little is known，但研究學者在此地的知識上每年都有所斬獲。

Words to Know

- **form** 形成 **be known as** 被叫做 **secret** 秘密 **palace** 宮殿 **grid pattern** 格子圖形
- **be laid out** 被規畫 **square** 正方形 **object** 物品 **copper** 銅 **bronze** 青銅
- **be based on** 以……為根據 **pictograph** 象形文字 **be translated** 被翻譯
- **civilized** 文明的；開化的 **researcher** 研究者

There were / many **city-states** / in ancient Greece. They **controlled** / the land around them. Two of the most famous / were Athens and Sparta. These two city-states / were very different / from each other.

First, / Athens was / the **birthplace** of **democracy**. It let **regular people** / **vote** and help **run** the city. Athens had / a very open society. There were slaves / in Athens, / but many people / were still free. Sparta was a lot different. It was / a very **warlike** city-state. The men there / trained to be soldiers / from a young age. And the Spartans owned / many slaves, / too. Sparta and Athens / sometimes fought wars / against each other.

Athens is also known for / its many **accomplishments**. There were / many great **thinkers** / in Athens. Socrates and Plato / were / two of the world's greatest **philosophers**. Plato recorded / many of his and Socrates's **thoughts**. People still read / his works / today.

古希臘 in ancient Greece 有許多城邦 city-states，這些城邦控制了它們四周的土地。其中兩個最有名的就是雅典 Athens 和斯巴達 Sparta，這兩個城邦彼此大相逕庭。

首先，雅典是民主的發源地 the birthplace of democracy，它讓平民 regular people 投票並協助城邦的運作。雅典是一個非常開放的社會 open society，它有奴隸 slaves 的存在，但許多人仍是自由的 many people are still free。斯巴達與雅典差異甚大，它是一個非常好戰的 very warlike 城邦，男人自幼 from a young age 便被訓練成為戰士 trained to be soldiers，斯巴達人也擁有許多自己的奴隸 own many slaves，有時候斯巴達和雅典之間會互相征戰 fight wars。

雅典以許多成就 accomplishments 而著名，雅典 in Athens 有許多大思想家 great thinkers，像蘇格拉底和柏拉圖 Socrates and Plato 就是世界上最偉大的兩位哲學家 two of the world's greatest philosophers。柏拉圖記錄了許多自己和蘇格拉底的思想，人們如今仍舊閱讀著他的著作 his works。

Words to Know

- **ancient** 古代的　　• **city-state** 城邦　　• **control** 管理；控制　　• **birthplace** 出生地；發源地
- **democracy** 民主政體　　• **regular people** 平民　　• **vote** 投票　　• **run** 經營；管理
- **warlike** 好戰的　　• **accomplishment** 成就　　• **thinker** 思想家　　• **philosopher** 哲學家
- **thought** 想法；觀點

26 **All Roads Lead to Rome** 條條大路通羅馬

EUROPE

Black Sea

Rome

Constantinople

Carthage

Mediterranean Sea

ARABIA

AFRICA

Red Sea

☐ the Western Empire

☐ the Eastern Empire (= the Byzantine Empire)

When it ruled the most land, / the Roman Empire was enormous. It covered / much of the known world. To the north, / it **stretched** / **as far as** England. To the west, / it ruled land / in Spain and western Africa. To the south, / it covered / much land in Africa. And to the east, / it stretched / far into the Middle East. However, / the most important city / in the empire / was always Rome.

There was / an important **saying**: / All roads lead to Rome. At that time, / the emperors were trying to be connected / to their **provinces** / far from the **capital**. So they built / many roads. And all of them / led back to the capital. When Rome was **powerful**, / the empire was powerful, / too. When Rome was weak, / the empire was weak. In later years, / Rome was defeated by **invaders** / from Germany. How did the invaders / get to Rome? They went there / on one of the Roman roads!

羅馬帝國 the Rome Empire 版圖擴張至最大時，幅員非常遼闊 enormous。它佔領了已知世界的眾多土地，往北延伸至英國 as far as England，往西控制了西班牙和西非的土地 land in Spain and western Africa，往南佔領了非洲大部分的土地 much land in Africa，往東延伸至中東 far into the Middle East。然而，整個帝國最重要的城市 the most important city 始終是羅馬 Rome。

有句重要的諺語 saying 説道：「條條大路通羅馬 All roads lead to Rome.。」在當時，羅馬皇帝想將各偏遠省分連結到首都，因此建築了許多條道路 build many roads。這些道路都通向首都 lead back to the capital。羅馬強盛時，帝國隨之強盛；羅馬衰敗時，帝國亦隨之衰敗。多年後 in later years，羅馬被來自日耳曼的入侵者擊敗 be defeated by invaders from Germany。這些入侵者是如何抵達羅馬 get to Rome 呢？他們靠的就是羅馬的其中一條道路 on one of the Roman roads！

Words to Know

• **stretch** 延伸；連綿　• **as far as** 遠至……　• **saying** 諺語　• **province** 行省（古羅馬行政單位）
• **capital** 首都　• **powerful** 強大的　• **invader** 侵略者

The Spanish Conquer the New World 西班牙人征服新世界

When Christopher Columbus discovered / America / in 1492, / there were already / millions of people / living in the Americas. Some of them / had **formed** / great empires. Two of these / were / the Aztecs and the Incas. However, / after a few years, / the Spanish defeated / both of them.

The Aztec Empire was / in the area of modern-day Mexico. The Aztecs were / very warlike. They had conquered / many of their neighbors. But they did not have / modern **weapons** / like guns and **cannons**. In 1519, / Hernando Cortés **invaded** / the Aztec Empire. He only had / about 500 soldiers. But many **neighboring** tribes / **allied with** him. They **disliked** the Aztecs / very much. There were several battles / as Cortés and his men / marched to Tenochtitlan, / the Aztec capital. In 1521, / Cortés captured the city / and conquered the empire.

The Inca Empire was in South America / in the Andes Mountains. In 1531, / Francisco Pissarro arrived there / with 182 soldiers. At that time, / the Inca Empire was already weak. There had just been / a civil war / in the empire. By 1532, / Pizarro and his men / had captured the Incan emperor. The next year, / they put their own emperor / on the **throne**. They had succeeded / in defeating the Incas.

克里斯多福‧哥倫布於 1492 年發現美洲 discover America 時，當地已有數百萬的居民。他們有的建立起偉大的帝國 great empires，其中兩個便是阿茲提克 the Aztecs 和印加 the Incas。然而幾年之後，西班牙人卻把他們雙雙擊敗。

阿茲提克帝國 the Aztec Empire 位於現在的墨西哥地區 in the area of modern-day Mexico，是一個非常好戰的 very warlike 民族，也曾征服許多鄰國，但是他們並沒有槍砲這類的現代武器。赫南多‧科特斯 Hernando Cortés 於 1519 年侵略阿茲提克帝國 invade the Aztec Empire，雖然只帶了五百名左右的士兵，許多鄰近部落 many neighboring tribes 卻與之結盟 ally，這些部落對阿茲提克恨之入骨。科特斯和他的士兵行軍前往阿茲提克首都特諾奇提特蘭的路上，爆發了多場戰役。他最終在 1521 年攻下這座城市 capture the city，征服了這個帝國 conquer the empire。

印加帝國 the Inca Empire 位於南美洲的安地斯山脈 in the Andes Mountains。1531 年，法蘭西斯克‧皮澤洛 Francisco Pissarro 帶著 182 名士兵抵達此地。當時的印加帝國已經非常衰弱，他們才剛經歷了一場內戰 civil war。就在 1532 年，皮澤洛和他的士兵俘虜了印加帝國的帝王 capture the Incan emperor。隔年，他們將自己的帝王拱上寶座 put on the throne，成功地擊敗印加帝國。

Words to Know

・**form** 組成　・**weapon** 武器　・**cannon** 大砲　・**invade** 入侵　・**neighboring** 鄰近的
・**ally with** 與⋯⋯結盟　・**dislike** 厭惡；不喜歡　・**throne** 君權；王位

For centuries, / the Catholic Church **dominated** life / in Europe. But many **priests** / in the Church / were **corrupt**. They were more interested in / money and living a good life / than in religion. Some people were upset / about that. One of them / was Martin Luther. In 1517, / he posted his 95 theses / on a church door / in Wittenberg, Germany. They were / a list of his complaints / about the Church. This was the beginning / of the Protestant Reformation.

Luther did not intend / to form a new church. He only wanted to **reform** / the Roman Catholic Church. But the Church / called him a **heretic** / and **excommunicated** him. This caused a split / in Germany. Many of the German people / disliked the Church. But they wanted / to remain Christians. The Reformation soon / turned violent. In Germany, / **Catholics** and **Protestants** / fought against each other. This happened / until 1555. That year, / the Peace of Augsburg / allowed every German prince / to choose / to be Catholic or Protestant.

At the same time / as the problems in Germany, / the Reformation quickly moved / across Europe. Men / like Jean Calvin and Ulrich Zwingli / led their own **protests** / against the Church. Soon, / new Protestant **sects** / were founded. There was / the Lutheran sect. There were / **Presbyterians** and **Baptists**. There were also / Calvinists. And, in England, / **the Anglican Church** was founded / when Henry VIII **broke away** / from the Roman Catholic Church.

數個世紀以來，天主教會 the Catholic Church 掌管了歐洲的生活。但教會裡許多的神父腐敗不堪，對利益與優沃生活的關注，遠勝過宗教。有些人對此感到不滿，其中一位就是馬丁·路德 Martin Luther。1517 年時，他在德國威登堡的教堂門上發表了 95 條論綱 post 95 theses，表達他對教會的不滿 his complaints，這就是新教徒宗教改革 the Protestant Reformation 的開始。

路德起初僅想整頓 reform 羅馬天主教會，並無意自立門戶。但教會視他為異教徒 heretic 並開除了他。此舉造成了德國的宗教分裂 cause a split，許多德國人對教會心生不滿，卻依舊想當基督教徒。很快地，宗教改革如火如荼地展開，在德國，天主教徒與新教徒 Catholics and Protestants 相互攻擊 fight against each other。直到 1555 年，該年，奧格斯堡宗教合約 the Peace of Augsburg 讓每位德國貴族可以選擇成為天主教徒或新教徒。

就當德國遭遇問題的同一時間，宗教改革也很快地橫掃整個歐洲。像是約翰·喀爾文和烏利希·慈運理也各自主導反抗教會。新教徒教派 new Protestant sects 很快便成立了。有路德教派 the Lutheran sect、長老教派 Presbyterians、浸信會 Baptists，還有喀爾文教派 Calvinists。而在英國 in England，當國王亨利八世脫離羅馬天主教會時，英國還創立了英國國教派 the Anglican Church。

Words to Know

- **the Reformation** 宗教改革　　• **dominate** 控制　　• **priest** 神父；神職人員　　• **corrupt** 貪污的；腐敗的
- **reform** 整頓；改革　　• **heretic** 異教徒　　• **excommunicate** 逐出教會　　• **Catholic** 天主教徒
- **Protestant** 新教徒　　• **protest** 示威；抗議　　• **sect** 派別　　• **Presbyterian** 長老教派
- **Baptist** 浸信會　　• **the Anglican Church** 英國國教　　• **break away from** 從……脫離

The French Revolution 法國大革命

In France / in the eighteenth century, / life was difficult / for most people. The **ruler** of France / was the king. He ruled / by **divine right**. This was the idea / that God had chosen the king / to be the ruler. This meant / that the king could do anything / he wanted. There were also **nobles** / with great power / in France. The **clergy** mostly lived good lives, / too. But the rest of the people / had difficult lives.

In the 1780s, / the world was changing. The Americans had won / their revolution with England / and become free. The French people wanted / the same thing. King Louis XVI / and his wife, Marie Antoinette, / were **oppressive** rulers. They taxed the people / too much. But the people **became tired of** / their poor lives. So, on July 14, 1789, / they **rebelled**. They **stormed** the Bastille / on that day. It was a **prison** / in Paris. They freed the **prisoners** / and took the weapons / that were there. The French Revolution / had begun.

The French Revolution / was very violent. Louis XVI **was beheaded** / during the revolution. More nobles and clergy / were killed, too. Thousands of people died / during the revolution. In the end, / the **monarchy** was destroyed. But France did not become a democracy / like the people had hoped. Instead, / Napoleon Bonaparte, a general, / became the emperor of France. He would then lead France to war / with many European nations / until he was finally defeated / in 1815.

法國 18 世紀時，生活對大部分人民來説是困苦的。法國的統治者 the ruler of France 是國王，他藉由神授君權來掌權 rule by divine right，也就是神選擇了國王來治理國家。這表示國王可以為所欲為。法國還有主掌龐大權力的貴族 nobles，大多神職人員 the clergy 也都生活富裕，而其他人 the rest of the people 則是生活困苦 have difficult lives。

在 1780 年間，世界正在改變。美國人贏得與英國革命的勝利，獲得自由。法國人也想要如此。路易十六 King Louis XVI 與妻子瑪麗・安東尼 Marie Antoinette 是暴虐的統治者，他們對人民課以重税，人民則對貧苦的生活感到厭倦。因此，他們在 1789 年的 7 月 14 日起義 rebel，猛烈攻擊位於巴黎的巴士底監獄 storm the Bastille。他們解放犯人 prisoner，奪取該地的武器，法國大革命 the French Revolution 已揭開序幕。

法國大革命非常激進暴力，路易十六在革命期間遭到斬首 be beheaded，還有更多的貴族與教士遭到殺害，數千人死於革命期間。最後，君主政體 the monarchy 崩解 destroyed，但法國卻無如人民所盼那樣成為民主國家。反而是由一名將軍——拿破崙・波拿巴 Napoleon Bonaparte 成為法國君王 become the emperor。他帶領法國與許多歐洲國家作戰 lead to war，一直到他在 1815 年遭到擊敗為止。

Words to Know

- **ruler** 統治者　• **divine right** 神賜予的權力　• **noble** 貴族　• **clergy** 神職人員；教士
- **oppressive** 專制的　• **become tired of** 對……厭煩　• **rebel** 反抗；造反　• **storm** 猛烈攻擊
- **prison** 監獄　• **prisoner** 囚犯　• **be beheaded** 被斬首　• **monarchy** 君主政治

30 The Great War 世界大戰

For centuries, / European countries / had fought each other. But, from 1914 to 1918, / there was a different kind of war. It was a world war. At that time, / people called it the Great War. Later, / it was called World War I (WWI). At first, / people thought / it would just be another war. By the time it ended, / millions were dead. And many people **were horrified** / by the **carnage** of war.

Before WWI began, / many European countries / **had alliances** with each other. They promised to **defend** other countries / if they were in trouble. On June 28, 1914, / **Archduke** Francis Ferdinand of Austria-Hungary / **was assassinated** / in Sarajevo. The Austrians quickly **declared** war / on Serbia. However, / because of the different alliances, / what should have been a small war / became an enormous one. The Central Powers / led by Germany, Austria-Hungary, and the Ottoman Empire / were on one side. The Allied Powers / led by England, France, and Russia / were on the other side. The Germans **swiftly** attacked France. However, / the German advance was stopped. Neither side could move / against the other. Thus **trench warfare** began. For four years, / each side succeeded / in killing many of the other's soldiers. Tanks and airplanes were used in war / for the first time. So were / **chemical weapons**.

Finally, the war ended. But it didn't end war. Around two **decades** later, / World War II began. It was an even worse war / than WWI had been.

幾世紀以來，歐洲國家互相征戰。但從 1914 年到 1918 年出現了一種截然不同的戰爭型態，也就是世界大戰。當時的人民將之稱為世界大戰 the Great War，也就是後來的第一次世界大戰 World War I。人民剛開始以為這僅是另一場戰爭，當戰爭結束時，數百萬人死亡 millions are dead，許多人被戰爭的屠殺給嚇壞了 be horrified by the carnage of war。

第一次世界大戰開始前，許多歐洲國家 many European countries 相互結盟 have alliances with each other，若其他國家遭遇到麻煩，承諾要彼此保護。在 1914 年的 6 月 28 日，奧匈帝國的斐迪南大公 Archduke Francis Ferdinand 於薩拉耶佛遭到暗殺 be assassinated，奧地利人很快就向塞爾維亞宣戰 declare war on Serbia。但由於不同的聯盟關係，原本小型的戰爭轉變成大規模的戰爭。一方 on one side 是由德國、奧匈帝國、鄂圖曼帝國主導的同盟國 the Central Powers，另一方 on the other side 則是由英國、法國、俄國領導的協約國 the Allied Powers。德國人迅速地偷襲了法國，卻無法再前進，雙方僵持不下，於是開始了塹壕戰 trench warfare。雙方在這四年來都成功殺害許多士兵，坦克車與飛機也首次被用在作戰上，當然也有化學武器 chemical weapons。

這場戰爭終於結束了，卻沒有真正結束掉戰爭。大概 20 年後又發生了第二次世界大戰 World War II，這一次的戰爭比第一次世界戰爭來的更加慘烈 even worse war。

Words to Know

- **be horrified** 被嚇壞　　• **carnage** 大屠殺　　• **have an alliance** 同盟　　• **defend** 保護；捍衛
- **archduke** 大公爵　　• **be assassinated** 遭到刺殺　　• **declare** 宣告　　• **swiftly** 迅速地
- **trench warfare** 塹壕戰　　• **chemical weapon** 化學武器　　• **decade** 十年

Chapter

2

Science

Life Science

Earth Science

Physical Science

Let's grow some plants / in a garden. First, / we need some **seeds**. We have to plant the seeds / in the **soil**, / and then / we should give them water. After a few days or weeks, / the plants will start growing / above the ground. First, / they will be tiny, / but they will become taller / every day.

Now, / the plants need / **plenty of** sunlight, water, and **nutrients** / **in order to** get bigger. Slowly, / the **stems** will grow higher, / and the plants will get / **branches** and **leaves**. Some of them / will start to **blossom**. These blossoms will **turn into** fruit / we can eat later. A part of these blossoms / makes seeds. They help plants / make new plants.

　　我們在花園裡種一些植物 grow some plants 吧。首先，我們需要一些種子 need some seeds。我們必須把種子種在土裡 plant the seeds in the soil，然後澆水 give them water。經過幾天或幾個星期後，植物會開始長 start growing 出地面 above the ground。它們一開始長得只有一點點 will be tiny，但會變得一天比一天還高大 become taller。

　　現在，植物需要充足的陽光、水分和養分 need sunlight, water, and nutrients 才能夠茁壯 in order to get bigger。莖會慢慢地越長越高 grow higher，而植物也會開始長出枝葉 get branches and leaves。有的還會開花 blossom，而這些花之後會變成我們所吃的果實 turn into fruit。其中一部分的花會產生種子 make seeds，之後又長成新的植物 make new plants。

Words to Know

- **seed** 種子　　• **soil** 土壤　　• **plenty of** 許多的　　• **nutrient** 養分　　• **in order to** 為了要……
- **stem** 莖　　• **branch** 枝幹　　• **leaf** 樹葉　　• **blossom** 花苞　　• **turn into** 變成

Roots, Stems, and Leaves 根、莖、葉

Plants are made up of / many parts. Three of the most important / are their roots, stems, and leaves. All three of them / have various functions.

The roots are found / at the bottom of the plant. Roots grow / underground. They help **anchor** the plant / to the ground. This **keeps** the plant / **from being washed away** / by rain / or **blown away** / by the wind. Also, / a plant's roots help it / **extract** nutrients / from the ground. These nutrients include / water and various **minerals**.

The stems have / several important **responsibilities**. First, / they move water and nutrients / from the roots / to the leaves. They also **store** / some nutrients and water / if the plant has / too much of them. And they **transport** food, / such as **sap**, / down from the leaves / to the roots. Finally, / they provide support / for the leaves.

The leaves have / a very important role. They contain **chloroplasts**. These let **photosynthesis** / take place. Because of this, / plants can create sugar, / which they use for food. And they also take **carbon dioxide** / and turn it into **oxygen**. This lets / all of the other animals on Earth / breathe.

植物有許多構造 parts，其中最重要的三個是根 root、莖 stem 以及葉 leaf，他們都具備了各種功能 have various functions。

根位於植物的底部 at the bottom，生長在地下 grow underground，負責把植物固定 anchor the plant 在土地上，防止 keep from 植物被雨水沖走或是被風吹走。同時，植物也藉由根部來吸收土裡的水和各種礦物質等養分 extract nutrients。

莖部擔負幾個重責大任 important responsibilities。首先，它們將水和養分從根部輸送 move water and nutrients 到葉子。如果水分和養分過剩，莖也會將它們儲存 store 起來。莖也負責將像汁液這樣的養料從葉子往下輸送 transport down 到根部，最後還有支撐葉子的功能 provide support for the leaves。

葉子也佔有非常重要的角色，其包含的葉綠體 contain chloroplasts，能夠行使光合作用 let photosynthesis take place，如此植物才能製造糖分 create sugar 作為養料。同時，葉子吸入二氧化碳 carbon dioxide，將其轉換成氧氣，讓地球上所有其他動物都能呼吸 breathe。

Words to Know

- **anchor** 使固定　• **keep . . . from** 讓……遠離　• **be washed away** 被沖走
- **be blown away** 被吹走　• **extract** 吸收　• **mineral** 礦物質　• **responsibility** 責任
- **store** 儲存　• **transport** 輸送　• **sap** 汁液　• **chloroplast** 葉綠體
- **photosynthesis** 光合作用　• **carbon dioxide** 二氧化碳　• **oxygen** 氧氣

An animal's **habitat** / is very important. It has everything / an animal needs to survive. Most animals can't live / in other habitats. Fish live / in the water. They can't survive / in the desert. Deer live / in the forest. They can't survive / in the **jungle**.

What makes a habitat **unique**? There are many things. Two of them / are more important / than the others. They are / weather and **temperature**. These two / help certain plants / grow. Many animals use / these plants / for food and **shelter**. Without them, / the animals could not live / in those habitats.

動物的棲息地 animal's habitat 非常重要，那裡有動物生存所需的一切。大部分的動物都無法居住在其棲息地之外的地方。魚兒住在水中 in the water，無法在沙漠中 in the desert 生存。鹿住在森林裡 in the forest，不能在叢林裡 in the jungle 生存。

是什麼讓棲息地變得如此獨特 make unique 呢？有許多原因，其中有兩項最為重要，也就是天氣和氣溫 weather and temperature。這兩項條件幫助特定的植物生長 help certain plants grow。許多動物都會把這些植物 use these plants 當作食物和棲身之處 for food and shelter。少了它們 without them，動物就無法在那些地方存活。

· **habitat** 棲息地　·**jungle** 熱帶叢林　·**unique** 獨特的；無可匹敵的　·**temperature** 溫度
·**shelter** 避難

Living Things vs. Nonliving Things 生物與非生物

Everything on Earth / is either living / or nonliving. A living thing / is alive. A nonliving thing / is not alive. Both animals and plants / are living things. Rocks, air, and water / are nonliving things.

There are / many kinds of animals and plants. But they are similar / in some ways. All of them / need oxygen / to survive. They also need / food and water. When they eat and drink, / they get nutrients. Nutrients provide energy / for them. Most plants and animals / need sunlight, / too. Living things also can / make new living things / **like** themselves.

Nonliving things / are not alive. They cannot move. They cannot breathe. They cannot / make new things / like themselves.

所有在地球上的事物不是「生物」就是「非生物」。生物 living thing 是活生生的 alive 事物，非生物 nonliving thing 則沒有生命 not alive。動物與植物兩類都屬於生物，石頭、空氣和水則是非生物。

動物與植物 **animals and plants** 的種類十分多樣，但兩者在某些地方具有相似性：他們都需要氧氣 **need oxygen** 以維生，同樣地，他們也需要食物與水 **need food and water**。當他們進食與喝水時，可以從中汲取養分 **get nutrients**，而養分提供了他們能量。大部分的動植物也需要陽光 **need sunlight**，他們還可以製造出跟自己一樣的新生物 **make new living things**。

非生物沒有生命，也無法移動 **cannot move** 和呼吸 **breathe**，他們無法製造出如同自己的新事物 **cannot make new things**。

Words to Know

• **living thing** 生物　• **nonliving thing** 非生物　• **like** 相似

There are / five types of animals. They are / **mammals**, birds, **reptiles**, **amphibians**, and fish. They are all different / from each other.

Mammals are animals / like dogs, cats, cows, lions, tigers, and humans. They **give birth to** / live young. And they feed their young / with milk / from their mothers.

Birds have feathers, / and most of them can fly. Penguins, **hawks**, and **sparrows** / are birds.

Reptiles and amphibians / are similar. Both of them / lay eggs. Snakes are reptiles, / and frogs and **toads** / are amphibians. Amphibians live / on land / and in the water.

Fish live / in the water. They lay eggs. They use **gills** / to **take in** oxygen / from the water. Sharks, **bass**, and **catfish** / are all fish.

所有動物可以分成五類 **five types of animals**，分別是哺乳類 **mammal**、鳥類 **bird**、爬蟲類 **reptile**、兩棲動物 **amphibian** 和魚類 **fish**，每一類動物都和其他動物不同 **be different from each other**。

哺乳類是像狗、貓、母牛、獅子、老虎和人類。他們會產下寶寶 **give birth to live young**，而媽媽們會餵母奶給自己的小寶寶 **feed their young with milk**。

鳥類擁有羽毛 **have feathers**，絕大部分的鳥會飛 **can fly**；企鵝、老鷹、麻雀都屬於鳥類。

爬蟲類和兩棲動物相似度高 **be similar**，兩者都會下蛋 **lay eggs**。蛇是爬蟲類，而青蛙和蟾蜍則屬於兩棲動物。兩棲類動物居住在陸地和水中 **on land and in the water**。

魚生長在水裡 **in the water**，會產卵 **lay eggs**，利用鰓吸入水中的氧氣 **use gills to take in oxygen from the water**；鯊魚、鱸魚和鯰魚都屬於魚類。

Words to Know

- **mammal** 哺乳類　　• **reptile** 爬蟲類　　• **amphibian** 兩棲類　　• **give birth to** 生產
- **hawk** 老鷹　　• **sparrow** 麻雀　　• **toad** 蟾蜍　　• **gill** 鰓　　• **take in** 讓……進入　　• **bass** 鱸魚
- **catfish** 鯰魚

Warm-Blooded vs. Cold-Blooded Animals

恆溫動物與變溫動物

All animals / are either warm-blooded / or cold-blooded. This **refers to** / how the animals **maintain** / their body temperature.

Warm-blooded animals / can **regulate** / their body temperature. So, / even if it is very cold outside, / their bodies will stay warm. But warm-blooded animals / have to eat / a lot of food. They use the food / to produce energy. That helps / keep their bodies warm. Mammals are warm-blooded, / and so are birds.

Cold-blooded animals / **rely upon** the sun / for heat. So their **internal** temperatures / can change / all the time. These animals often / rest in the sun / for hours. This lets their bodies / **soak up** heat / and become warm. Most cold-blooded animals / don't live / in cold places. They prefer hot places / instead. Reptiles, amphibians, and fish / are all cold-blooded.

所有的動物 **all animals** 不是恆溫動物就是變溫動物 **warm-blooded or cold-blooded**，主要視他們如何維持體溫 **body temperature** 而定。

恆溫動物 **warm-blooded animal** 可以控制 **regulate** 自己的體溫，所以，就算室外很冷，牠們的身體仍能保持溫暖 **stay warm**，但恆溫動物需要大量進食 **eat a lot of food**，牠們利用食物產生能量 **to produce energy** 來維持體溫 **keep their bodies warm**，哺乳類 **mammal** 和鳥類 **bird** 都屬於恆溫動物。

變溫動物 **cold-blooded animal** 則靠陽光 **rely upon the sun** 來獲取熱能，因此牠們的體溫 **internal temperature** 一直隨著時間而變化 **change all the time**，這些動物通常會在太陽底下休息 **rest in the sun** 好幾個小時 **for hours**，讓身體吸收熱能 **soak up heat**、變得溫暖。大部分的變溫動物不會居住在寒冷的地方，反之，它們會選擇溫暖的地方 **prefer hot places**。爬蟲類 **reptile**、兩棲類 **amphibian** 以及魚類 **fish** 都屬於變溫動物。

Words to Know

- **warm-blooded** 溫血的；恆溫的　　• **cold-blooded** 冷血的；變溫的　　• **refer to** 指的是
- **maintain** 維持　　• **regulate** 調節　　• **rely upon** 依賴　　• **internal** 內部的　　• **soak up** 吸收

There are / many kinds of insects. They **include** / ants, bees, butterflies, **grasshoppers**, and **crickets**. They look different / from each other. But they have / the same body parts / **in common**.

All insects have / three main body parts. They are / the head, **thorax**, and **abdomen**. The head has / the insect's mouth, eyes, and **antennae**. An insect uses / its antennae / to feel and taste things. The thorax is / the middle body part. It has / three pairs of legs. Adult insects have / six legs. Some insects have / wings / on their bodies. The abdomen is / the third and final part / of the insect.

　　昆蟲有許多種類 many kinds of insects，包括螞蟻、蜂、蝴蝶、蚱蜢和蟋蟀，每一種的外觀皆不相同 look different from each other，然而身體部分的結構卻一樣 the same body parts。

　　所有昆蟲的身體主要分成三部分 three main body parts，分別是頭部 head、胸部 thorax 和腹部 abdomen。頭部包括昆蟲的嘴、眼睛和觸角。昆蟲利用觸角來感覺與辨識事物的味道。胸部是身體的中間部位 the middle body part，包含有三對腳 three pairs of legs。成蟲 adult insect 擁有六隻腳 six legs，有些昆蟲身體上還附有翅膀 wings。腹部是第三個部分，也是昆蟲的最後一個部位 the third and final part。

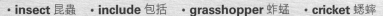

Words to Know

· **insect** 昆蟲　　· **include** 包括　　· **grasshopper** 蚱蜢　　· **cricket** 蟋蟀
· **in common** 相同的；共有的　　· **thorax** 胸　　· **abdomen** 腹　　· **antenna** 觸角

44

The Life Cycles of Cats and Frogs 貓和青蛙的生命週期

Every animal has / a life cycle. This is the **period** / from birth to death.

Cats are mammals, / so they are born / **alive**. Baby cats are called / kittens. A mother cat / **takes care of** / her kittens / for many weeks. The mother cat / feeds her kittens / with milk / from her body. As the kittens get bigger, / they become / more **independent**. After about one year, / they become **adult** cats, / and they can take care of / themselves.

Frogs have / different life cycles. Frogs are born / in eggs. When they **hatch**, / they are called / **tadpoles**. Tadpoles have / long tails and no legs. They use gills / to breathe / in the water. Soon, / they grow legs / and start to use **lungs** / to breathe. Later, / they can leave the water. When this happens, / they become adult frogs.

每種動物都擁有生命週期 life cycle，一個從出生到死亡 from birth to death 的階段。

貓 cat 屬於哺乳動物，能直接產下幼兒 born alive。貓寶寶被稱為小貓 kitten，貓媽媽會照顧小貓數週，用身體產生的母奶餵養自己的寶寶 feed her kitten with milk。當小貓越長越大時，會漸漸變得獨立 become independent。大約一年後，小貓長成成貓 adult cat，便可以照顧好自己 take care of themselves。

青蛙 frog 擁有不同的生命週期。青蛙從卵裡面出生 born in eggs，它們被孵化後，稱作「蝌蚪」tadpole。蝌蚪有長尾巴，沒有腳 long tail and no legs，它們使用鰓在水中呼吸 use gills to breathe。不久，蝌蚪長出了腳 grow legs，開始用肺呼吸 use lungs to breathe，之後它們便可以離開水 leave the water。當這個情況發生了，它們就變成了成蛙 adult frog。

Words to Know

- **life cycle** 生命週期　· **period** 時期　· **alive** 活著的　· **take care of** 照顧
- **independent** 獨立的　· **adult** 成熟的　· **hatch** 孵化　· **tadpole** 蝌蚪　· **lung** 肺

Every plant, / like pine trees, / has its own life cycle. A pine tree's life cycle / begins with a seed. Adult pine trees / have **pine cones**. Inside the pine cones / are tiny seeds. Every year, / many pine cones / fall to the ground. Some of them / stay near the pine tree, / but other times, / animals pick them up / and move them. The wind and rain / might move them, / too. Sometimes, / the seeds fall out of the pine cones / and **get buried** / in the ground. They often start to **sprout**. These are called / **seedlings**. These seedlings / get bigger and bigger. After many years, / they become / adult pine trees. Then they too / have pine cones / with seeds. So a new life cycle / begins again.

每一棵植物，如松樹，都有自己的生命週期 its own life cycle。松樹的生命週期 a pine tree's life cycle 從一顆種子開始 begin with a seed。長大的松樹會結松果 pine cone，松果內部全都是微小的種子 tiny seeds。每一年都有許多松果掉落在地上 pine cones fall to the ground，有些會停留在原本的松樹附近，但有時會有動物將它們拾起，帶到不同地方去，風和雨水也可能使松果移動。有時候，種子會從松果裡掉出來 fall out of the pine cone，埋入泥土中 get buried in the ground。通常這些種子會開始發芽 sprout，它們也稱為「幼苗」seedling。幼苗越長越大 get bigger and bigger，經過數年之後，長成了成松 adult pine tree，又可以結成含有種子的松果 have pine cones with seeds。新的生命週期 a new life cycle 便又展開了 begins again。

40 **Photosynthesis** 光合作用

Every living creature / needs food and water / to survive. Without food and water, / a creature would die. Plants are also / living creatures. So they need to / have these things, / too. Plants can create / their own food. They do this / in a **process** / called photosynthesis.

Plants need sunlight / in order to make energy. First, / when the sun **shines**, / **chlorophyll** in the plants / captures the sunlight. Sunlight is just energy. So the chlorophyll / is capturing energy. Then a plant needs / two more things: / water and carbon dioxide. That is / when photosynthesis can take place. In photosynthesis, / a plant **undergoes** / a **chemical reaction**. Thanks to the chlorophyll, / it creates sugar. The plant **feeds on** / the sugar. The reaction also produces / oxygen. The plant **releases** oxygen / into the air, / and people breathe it. So, / without photosynthesis, / people could not survive / either.

　　每一個生物體 living creature 都需要水和食物來生存，缺乏水和食物 without water and food，生物就會死亡。植物也是生物體，因此也需要這些東西。植物可以自行製造食物 create their own food，而這個製造的過程 in a process 稱作「光合作用」photosynthesis。

　　植物需要陽光 need sunlight 來產生能量。首先，當太陽照射時，植物體中的葉綠素 chlorophyll 會汲取陽光 capture the sunlight，陽光就是能量，也就是說葉綠素是在吸收能量。接著，植物還需要另外兩個東西 need two more things：水以及二氧化碳 water and carbon dioxide。這就是光合作用發生的時候。光合作用中，植物會經歷一種化學反應 chemical reaction，由於有葉綠素，光合作用產生了糖分 create sugar，植物也從中得到滋養。這個反應也會產生氧氣 produce oxygen，植物釋放氧氣 release oxygen 到空氣中，人們才得以吸入 people breathe it。所以，沒有光合作用 without photosynthesis，人們也無法存活 cannot survive。

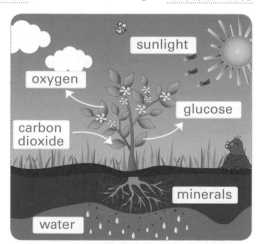

Words to Know

- **process** 過程　• **shine** 發光；照耀　• **chlorophyll** 葉綠素　• **undergo** 經歷　• **chemical** 化學的
- **reaction** 反應　• **feed on** 以……為食；得到養分　• **release** 釋放

What Is a <u>Food Chain</u> 何謂食物鏈

All animals must eat / to survive. Some eat plants. Some eat animals. And others eat / both plants and animals. A food chain shows / the relationship of each animal / to the others.

At the bottom of a food chain / are the **plant eaters**. They are often / **prey animals**. They are usually / small animals / like **squirrels** and rabbits. Sometimes / they are / bigger animals / like deer. Animals / higher on the food chain / eat these animals. They might be / **owls**, snakes, and **raccoons**. Then, / bigger animals / like bears and wolves / eat these animals. Finally, / we **reach** / the top of the food chain. The most dangerous animal / of all / is here: / man.

所有的動物必須藉由進食來維生。有些動物吃植物，有些吃動物，還有些既會吃植物也會吃動物。食物鏈 food chain 呈現其中每種動物和其他動物的關係 relationship of each animal to the others。

食物鏈的最底端 at the bottom 是草食動物 plant eater，他們通常也是獵物 prey animals，像松鼠和兔子 squirrels and rabbits 之類的小型動物都屬於此類；有時如鹿 deer 這種體型較大的動物也算在內。食物鏈中層級較高的 higher on the food chain 動物會以這些草食動物為食，像是貓頭鷹、蛇和浣熊 owls, snakes, and raccoons；而 then 更大型的動物如熊和狼 bears and wolves，會吃掉上述這些動物。最後便來到了食物鏈的最頂端 the top of the food chain，也就是最危險的動物 the most dangerous animal：人類 man。

hawk

snake

frog

grasshopper

grass

Words to Know

- **food chain** 食物鏈　• **plant eater** 草食動物　• **prey (animals)** 被捕食的動物；獵物
- **squirrel** 松鼠　• **owl** 貓頭鷹　• **raccoon** 浣熊　• **reach** 到達

42 **Fishing and <u>Overfishing</u>** 捕魚與過度捕撈

The ocean has / many different habitats / for many plants and animals. It helps the earth / stay healthy. So we have to be careful / not to hurt the ocean.

Many people / around the world / enjoy eating seafood. Fishermen catch food / in the ocean / for us to eat. This includes **shellfish** / **as well as** fish. Shellfish are animals / like **shrimp**, **clams**, **crabs**, and **lobsters**. Because people eat / so much seafood, / there are many fishermen.

Unfortunately, / the fishermen are catching / too many fish / these days. So the number of fish / in the oceans / is **decreasing**. Many fishing grounds / are getting / smaller and smaller. Fishermen need to stop catching / so many fish. They must give the fish / time / to **increase** their numbers.

海洋 ocean 為許多植物和動物提供了<u>很多不同的棲息地 many different habitats</u>，幫助地球<u>保持健康 stay healthy</u>。因此，我們必須小心<u>別傷害了 not to hurt</u> 海洋。

世界上有很多人<u>喜歡吃海產 enjoy eating seafood</u>，漁夫從海裡<u>捕撈食物 catch food</u> 供我們食用，其中包括<u>水生有殼動物和魚類 shellfish as well as fish</u>。水生有殼動物是指蝦子、蛤蜊、螃蟹和龍蝦這類的動物。由於人們吃很多海產，所以也有很多漁夫。

<u>不幸的是 unfortunately</u>，近年來漁夫<u>捕捉過量的魚類 catch too many fish</u>，造成海洋中<u>魚兒的數目 the number of fish</u> <u>逐漸減少 be decreasing</u>。<u>許多捕魚場 many fishing grounds</u> 的面積<u>變得越來越小 get smaller and smaller</u>。漁夫必須要<u>停止大量捕捉魚類 stop catching so many fish</u>，他們必須給魚兒們繁殖的時間。

Words to Know

• **overfishing** 過度捕撈　• **shellfish** 水生有殼動物　• **as well as** 和　• **shrimp** 蝦　• **clam** 蛤蜊
• **crab** 螃蟹　• **lobster** 龍蝦　• **decrease** 減少　• **increase** 提高；增加

There has been life / on Earth / for billions of years. These **organisms** / are always changing. In fact, / many organisms / no longer / live on Earth. They all died. So people say / that they are extinct. Many animals / are extinct. The dinosaurs / are extinct. The **dodo bird** / is extinct. The **woolly mammoth** / is also no longer alive.

Why do animals / become extinct? There are / many reasons. Natural disasters / such as fires, floods, **droughts**, and earthquakes / can **destroy** habitats. People can destroy habitats, / too. **Pollution** can also / harm organisms. Some animals are hunted / by people. All these things are **harmful** / to plants and animals, / and they can cause the changes / to **ecosystems**.

When a large change occurs / in an ecosystem, / some organisms / have trouble surviving. Then they can be **endangered** / and may become extinct. So, / it is important / to protect our natural environment and ecosystems. What do you think / we can do / for endangered animals?

生命自數十億年前便已存在於地球上,這些生物一直在改變。事實上,許多生物已經從地球上消失 no longer live on Earth,它們全都死了 die,所以人們稱這些動物絕種 be extinct 了。許多動物都已絕種,恐龍 dinosaur、渡渡鳥 dodo bird 以及長毛象 woolly mammoth 都絕種了。

為什麼動物會滅絕 become extinct 呢?這其中有很多的原因 many reasons,火災、洪水、旱災以及地震這樣的天災 natural disasters 會摧毀棲息地 destroy habitats,人類 people 也會摧毀棲息地。汙染 pollution 也會危害到生物 harm organisms,有些動物被人類獵殺 be hunted by people,這些都會傷害動植物,造成生態系統 ecosystem 的改變。

一旦生態系統發生巨大的變化,有些生物便難以生存 have trouble surviving,接著牠們會瀕臨絕種 be endangered,並可能繼而滅絕 become extinct。因此,保護我們的自然環境和生態系統是很重要的。你認為我們能為瀕臨絕種的動物做些什麼事呢 what we can do ?

Words to Know

- **become extinct** 絕種　　• **organism** 生物;有機體　　• **dodo bird** 渡渡鳥
- **woolly mammoth** 長毛象　　• **drought** 旱災　　• **destroy** 破壞　　• **pollution** 污染
- **harmful** 有害的　　• **ecosystem** 生態系統　　• **endangered** 瀕臨絕種的

44 Staying Healthy 保持健康

A person's body / is like a machine. It has many parts / that help keep it running. If these parts / are running well, / a person will be healthy. But sometimes / a person's body / **breaks down**. Then / that person gets sick.

Many times, / **germs** make a person sick. When germs attack a body, / it needs to **fight back**. Sometimes, / the person's body alone / can defeat the germs. Other times, / the person might need medicine / from a doctor / to get better. Fortunately, / many medicines can kill germs / and help bodies / become healthy again.

人體 body 就像是機器 like a machine，許多部位都有助於身體維持運作。如果這些部位正常運轉 run well，這個人就很健康 healthy。但人類的身體有時也會故障 break down，這時這個人也就生病 get sick 了。

細菌 germs 常常會使人生病。當細菌攻擊人體 germs attack a body 時，身體必須反擊 fight back。人體有時 sometimes 能夠獨自對抗細菌 defeat the germs，但有時 other times 可能會需要藉由醫生所開的藥物 need medicine 使身體好轉。幸虧 fortunately 許多藥物都能夠殺死細菌，並且幫助身體再度恢復健康 become healthy again。

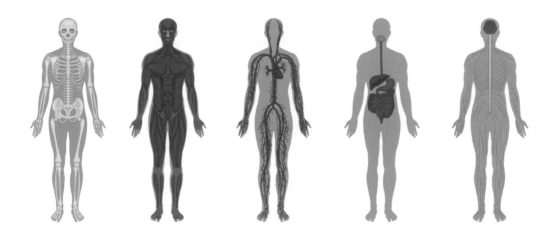

Everyone has / five senses. The five senses / are **sight**, **hearing**, smell, taste, and touch. We use different body parts / for different senses. We need to take care of / the parts of our bodies / that let us use our senses.

For example, / you use your eyes / for seeing. You should protect your eyes / and have a doctor / **regularly** check your **eyesight**. Don't sit too close / to the TV or computer monitor, / and don't read / in the dark or in **dim** light. Never look **directly** / at the sun / or at very bright lights.

Your ears / let you hear the things / around you. You should clean your ears / all the time. Don't listen to loud music, / and try to avoid places / that are really loud. Protect your ears / when you play sports.

Your nose / cleans the air / you breathe / and lets you smell things. Avoid things / that have very strong smells.

Your **tongue** / help you taste things / you eat and drink. Your skin protects your body / from germs / and gives you / your sense of touch. Always wash your hands / after **blowing your nose**, / playing outside, / or using the restroom. Protect your skin / from **sunburns**. Use **sunscreen** / to protect your skin / from the sun.

每個人都有五種感官 five senses：視覺 sight、聽覺 hearing、嗅覺 smell、味覺 taste 以及觸覺 touch，我們利用不同的身體部位來感受不一樣的感覺，必須照顧好這些能讓我們運用感官的身體部位 take care of the parts of our bodies。

舉例來說，你用眼睛來看東西，因此要好好保護眼睛 protect your eyes 並定期就醫、檢查視力 check your eyesight，不要坐在離電視或電腦螢幕太近，不可在昏暗或是微弱的燈光下閱讀，絕不直視太陽或強光。

你的耳朵讓你能聽見周遭的聲音，應該要時常清耳朵 clean your ears，不要聽音量太大的音樂 don't listen to loud music，避免待在過於喧鬧的地方，運動時也要保護你的耳朵 protect your ears。

你的鼻子幫助你清理吸入的空氣，並使你能聞到氣味，應避免 avoid 過於刺鼻的氣味 very strong smells。

你的舌頭 tongue 幫助你品嚐食物和飲料的味道。你的皮膚保護身體不讓細菌侵入，也讓你產生觸覺。擤完鼻子、在室外玩耍及上完廁所後，記得要洗手 wash your hands。小心不要讓皮膚曬傷 protect your skin from sunburns，要擦防曬油 use sunscreen 以避免皮膚受到日照的傷害。

Words to Know

· **sight** 視覺　· **hearing** 聽覺　· **regularly** 定期地　· **eyesight** 視力　· **dim** 昏暗的
· **directly** 直接地　· **tongue** 舌頭　· **blow one's nose** 擤鼻涕　· **sunburn** 曬傷
· **sunscreen** 防曬乳

The Organs of the Human Body 人體的器官

46

Organs are very important parts / of the human body. They help do / certain body functions. There are / many different organs.

One important organ / is the heart. It **pumps** blood / all throughout the body. Without a heart, / a person cannot live. The brain runs / the body's **nervous system**. It controls / both mental and physical activities. People can breathe / thanks to their **lungs**. A person has / two lungs. The **stomach** helps / digest food. It breaks food down / into nutrients / so that **the rest** of the body / can use it. The **liver** also helps with digestion. One of the most important organs / is the biggest. It's the skin. It covers / a person's entire body!

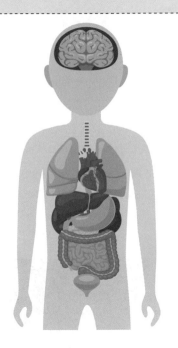

器官 organ 是人體 human body 非常重要的部分 very important parts，它們協助進行特定的身體功能 body functions，人體有許多不同的器官。

其中一個重要的器官就是心臟 heart。心臟打出血液 pump blood 輸送全身，如果沒有心臟，人也無法存活。大腦 brain 控制身體的神經系統 run the nervous system，凡是心理與身體的活動都受它主宰。人因有了肺 thanks to their lungs，才得以呼吸 breathe，一個人有兩個肺。胃部 stomach 幫助消化食物 help digest food，將食物分解成身體其他部分也能吸收的營養素；肝臟 liver 同樣也能幫助消化 help with digestion。人最重要且最大的器官是皮膚。皮膚覆蓋了人體的全身 cover a person's entire body ！

Words to Know

• **pump** 抽送（液體或氣體） • **nervous system** 神經系統 • **lung** 肺臟 • **stomach** 胃
• **the rest** 其餘 • **liver** 肝臟

Seasons and Weather 季節與氣候

There are / four seasons / in a year. They are / spring, summer, fall, and winter. Sometimes / people say "**autumn**" / **instead of** fall.

Each season has / different kinds of weather. In spring, / the air gets warmer, / and the weather is often rainy. Everything / **comes back to life**. Flowers start to **bloom**, / and leaves start growing / on trees. In summer, / the weather is usually / very hot and sunny. In fall, / the temperature starts to **decrease**. The weather gets cooler. The leaves on trees / start changing colors. Winter is the coldest season. It usually snows / during the winter.

　　一年有四季 four seasons，分別是春天 spring、夏天 summer、秋天 fall 和冬天 winter。人們有時候會用 autumn 取代 fall 的說法。

　　每個季節的天氣都不相同。春天的氣溫變得暖和 get warmer，常常都是下雨天 often rainy。一切事物都恢復了生命力 come back to life，花兒開始綻放，樹葉也開始茂盛起來。在夏天，天氣通常都很炎熱晴朗 very hot and sunny。到了秋天，氣溫開始下降，天氣變得比較涼爽 get cooler，樹葉的顏色也開始改變 change colors。冬天是最寒冷的 the coldest 季節，通常都會下雪 snow。

Words to Know

- **autumn** 秋天　- **instead of** 取代　- **come back to life** 恢復生氣　- **bloom** 開花
- **decrease** 下降；減少

How Can Water Change 水如何變化

Water has / three **forms**. It can be / a **solid**, a liquid, or a **gas**. Why does it change? It changes / because of the temperature.

Water's **normal state** / is liquid. But water sometimes / becomes a solid. Why? It gets / too cold. Water **freezes** / when heat **is taken away** / from it. Water / in its solid form / is called / ice. Also, / sometimes / water becomes a gas. Why? It gets / too hot. Water **boils** / when its temperature / gets high enough. Then / it turns into **steam**. This steam is a gas. When water is a gas, / it is called water vapor.

水有三種狀態 three forms：固體 solid、液體 liquid 或氣體 gas。為何它會改變呢？因為「溫度」because of the temperature。

水 water 的正常狀態 normal state 為液體，但有時也會變成固體。為什麼呢？因為過冷 get too cold。當熱能被帶走時，水就會結冰 freeze。固態的水稱為「冰」ice。還有，水有時也會變成氣體。為什麼呢？因為過熱 get too hot。當溫度夠高的時候，水就會沸騰 boil，然後變成蒸氣 turn into steam，而這種蒸氣就是氣體。當水變成氣體時，稱為「水蒸氣」water vapor。

Words to Know

- **form** 型態 • **solid** 固體 • **gas** 氣體 • **normal** 正常的 • **state** 狀態 • **freeze** 結冰
- **be taken away** 被帶走 • **boil** 沸騰 • **steam** 蒸氣

The earth is a huge **planet**. But it is divided / into three parts. They are / the **crust**, mantle, and **core**. Each **section** / is different from the others.

The crust / is the **outermost** part / of the earth. That's the **surface** / of the earth. Everything / on top of the earth / —the oceans, seas, rivers, mountains, deserts, and forests— / is part of the crust. **Beneath** the crust, / there is a **thick** layer / of hot, **melted** rock. It's called / the mantle. The mantle / is the biggest section. The mantle is extremely hot. The **innermost** part / of the earth / is the core. Part of it is solid, / and part is liquid.

地球是一顆巨大的行星，總共分為三部分 divided into three parts：地殼 crust、地幔 mantle 和地核 core，每個部分都不相同。

地殼是地球的最外層 the outermost part，也就是地球的表面 the surface of the earth。海洋、河流、山、沙漠和森林等所有在地球表面的東西都是地殼的一部分。地殼下 beneath the crust 有一層高溫、熔化的厚岩石 a thick layer of hot, melted rock，稱為地幔。地幔佔了最大的比例 the biggest section，其溫度非常高 extremely hot。地球最內層的部分 the innermost part 稱為「核心」，其中有些部分是固態 part is solid，而有些是液態 part is liquid。

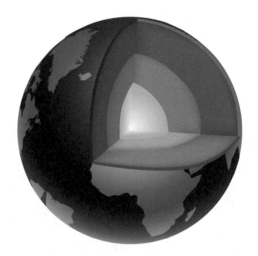

50 How to Conserve Our Resources 如何保存我們的資源

Earth has / many natural resources. But many of them / are resources / that cannot be **reused** or **replaced** / easily. Once **nonrenewable** resources / are used up, / they are gone / forever. That means / we should conserve / our resources / **as much as possible**. Everyone can help do this / in many ways.

Water is a **valuable** resource. So we shouldn't **waste** it. When you're brushing your teeth, / turn the water off. Don't take / really long showers / either. We should also be careful / about using **electricity**. Don't turn on any lights / if you aren't going to use them. Don't leave your computer on / all night long. Recycling is another way / to **save** natural resources. Try to reuse things / like papers and boxes. **Reducing** the amount of energy / you use / is also a good way / to conserve our resources.

地球有許多自然資源,但其中有很多資源都不易重複使用或是取代。不可再生資源 nonrenewable resources 一旦 once 被用盡 be used up,就是永遠消失 gone forever,因此我們要盡量保存我們的資源 conserve our resources,每個人都可以在許多方面 in many ways 盡自己的一份力。

水是珍貴的 valuable 資源,所以我們不可以浪費水 shouldn't waste water,刷牙時請把水關上 turn the water off,洗澡也不要洗太久。我們也要節約用電 be careful about using electricity,電燈不使用時不要開燈 don't turn on,電腦也不要整夜都開著。回收再利用 recycling 是節省自然資源的另一個方法,盡量重複使用 to reuse 紙和盒子這樣的物品。節能 reducing the amount of energy 也是維護自然資源的另一個好方法。

Words to Know

• **conserve** 保存 • **reuse** 重複使用 • **replace** 取代 • **nonrenewable** 不可再生的
• **as…as possible** 盡可能 • **valuable** 有價值的;貴重的 • **waste** 浪費 • **electricity** 電力
• **save** 節省 • **reduce** 減少

The surface of the earth / is constantly changing. Mountains and hills / **break down**. Rocks and soil / move / from one place to another. Some changes are / very slow. **Weathering** and **erosion** / can cause these changes.

Weathering **occurs** / when wind and water / break down rocks / into pieces. Erosion occurs / when weathered rocks or sand / **are carried away**. There are / many types of erosion. The most powerful / is water. Water can / break down mountains / and form **canyons**. Water erosion / made the Grand Canyon / over millions of years. Water also moves / **dirt** and soil / to oceans and seas. The wind can move / sand in deserts / from place to place. And it can / erode valuable **topsoil** / and make deserts that way.

Earthquakes, volcanoes, and violent storms / can change / the earth's surface / quickly. Earthquakes can make / huge **cracks** in the land. Volcanoes can cover / entire cities / in **ash** and **lava**. And storms can drop / huge amounts of water / and causes floods.

地表 the surface of the earth 一直在改變 constantly change，高山和丘陵會崩落，岩石和土壤會位移。有些改變非常緩慢，像是風化 weathering 和侵蝕 erosion。

風和水 wind and water 將岩石瓦解為小碎塊 break down rocks into pieces 的過程稱為風化，風化的岩石或沙粒 weathered rocks and sand 被帶走 be carried away 則稱為「侵蝕」。侵蝕可分為很多種，其中水是作用最大的一種，水可以侵蝕高山使其形成峽谷 form canyon，數百萬年的水侵蝕 water erosion 造就了大峽谷 make the Grand Canyon，河水亦可將塵土沖至海洋。風 wind 能將沙漠中的沙四處搬移，亦能以此方式侵蝕珍貴的表土 erode topsoil 使之成為沙漠 make deserts。

地震 earthquake、火山 volcano 以及劇烈的暴風雨 violent storm 都能迅速改變地表，地震會在陸地上造成巨大的裂縫 make huge cracks in the land，火山用灰燼和熔岩覆蓋整座城市 cover entire cities in ash and lava，暴風雨挾帶豪雨造成水患 cause flood。

Words to Know

- **break down** 分解　・**weathering** 風化（作用）　・**erosion** 侵蝕　・**occur** 發生
- **be carried away** 被帶走　・**canyon** 峽谷　・**dirt** 灰塵　・**topsoil** 表土　・**crack** 裂縫
- **ash** 灰燼　・**lava** 熔岩

Sometimes / people go to the museum. They see / many bones / of **dinosaurs** or other animals. There are even / some plant fossils! But, / what exactly are fossils? And how do fossils form?

Fossils are / the **imprints** or **remains** / of dead animals or plants. They can form / in many ways. The most common way / is like this: / a long time ago, / an animal died. Then it got buried / in the ground. Over time, / the skin and **muscles** / **rotted** away. But the bones remained. Then, / **minerals** entered / the animal's bones. The bones then became / as hard as rock. This might have taken / thousands or millions of years / to occur.

Scientists like to / study fossils. They can learn a lot / about the animals and plants / that lived a long time ago. Scientists can learn / how big they are. Scientists can even learn / what kind of food they ate. **Thanks to** fossils, / scientists today / know a lot / about dinosaurs and other animals.

有時候人們到博物館參觀，可以看到許多恐龍和其他動物的骨頭，甚至還有一些植物的化石 fossils ！但是，化石到底是什麼呢？化石是如何形成的呢？

所謂的化石是動植物死後留下的印痕或遺骸 the imprints or remains，其成因有很多種，最常見的方式 the most common way 如下：很久以前，某隻動物死後 an animal dies 被埋 get buried 入土壤中。牠的皮膚和肌肉隨著時間逐漸腐爛 rot away，不過骨頭還在 the bones remain，接著礦物質進入動物的骨頭中 minerals enter the bones，骨頭隨之變得像岩石一樣硬 become as hard as rock，這過程通常要耗時數千年或數百萬年才會發生。

科學家 scientists 喜歡研究化石 study fossils，他們可以從中瞭解很久以前的動植物。從化石中，科學家可以得知動植物的大小、甚至是牠們吃的食物。由於化石的存在，現今的科學家才能對恐龍和其他動物 about dinosaurs and other animals 有深入的了解。

Words to Know

- **dinosaur** 恐龍　• **imprint** 印記；痕跡　• **remains** 遺骸　• **muscle** 肌肉　• **rot** 腐壞
- **mineral** 礦物　• **thanks to** 由於；多虧

The solar system / is the sun and the planets / going around the sun. There are eight planets / in it. In order of **distance** / from the sun, / they are: / **Mercury**, **Venus**, Earth, **Mars**, **Jupiter**, **Saturn**, **Uranus**, and **Neptune**. Scientists **used to** / consider Pluto / the ninth planet / in the solar system. But they do not think / that way / now. Instead, / they consider Pluto / to be a **minor planet**. There are many objects / like Pluto / in **the outer solar system**. And scientists don't think / they are planets. So they don't consider Pluto / a planet anymore.

太陽系 the solar system 是指太陽 the sun 和圍繞著太陽運轉的行星 the planets going around the sun，共有八大行星 eight planets。與太陽的距離從近到遠依序為：水星 Mercury、金星 Venus、地球 Earth、火星 Mars、木星 Jupiter、土星 Saturn、天王星 Uranus 和海王星 Neptune。科學家曾認為冥王星 Pluto 是太陽系中的第九大行星 the ninth planet，但他們現在改變了看法。他們認為冥王星是顆小行星 minor planet。外太陽系 in the outer solar system 有許多類似冥王星的物體，而科學家並不認為它們是行星 planet。因此，他們不再把冥王星當作是行星。

Words to Know

- **Pluto** 冥王星　　- **distance** 距離　　- **Mercury** 水星　　- **Venus** 金星　　- **Mars** 火星
- **Jupiter** 木星　　- **Saturn** 土星　　- **Uranus** 天王星　　- **Neptune** 海王星　　- **used to** 過去習慣……
- **minor planet** 小行星　　- **the outer solar system** 外太陽系

The <u>Phases</u> of the Moon 月相

The moon takes / about 29 days / to **orbit** the earth. During this time, / the moon **seems to** / change shapes. We call / these looks / "phases." The phases change / as the moon moves / around the earth.

The first phase / is the new moon. The moon is **invisible** / now. However, / it starts to get brighter. It looks like a **crescent**. This next phase / is called / **waxing** crescent. Waxing means / it is getting bigger. Soon, / it is / at the first quarter phase. Half the moon / is visible. Then / it becomes / a full moon. The entire moon / is visible. Now, / the moon starts to **wane**. It is beginning to disappear. It goes / to the last quarter stage. Then / it is / a waning crescent. Finally, / it becomes a new moon / again.

月亮 **the moon** 繞行地球 **orbit the earth** 需要約 29 天。在此期間，月亮會改變形狀 **change shapes**，我們便把月亮呈現的不同面貌稱為「月相」**phase**。隨著月亮繞行地球，月相也會有所改變。

第一個月相稱作「新月」**new moon**，這個階段的月亮肉眼是看不見的 **invisible**，但是月亮的亮度會越變越強，形狀就如同月牙般。下一個月相稱作「娥眉月」**waxing crescent**，英文 waxing 的意思是「越來越大」**get bigger**。很快地，月相就轉變成上弦月 **first quarter phase**，能看到一半的月亮 **half the moon** 形狀。接著滿月 **full moon** 便出現了，這時能看到整個月亮。之後月亮開始轉虧，逐漸地消失，到最後的下弦月月相 **the last quarter stage**，然後變成虧眉月 **waning crescent**，最後又再次回到了新月 **new moon again**。

Words to Know

· **phase**（天體）相　· **orbit** 繞軌道運行　· **seem to** 看起來好像；似乎　· **invisible** 看不到的
· **crescent** 新月；弦月；蛾眉月　· **waxing**（月亮）漸圓　· **wane**（月亮）缺；虧

It's time / to make some cookies. We have / all the **ingredients**. Now, / we need to measure everything / before we start cooking.

First, / we need / 1 cup of **butter**. After that, / we need / $\frac{3}{4}$ cup of white sugar, / the same amount of brown sugar, / and $2\frac{1}{4}$ cups of **flour**. We also need / $1\frac{1}{2}$ **teaspoons** of vanilla **extract**, / 1 teaspoon of **baking soda**, / and $\frac{1}{2}$ teaspoon of salt. We have to measure / $1\frac{1}{2}$ cups of **chocolate chips**, / too. Finally, / we need 2 eggs. Now we have measured / all of our ingredients. Let's start cooking.

來做一些餅乾 make some cookies 吧。我們備齊了所有的食材 all the ingredients。現在，在開始製作前，我們必須先測量所有食材 measure everything。

首先，我們需要一杯奶油 1 cup of butter。然後我們需要四分之三杯的白糖 $\frac{3}{4}$ cup of white sugar，還有等量的紅糖 the same amount of brown sugar，以及二又四分之一杯的麵粉 $2\frac{1}{4}$ cups of flour。我們還需要一又二分之一茶匙的香草精 $1\frac{1}{2}$ teaspoons of vanilla extract、1 茶匙的蘇打粉 1 teaspoon of baking soda，和二分之一茶匙的鹽 $\frac{1}{2}$ teaspoon of salt。我們同時也需要量出一又二分之一杯的巧克力碎片 $1\frac{1}{2}$ cups of chocolate chips。最後，我們需要 2 顆雞蛋 2 eggs。現在，我們已經量好所有的食材了。開始製作吧。

Words to Know

- **ingredient**（烹調）原料；內容物　• **butter** 奶油　• **flour** 麵粉　• **teaspoon** 茶匙
- **extract** 提取物；精　• **baking soda** 小蘇打　• **chocolate chip** 巧克力碎片

56 **Benjamin Franklin** 班傑明·富蘭克林

Benjamin Franklin / was a great American scientist. He lived / more than 200 years ago. He was very **curious** / about **lightning**. He thought / that it was **electricity**. But he wasn't sure. So he decided to do / an **experiment**.

Franklin tied / a metal key / to a kite. Then he waited for a **storm** / to begin. He flew the kite / in the storm. Lightning was striking / in the **area**. **Electric charges** / from the lightning / got on the key. When Franklin **touched** the key, / he got shocked. He had just **proved** / that lightning was / a form of electricity!

　　班傑明·富蘭克林 Benjamin Franklin 是一位偉大的美國科學家 American scientist，他活在 200 多年前。他對閃電非常好奇 very curious about lightning。他認為那是電，但他並不確定。因此，他決定做一項實驗 do an experiment。

　　富蘭克林在風箏上綁了一支金屬製的鑰匙 tie a metal key to a kite，然後等著暴風雨的來臨。他在暴風雨中放風箏 fly the kite in the storm，而閃電打中了那個地方。閃電產生的電荷 electric charges 擊中了鑰匙 get on the key。當富蘭克林觸摸鑰匙 touch the key 時，他被電擊 get shocked 了。他證實 prove 了閃電是電的一種形式 lightning is a form of electricity ！

Words to Know

- **curious** 好奇的　· **lightning** 閃電　· **electricity** 電流；電　· **experiment** 實驗
- **storm** 暴風雨　· **area** 地區；區域　· **electric charge** 電荷　· **touch** 碰觸；接觸
- **prove** 證明

Some objects are **attracted** / to each other. And some objects / **repel** each other. A magnet is an object / that can attract or repel / other objects. Magnets can move things / like **iron** or **steel** / without touching them. How does a magnet work?

A magnet is / a piece of **magnetized** metal / like iron or **nickel**. It has / two separate poles. It has / a **north-seeking** pole, or N pole, / and a **south-seeking** pole, or S pole. This creates / a **magnetic field**. So it can attract or repel / different metals. If the north pole of a magnet / is near / the south pole of another one, / the two will be attracted. But if two north poles / of two magnets / are near each other, / they will repel each other.

　　某些物件會相互吸引 be attracted，某些則是彼此排斥 repel。磁鐵 magnet 擁有能夠吸引或排斥 attract or repel 其他物品的能力，不需要碰觸到 without touching 鋼或鐵之類的物品 things like iron or steel，便可以使它們移動。磁鐵是如何產生磁性的呢？

　　磁鐵是一塊帶有磁性的金屬 magnetized metal 如鐵或鎳，擁有兩個相異的磁極 two separate poles，一端是向著北極（稱為 N 極）north-seeking pore, or N pole，另一端向著南極（稱為 S 極）south-seeking pole, or S pole，兩極產生一個磁場 create a magnetic field，能夠吸引或排斥不同的金屬。假設某塊磁鐵的北極鄰近另一塊磁鐵的南極 north pole of a magnet is near the south pole，兩塊磁鐵會互相吸引 the two will be attracted；但要是兩塊磁鐵的北極相鄰 two north poles of two magnets are near each other，彼此則會產生排斥 repel each other。

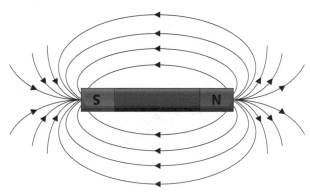

Words to Know

· **magnet** 磁鐵　· **attract** 吸引　· **repel** 排斥　· **iron** 鐵　· **steel** 鋼　· **magnetized** 有磁性的
· **nickel** 鎳　· **north-seeking** 朝北的　· **south-seeking** 朝南的　· **magnetic field** 磁場

58 The <u>Invention</u> of the Telephone 電話的發明

A long time ago, / there were / no telephones. But people knew / that sound travels by **vibrations**. So many people tried to **invent** / the telephone.

Alexander Graham Bell / was one of these people. He wanted to use electricity / to **transmit** sound. He thought / he could turn sound / into **electric pulses**. Then it could move / through **wires**. He worked very hard / on his project. One day in 1876, / he had an accident / in his office. He needed / his **assistant** Watson. He said, / "Watson, come here. I want you." Watson was / in another part of the house. But he heard Bell / over the telephone. Finally, / Bell was successful. He had invented / the telephone!

在很久之前，<u>電話 telephone</u> 還沒出現。不過那時候人們知道，<u>藉由振動可以傳導聲音 sound travels by vibrations</u>，因此有很多人嘗試發明電話。

<u>亞歷山大‧葛拉罕‧貝爾 Alexander Graham Bell</u> 正是其中一位。貝爾希望利用<u>電力傳導聲音 use electricity to transmit sound</u>，他認為自己能夠<u>將聲音轉為電脈衝 turn sound into electric pulses</u>，聲音便可以<u>經由金屬線傳送 move through wires</u>。貝爾對這<u>個計畫投入許多努力 work very hard on his project</u>。在 1876 年的<u>某日 one day</u>，貝爾<u>在辦公室發生了一個意外 have an accident</u>，<u>需要求助助手 need his assistant</u> 華森。貝爾說：「華森，快來，我需要你。」華森當時在房子的另一頭，但他卻透過電話聽到了<u>貝爾的聲音 hear Bell over the telephone</u>。最終貝爾成功了，他<u>發明了電話 invent the telephone</u>！

Words to Know

· **invention** 發明（物） · **vibration** 振動；搖動 · **invent** 發明 · **transmit** 傳導；傳送
· **electric pulse** 電脈衝 · **wire** 金屬線；電線 · **assistant** 助理

Physical and Chemical Changes 物理變化與化學變化

Matter often undergoes / many changes. There are / two main types of changes. They are / physical and chemical changes.

There are / a lot of physical changes. In a physical change, / matter changes / in size, shape, or state. But it does not change / a **substance** / into a new one. For instance, / melting ice / to get water / is a physical change. And boiling water / to get water vapor / is another one. The states are changed, / but ice, water, and steam / are all different forms / of the same thing. So a new substance / is not made. It is also possible / to make physical changes / in other ways. For instance, / put some sugar in water / and then **stir** it. The sugar **dissolves**. That is / a physical change. Or, / simply **tear up** / a piece of paper. That is / another physical change.

Chemical changes are different. Chemical changes / involve the forming / of a new substance or **compound**. A chemical change / is also called / a chemical **reaction**. For instance, / if **sodium** and **chlorine** / come together, / they undergo / a chemical reaction. The result is / the creation of salt. Photosynthesis is another chemical reaction. Water and carbon dioxide / change into sugar and oxygen.

物質通常會經過 undergo 許多種變化。主要的改變有兩種：物理變化 physical change 和化學變化 chemical change。

物理變化有許多種，發生物理變化時，物質 matter 的大小、形狀或狀態會改變 change in size, shape, or state，但是不會將一種物質變成另一種新的物質。舉例來說，將冰融化得到水 melting ice to get water 是一種物理變化；將水煮沸產生水蒸氣 boiling water to get water vapor 也是一種物理變化。它們的形態改變了，但是冰、水和水蒸氣只是同一種東西的不同形態，並沒有生成新的物質 new substance is not made。不過物理變化還是有其他可能的形式。譬如，將一些糖放入水中並攪拌它，糖會溶解，這就是物理變化。或是，單純把一張紙撕碎，這也是另一種物理變化。

化學變化則有所差別，它涉及到新物質或化合物的生成 forming of a new substance or compound。化學變化也稱為「化學反應」chemical reaction。舉例來說，鈉和氯 sodium and chlorine 結合 come together 會經過一個化學反應，反應的結果就是鹽的生成 creation of salt。光合作用是另一種化學反應，水加上二氧化碳會變成糖和氧氣。

Words to Know

- **physical** 物理的
- **chemical** 化學的
- **substance** 物質
- **stir** 攪拌
- **dissolve** 溶解
- **tear up** 撕破
- **compound** 化合物
- **reaction** 反應
- **sodium** 鈉
- **chlorine** 氯

Heat is / a form of energy. It can move / from place to place. There are three ways / it can move: / conduction, convection, and radiation.

When heat touches matter, / it makes / the **particles** in that matter / move. These particles / then / touch other nearby ones. They start moving, / too. This is conduction, / and it is the reason / why the **pot handle** gets hot. Conduction usually occurs / in solids / and between objects / that are touching.

Convection is the second way / that heat moves. Convection happens / because of temperature differences / in different parts / of the liquids or gases. In convection, / warm liquid or gas / **is forced up** / by cooler liquid or gas. Then, / the cooler liquid or gas / is heated / and is forced up. This happens / over and over / **in a circular flow**. Ovens work by convection. **Coils** in the oven / heat the air. The air rises, / where it cooks the food. The air then cools, / so it goes down. Then, / the coils heat it again, / so it rises once more.

Radiation is the third way / that heat moves. This occurs / when heat moves as waves, / so it does not require matter at all. The sun heats the earth / by radiation. The sun **sends out** heat / in the form of waves. The waves reach the earth, / where they provide heat.

熱 heat 是能量的一種形式 a form of energy，可以四處移動 move。熱移動的方式可分為三種：傳導 conduction、對流 convection 與輻射 radiation。

當熱接觸到物質 heat touches matter，會使物質中的粒子移動 the particles move。這些粒子接著碰到周遭其他的粒子 touch other nearby ones，它們也跟著移動 they move too。這就是傳導，也是鍋柄會發熱 pot handle gets hot 的原因。傳導通常發生在固體中，以及互相接觸的物品中。

對流是熱移動的第二種形式。當液體或氣體中的不同部位產生溫差 because of temperature differences 時，就會造成對流。對流時，溫暖的液體或氣體 warm liquid or gas 會被較冷的液體或氣體抬升 forced up by cooler liquid or gas，然後較冷的液體或氣體 the cooler liquid or gas 受熱又被抬升 be heated and be forced up，以一種循環流動的方式反覆進行。烤箱就是靠對流來運作 ovens work by convection。烤箱裡的線圈加熱了空氣，致使空氣上升，食物正是在此處烹煮。接著空氣冷卻下降，而線圈再度將其加熱，所以空氣又再次上升。

輻射是熱移動的第三種形式，當熱能以波的形式移動 heat moves as waves 時，便產生輻射，因此完全不需要依靠物質 do not require matter。太陽便是以輻射的方式使地球溫暖 the sun heats the earth by radiation，它以波的形式散發出熱能，波抵達地球並帶來熱能。

Words to Know

- **conduction** 傳導　• **convection** 對流　• **radiation** 輻射　• **particle**（物理）粒子；微粒
- **pot handle** 鍋柄　• **be forced up** 往上推　• **in a circular flow** 循環方式的流動
- **coil**（電子）線圈　• **send out** 發出

Chapter 3

Mathematics

Geometry

Numbers and Computation

There are / five basic shapes: / the square, **rectangle**, **triangle**, **circle**, and **oval**. There are / many other shapes, / but they all resemble / these five basic ones.

Every object / has a certain shape. For example, / a box may look like / a square or rectangle. A piece of pizza / might resemble / a triangle. A soccer ball and a baseball / are both circles. And eggs / are oval-shaped.

There are also / other more **complicated** shapes. A mountain might resemble / a **pyramid**. A **funnel** looks like / a **cone**.

基本形狀有五種 five basic shapes：正方形 square、長方形 rectangle、三角形 triangle、圓形 circle 和橢圓形 oval。還有許多其他的形狀，但都和這五種基本形狀相似。

每個物體 every object 都有一定的形狀 have a certain shape。例如，一個盒子可能看起來像正方形或長方形；一片披薩可能會像三角形；足球和棒球都是圓形的；雞蛋則是橢圓形的。

還有其他更複雜的形狀 other more complicated shapes。一座山可能像是一座角錐形 pyramid；漏斗看起來像是圓錐形 cone。

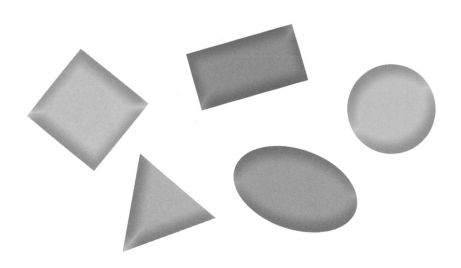

Words to Know

• **shape** 形狀　• **rectangle** 長方形　• **triangle** 三角形　• **circle** 圓形　• **oval** 橢圓形
• **complicated** 複雜的　• **pyramid** 角錐形　• **funnel** 漏斗　• **cone** 圓錐形

62 Plane Figures and Solid Figures 平面圖形與立體圖形

Geometry is / the study / of regular shapes. We can divide these shapes / into two kinds: / plane figures / and solid figures.

There are / many kinds of / plane figures. Squares, rectangles, triangles, and circles / are all plane figures. Plane figures have / both **length** and **width**. They are **flat surfaces**, / so you can draw them / on a piece of paper.

Solid figures are different / from plane figures. They have / length, width, and **height**. A box is a solid figure. We call that a cube / in geometry. A **globe** is a solid figure. That's a **sphere**. Also, / a pyramid and a cone / are two more solid figures.

幾何學 **geometry** 是對規則形狀的研究 **the study of regular shapes**。我們可以將這些形狀分為兩大類:平面圖形與立體圖形。

平面圖形 **plane figures** 有許多種,像正方形、長方形、三角形,和圓形都屬與此類。平面圖形有長與寬 **length and width**,因為由平面組成,所以可以將它們畫在紙上。

立體圖形 **solid figures** 與平面圖形不同,它有長、寬與高 **length, width, and height**。箱子就是立體圖形,在幾何學上被稱作立方體 **cube**。地球儀也是立體圖形,它是一個球體 **sphere**;此外,角錐體 **pyramid** 和圓錐體 **cone** 是另外兩種立體圖形。

- **plane figure** 平面圖形　- **solid figure** 立體圖形　- **length** 長度　- **width** 寬度　- **flat** 平坦的
- **surface** 表面　- **height** 高度　- **globe** 地球儀　- **sphere** 球形;球體

There are / many different types / of polygons. There are / two **requirements** / for an object to be a polygon. It must be made of / three or more **line segments**. And it must be / a **closed** figure. That means / that all of the lines / in the polygon / meet each other.

A three-sided polygon / is a triangle. Some four-sided polygons / are squares, rectangles, or **rhombuses**. A five-sided one / is a **pentagon**. An **octagon** has / eight sides. A polygon can have / any number of sides. It could have / 10, 100, or even 1,000 sides! But circles are not polygons.

Sometimes / two polygons / are congruent figures. This means / they have / the same shape and size. For example, / two squares have sides / that are three inches long. They are **identical**. So they are / congruent figures. But / if one square's sides / are two inches long / while the other's sides / are three inches long, / they are not congruent. Also, / a triangle and a square / can never be congruent.

多邊形 polygon 有許多種，物體要構成多邊形有**兩個必要條件 two requirements**：必須由三條或三條以上的線段 three or more line segments 組成，而且要是一個封閉圖形 closed figure。也就是說，多邊形的所有線段都會交會。

三個邊的 three-sided 多邊形稱為三角形，四個邊的 four-sided 多邊形是正方形、長方形或是菱形，五個邊的 five-sided 多邊形稱為五角形，八邊形有八個邊 eight sides。多邊形可以有任何數量的邊 any number of sides，例如 10 個、100 個，甚至 1,000 個邊！然而，圓形則不屬於多邊形。

有時候兩個多邊形會是全等圖形 congruent figures，亦即它們的形狀相同、大小相等 the same shape and size。舉例來說，兩個邊長皆為三英寸的正方形，它們完全相同 identical，因此是全等圖形。但如果一個正方形的邊長為二英寸，另一個正方形的邊長為三英寸，那它們就不是全等 not congruent。同樣地，三角形和正方形也絕不會是全等圖形。

64 Addition and Subtraction 加法和減法

Addition is **adding** / two or more numbers together. When you add numbers together, / the **answer** / you get / is called the *sum*. For example, / the sum of 5+2 / is 7.

Subtraction is **taking a number away** / **from** another. **Imagine** / you have 5 apples. You take away 2 apples /

and give them to your brother. How many are left? There were 5 apples, / but you took away 2, / so now you have 3 apples. 5−2=3. The number / you have left / is called the *difference*. So, / the difference of 5−2 / is 3.

加法 addition 就是把兩個或兩個以上的數字相加 add together。在做加法的時候，所得到的答案稱為「和」sum。舉例來說，5 ＋ 2 的和為 7。

減法 subtraction 就是把一個數字從另一個數字中減去 take away。假設你有 5 顆蘋果 have five apples，你拿了 2 顆 take away two apples 給你的弟弟。還剩下幾顆 how many are left？原本有 5 顆，但你拿走了 2 顆，所以現在還有 3 顆。5−2=3。剩下的數字稱為「差」difference，所以 5−2 的差為 3。

Words to Know

- **add . . .** 將……相加　　• **answer** 答案　　• **sum** 總和　　• **take . . . away from** 從……減去
- **imagine** 想像　　• **difference** 差

People use money / to buy / many different **goods** and services. Money can be / both **paper bills** and **coins**. All bills and coins / have different **values**.

Learn to recognize the coins / so that you can know / how much they are worth. You might buy some candy / at a store. It **costs** seventy-five cents, / so you give the **clerk** a dollar. One dollar / is worth 100 cents. How much change / will you **get back**? Twenty-five cents. You'll receive one **quarter**. But maybe you don't want / a quarter. Tell the clerk, / "I'd like two **dimes** / and a **nickel**, please." That is / how you make change.

人們用錢來購買許多不同的物品和服務。紙鈔和硬幣 paper bills and coins 都屬於錢 money，所有的紙鈔和硬幣幣值都不相同 have different values。

學著辨別硬幣 recognize the coins，就能夠知道其價值。你可能在商店買些糖果 buy some candy，花了 75 分錢 seventy-five cents，因此你可以給店員一元 give the clerk a dollar。一元 one dollar 值 100 分錢 worth 100 cents。你會找回多少零錢呢 how much change ？25 分錢 twenty-five cents。你會拿到一個 25 分硬幣，但也許你並不想要 25 分硬幣 don't want a quarter。因此，告訴店員：「請給我兩個十分錢和一個五分錢 two dimes and a nickel。」這就是換零錢 make change 的方式。

66 **Greater and Less Than** 大於和小於

All numbers have / a certain value. So some numbers are / **greater than** others. And some numbers are / **less than** others.

A number / that **comes after** another number / is greater than it. For example, / 6 comes after 5. So we can say, / "6 is greater than 5." In **math terms**, / we write it / like this: / 6 > 5.

A number / that **comes before** another number / is less than it. For example, / 2 comes before 3. So we can say, / "2 is less than 3." In math terms, / we write it / like this: / 2 < 3.

所有的數字都有一定的數值 certain value，因此有些數字 some numbers 會比其他數字大 greater than others，而有些數字會比其他數字小 less than others。

在後面的數字會比前面的數字大。舉例來説，6 在 5 的後面 6 comes after 5，所以我們會説：「6 比 5 大」6 is grater than 5。在數學的術語中 in math terms，我們會寫成：「6 > 5」。

在前面的數字會比後面的數字小。舉例來説，2 在 3 的前面 2 comes before 3，所以我們會説：「2 比 3 小」2 is less than 3。在數學的術語中 in math terms，我們會寫成：「2 < 3」。

Words to Know

- **greater than** 大於　　• **less than** 小於　　• **come after** 在……之後　　• **math** 數學　　• **term** 術語
- **come before** 在……之前

People use sentences / when they speak, / but they can also use sentences / when they do math. How can they do this? It's easy. They use / number sentences.

Let's **think of** / a math **problem**. You have four apples, / but then / you add two more. That gives you / **a total of** six apples. Now, / let's make that / a number sentence. It would look like this: / 4+2=6. You can make number sentences / for **addition**, / and you can make them / for **subtraction**, / too. Your friend has / ten pieces of candy, / but he eats five pieces. Now / he **has** five pieces **left**. Let's make a number sentence / for that. Here it is: / 10−5=5.

　　人們說話時會運用句子，但算數學 do math 時也有「句子」（算式）可以套用。人們要怎麼用句子來算數學呢？方法其實很簡單，只要運用算式 use number sentences 即可。

　　我們試想一則數學題 math problem：你有四顆蘋果 have four apples，然後你再加上兩顆 add two more，總共有六顆蘋果 a total of six apples。現在，我們用這個例子來形成一個算式，就會得到 4+2=6。你可以用算式來做加法或減法。例如你的朋友有 10 顆糖果 have ten pieces of candy，他吃了 5 顆 eat five pieces 了，所以只剩下 5 顆 have five pieces left，用這個例子來形成算式，就會得到 10-5=5。

Words to Know

• **sentence** 句子　• **think of** 思考；設想　• **problem** 問題　• **a total of** 總共　• **addition** 加法
• **subtraction** 減法　• **have . . . left** 剩下

John **wakes up** / in the morning / at seven A.M. School starts at eight o'clock, / so he has one **hour** / to get there. When he **arrives** at school, / it's seven forty-five. School will begin / in fifteen **minutes**. School runs / from eight / until three o'clock. That's / a total of seven hours.

In the morning, / John has class / from eight until **noon**, / so he has / a total of four hours / of class. Then he has lunch / from twelve o'clock / until a **quarter** to one. After that, / from twelve forty-five / until three P.M., / he has more classes. That's / a total of two hours and fifteen minutes. Finally, / at three, / school finishes, / and John can go home.

約翰早上七點 **at seven A.M.** 醒來，學校上課時間是八點 **at eight o'clock**，所以他有一個鐘頭 **one hour** 要到校。約翰抵達學校的時間是 7 點 45 分 **seven forty-five**，再 15 分鐘 **in fifteen minutes** 課就要開始了。學校時間從八點 **from eight** 到三點 **until three o'clock**，總共是七個鐘頭 **a total of seven hours**。

約翰早上的課從八點排到中午 **noon**，上課時數共是四個鐘頭。接著，從 12 點到 12 點 45 分 **a quarter to one** 是午餐時間。接著從 12 點 45 分到下午三點 **three P.M.**，他還有其他課程，共計是兩個鐘頭又 15 分 **two hours and fifteen minutes**。最後下午三點是放學時間，約翰就可以回家了。

Words to Know

• **wake up** 醒來　• **hour** 小時　• **arrive** 到達；抵達　• **minute** 分鐘　• **noon** 中午
• **quarter**（時間上）十五分鐘

Sometimes, / you might want to / add many groups of things together. For example, / you might have / five groups of apples. Each group has / two apples. You could add 2 / five times / like this: / 2+2+2+2+2=10. But that's too long. Instead, / use **multiplication**. You can write that / as a multiplication problem / like this: / 2×5=10. When you multiply, / you add / equal groups of numbers / **many times**.

Multiplication is **useful** / because it makes math easier. However, / remember a couple of things / about it. First, / when you multiply any number / by 1, / the **product** is / always the same / as that number: / 5×1=5. 100×1=100. Also, / when you multiply any number / by 0, the product is always 0: / 2×0=0. 100×0=0.

有時候你或許需要將很多組事物相加，舉例來說，你有 5 袋蘋果 **five groups of apples**，每一袋都有兩顆蘋果。你可以將一袋的兩顆蘋果相加 5 次 **add 2 five times**，得到算式 2 ＋ 2 ＋ 2 ＋ 2 ＋ 2 ＝ 10。但是那樣的算式太長 **too long** 了，所以你可以改用乘法 **use multiplication** 來替代。你可以把上述的加法算式寫成 2 × 5 ＝ 10 的乘法題 **multiplication problem**。當你將數字相乘 **multiply**，等於把相等的數字組進行多次相加 **add equal groups of numbers many times**。

乘法很有用，因為它讓數學變得更簡單 **make math easier**。然而，有幾件事情要謹記：第一、當你將任何數字乘以 1 **multiply any number by 1** 時，得到的乘積 **the product** 一定和那個數字相同 **always the same as that number**，例如 5 × 1 ＝ 5，而 100 × 1 ＝ 100。另外，當你將任何數字乘以 0 **multiply any number by 0** 時，乘積 **the product** 必定永遠是 0 **always 0**，例如 2 × 0 ＝ 0、100 × 0 ＝ 0。

Words to Know

・**multiplication** 乘法　・**many times** 許多次　・**useful** 有用的　・**product**（乘）積

1. Mrs. White is a teacher. She is **giving a test** / to the students. Each test has / 3 **sheets** of paper. She has 10 students / in her class. How many sheets of paper / does she need? ➡ The answer is 30 / because 3×10=30.

2. Some families are going to **go** / **on a picnic** together. Each family has / a mother, father, and two children. There are / 8 families. How many people / are going on the picnic? ➡ The answer is 32 / because 4×8=32.

3. Jenny has / 24 pieces of candy. She wants to **share** / all of the candy / with her friends. There are / 5 people plus Jenny. How many pieces of candy / should each person get? ➡ The answer is 4 / because 24÷6=4.

4. 5 students find some coins / in a **jar**. They want to share the coins / with each other. They **count** the coins / and see / that there are 25 coins. How many coins / does each student get? ➡ The answer is 5 / because 25÷5=5.

1. 懷特太太是一位老師，她要給學生考試 **give a test**，每份考卷有三張 **3 sheets of paper**，她的班上有 10 個學生，請問她需要多少張紙 **how many sheets of paper**？ ➡ 答案是 30，因為 3 × 10 = 30。

2. 有幾個家庭要一起去野餐 **go on a picnic**，每個家庭都有媽媽、爸爸以及兩個小孩，一共有八個家庭要參加，請問會有多少人 **how many people** 去野餐？ ➡ 答案是 32，因為 4 × 8 = 32。

3. 珍妮有 24 顆糖果 **24 pieces of candy**，她想把糖果全分給 **share all of the candy** 她的朋友，一共有五個朋友再加上珍妮，請問每個人可以分到幾顆糖果 **how many pieces of candy**？ ➡ 答案是 4，因為 24 ÷ 6 = 4。

4. 五個學生找到一罐硬幣 **find some coins**，他們想把硬幣分一分 **share the coins**。他們數了一共有 25 個硬幣 **count the coins**，請問每個學生可以分到幾個硬幣 **how many coins**？ ➡ 答案是 5，因為 25 ÷ 5 = 5。

• **give a test** 考試　• **sheet** 一張（紙）　• **go on a picnic** 去野餐　• **share** 分享　• **jar** 罐子
• **count** 計算；數

1. Mary is **baking** a cake. She needs to use **flour** / to make the cake. She needs / 2 **pints** of flour. But her **measuring cup** / can only **fill** 1 cup / **at a time**. How many cups of flour / does she need?
   ➡ She needs 4 cups. 2 cups is 1 pint. So 4 cups is 2 pints.

2. Chris likes to run. Today, / he ran 2,500 meters. How many kilometers / did he run? ➡ He ran 2.5 kilometers. There are / 1,000 meters / in 1 kilometer.

3. Peter gets a ruler / and measures himself. He is / 60 **inches** tall. How many feet tall / is he? ➡ He is / 5 feet tall. There are / 12 inches / in one foot. So 60÷12=5.

4. Lucy steps on a scale. She sees / that she weighs 38 kilograms. How many grams / does she weigh? ➡ She weighs 38,000 grams. There are / 1,000 grams / in one kilogram. So 1,000×38＝38,000.

1. 瑪麗正在烘焙蛋糕 bake a cake，她需要用些麵粉 use flour 來作蛋糕。瑪麗需要兩品脱的麵粉 2 pints of flour，但她的量杯一次只能裝一杯 one cup at a time，請問她一共需要幾杯麵粉 how many cups of flour？ ➡ 她需要四杯。因為兩杯是一品脱，所以四杯是兩品脱。

2. 克里斯喜歡跑步 like to run。今天他跑了 2,500 公尺，請問他跑了幾公里 how many kilometers？ ➡ 他跑了 2.5 公里，因為 1,000 公尺為一公里。

3. 彼德拿了一把尺測量自己 measure himself，他的高度為 60 英寸 60 inches tall，請問他高幾英尺 how many feet tall？ ➡ 他有五英尺高。因為 12 英寸為一英尺，所以 60 ÷ 12 ＝ 5。

4. 露西站在體重計上 step on a scale，她看見她的體重為 38 公斤 weigh 38 kilograms。請問她重幾公克 how many grams？ ➡ 她重 38,000 克。因為 1,000 克為一公斤，所以 1,000 × 38 ＝ 38,000。

Words to Know

• **bake** 烘烤　• **flour** 麵粉　• **pint** 品脱　• **measuring cup** 量杯　• **fill** 充滿
• **at a time** 每次；一次　• **inch** 英寸

Reading and Writing Fractions and Decimals
分數與小數的讀寫

You can write / both fractions and decimals / as numbers and words. There are many ways / to do this.

For example, / write the fraction two-thirds / as $\frac{2}{3}$. However, / there are / other ways / to say fractions. You can say / that $\frac{1}{6}$ is one-sixth / or one out of six. And the fraction $\frac{5}{8}$ / could be / five divided by eight.

As for decimals, / usually just say / the **individual** numbers / to the right of the **decimal point**. For example, / 1.1 is / one point one. 2.45 is / two point four five. However, / for some decimals, / you can say them / as fractions. 0.1 is / zero point one / or one-tenth. 0.7 is / zero point seven / or seven tenths.

Sometimes, / you can write a fraction / in easier terms. This is called / its **simplest form**. For instance, / think about the fraction $\frac{4}{8}$. In its simplest form, / it is $\frac{1}{2}$. And the simplest form of $\frac{3}{9}$ / is $\frac{1}{3}$.

Finally, / you can sometimes / write fractions / as decimals. The fraction $\frac{2}{10}$ / can be 0.2. The fraction $\frac{9}{10}$ / can be 0.9. This is / why you can read / the decimal 0.1 / as one-tenth.

你可以用數字或文字來表達分數 fraction 與小數 decimal。它們有許多的表達方式。

舉例來說，你可以把三分之二 two-thirds 寫成 $\frac{2}{3}$。然而，分數也有別的唸法。$\frac{1}{6}$ 可以唸成 one-sixth 或是 one out of six。分數 $\frac{5}{8}$ 可以唸成 five divided by eight。

至於小數，通常只要將小數點 decimal point 右邊的數字個別唸出即可。舉例來說，1.1 唸作一點一 one point one；2.45 唸作二點四五 two point four five。然而有些小數是可以以分數的說法來唸。0.1 唸作零點一 zero point one 或是十分之一 one-tenth；0.7 唸作零點七 zero point seven 或是十分之七 seven-tenths。

有時候你可以用比較簡單的方式來書寫分數，這稱為最簡分數 simplest form。例如，分數 $\frac{4}{8}$ 的最簡分數是 $\frac{1}{2}$；$\frac{3}{9}$ 的最簡分數 the simplest form of $\frac{3}{9}$ 是 $\frac{1}{3}$ is $\frac{1}{3}$。

最後，有時候你可以將分數寫成小數。分數 $\frac{2}{10}$ 可以寫成 0.2；分數 $\frac{9}{10}$ 可以寫成 0.9。這就是為什麼你可以將小數 0.1 讀作十分之一的原因。

Words to Know

- **decimal** 小數　　- **as for** 至於；說到　　- **individual** 單獨的　　- **decimal point** 小數點
- **simplest form** 最簡分數

Chapter

4

Language •
Visual Arts •
Music

Language and
Literature

Visual Arts

Music

Aesop was a slave / who lived in ancient Greece. He lived / more than 2,000 years ago. He is famous / because of the **collection** of stories / he told. Today, / we call them / *Aesop's Fables*.

Aesop's Fables / are short stories. Often, / animals are the main characters. Through the stories about animals, / Aesop teaches us / how we should act / as people. At the end of the fable, / Aesop always tells us / a lesson. The lesson is called / the **moral** of the story. Many of his stories / are still famous / today. *The Tortoise and the Hare* / is very popular. So is / *The Ant and the Grasshopper*. *The Lion and the Mouse* / and *The Fox and the Grapes* / are also well-known.

伊索 **Aesop** 是古希臘時期的 **live in ancient Greece** 一名奴隸 **slave**，他活在二千多年前。他因講述他所蒐集的故事 **the collection of stories** 而聞名。現今，我們稱之為《伊索寓言》**Aesop's Fables**。

《伊索寓言》是短篇故事 **short stories**，通常以動物 **animals** 為主角 **characters**。透過關於動物的故事，伊索教導我們人類該有何種行為舉止 **how we should act as people**。在寓言的結尾，伊索通常會告訴我們一個教訓，而這個教訓又稱為故事的寓意 **the moral of the story**。他有許多故事至今仍非常膾炙人口。《龜兔賽跑》*The Tortoise and the Hare* 非常受歡迎，《螞蟻與蚱蜢》*The Ant and the Grasshopper* 也一樣，而《獅子與老鼠》*The Lion and the Mouse* 和《狐狸與葡萄》*The Fox and the Grapes* 也都很有名。

The Greek Gods and Goddesses 希臘眾神

Myths are stories / that have been around / for thousands of years or more. Myths tell / about **brave** heroes, / great battles, / monsters, / and gods and goddesses. Some wonderful myths / come to us / from ancient Greece. These tales / are a part of Greek **mythology**. Now, / let's meet / some of the main Greek gods and goddesses.

The Greeks believed / that the gods lived / on Mount Olympus, / a mountain in Greece. At Mount Olympus, / Zeus was / the most powerful god. He was / the king of the gods. He controlled the heavens / and decided arguments / among the gods. Poseidon was / the god of the sea, / and Hades was / the god of **the underworld**. They were / the three strongest gods. Hera was / Zeus's wife. She was / the goddess of **marriage**. Athena was / Zeus's daughter. She was / the goddess of **wisdom**. Apollo and Artemis / were twins. Apollo was / the god of light, / and Artemis was / the goddess of the hunt. Ares was / the god of war. And Aphrodite was / the goddess of love. There were / some other gods. But they were / the most powerful of all.

神話 **myth** 是指流傳數千年以上的故事，它述說著勇敢的英雄、偉大的戰役、怪物以及眾神們的事蹟。有些我們熟知的美麗神話來自古希臘，這些故事都是希臘神話 **Greek mythology** 的一部分。現在，就讓我們與希臘眾主神相遇吧。

希臘人相信眾神 **the gods** 住在希臘的奧林帕斯山 **live on Mount Olympus**。在奧林帕斯山上，宙斯 **Zeus** 是權力最大的神，也是眾神之王 **the king of the gods**。宙斯掌管天國並裁決眾神的紛爭。波塞頓 **Poseidon** 為海神 **the god of the sea**，哈帝斯 **Hades** 為冥府之神 **the god of the underworld**，他們三個同為希臘最強大的神。赫拉 **Hera** 是宙斯之妻，也是掌管婚姻的女神 **the goddess of marriage**。雅典娜是宙斯之女，也是智慧之女神 **the goddess of wisdom**。阿波羅 **Apollo** 和阿耳忒彌斯 **Artemis** 為雙胞胎，阿波羅是光明之神 **the god of light**，阿耳忒彌斯則是狩獵之女神 **the goddess of the hunt**。阿瑞斯 **Ares** 為戰神 **the god of the war**，阿芙蘿黛蒂 **Aphrodite** 為愛之女神 **the goddess of love**。還有其他希臘神，但上述的權力則凌駕於其他之上。

Words to Know

- **myth** 神話　• **brave** 勇敢的　• **mythology**（總稱）神話　• **the underworld** 陰間；冥府
- **marriage** 婚姻　• **wisdom** 智慧

August 31, 2012

Dear John,

My name is Sara.

I live in Seoul, / Korea.
Where do you live?

I go to / Central Elementary School.
I like to / ride my bike. Please write
me back / and tell me about yourself.

Sincerely,

Sara

Date: Begin with the date at the top. Use a capital letter for the name of the month.

Greeting: Start your greeting with "Dear." Use a capital D.

Capitalization: Use capital letters to begin a sentence.

Question: Use question marks at the end of questions.

Names: Capitalize the names of people, places, and things.

Closing: End the letter with a closing and your name.
Use a capital letter to begin the closing and put a comma after the closing.
Don't forget that your name should start with a capital letter, too.

2012/8/31

親愛的約翰：

我的名字叫做莎拉。
我住在韓國首爾。
你住在哪裡呢？

我就讀於中央國小。
我喜歡騎腳踏車。
請回信給我，並且告訴我關於你的事情。

敬祝 順心
莎拉

- **日期**：先在最上方寫上日期。月分的字首要大寫。
- **問候**：以 Dear 作為問候語的開頭，要用大寫字母 D。
- **大寫**：句首的字母要大寫。
- **問句**：問句句末要放問號。
- **名字**：人名、地名或特定事物的名稱字首要大寫。
- **結尾**：信末以結尾敬辭和自己的名字作結。
  結尾敬辭的字首要大寫，後面要放逗號。
  別忘了你的名字字首也要用大寫。

Words to Know

- **sincerely** 誠懇地　　• **date** 日期　　• **capital letter** 大寫字母　　• **capitalization** 首字母大寫
- **question mark** 問號　　• **comma** 逗號

There are / many words / in the English **language**. We use words / to make **sentences**. But there are also / many types of words. We call these / "parts of speech," / and we make sentences / with them. Nouns, verbs, **adjectives**, and **prepositions** / are all / parts of speech.

Every sentence needs / a subject and a verb. The subject / is often a noun. Nouns are / words / that name a person, place, or thing. Look around your room. Think of the names / of everything / you see. All those words / are nouns. Verbs **describe** actions. Think of / some activities / you do. The names / of those activities / are verbs.

Sometimes / we also use / other parts of speech. Adjectives describe / other words / like nouns and **pronouns**. *Hot, cold, white, black, windy, rainy,* and *sunny* / are all / adjectives.

英語中有許多單字，我們用單字 use words 來造句 make sentences。然而這些單字也有許多類型，我們把它們稱為「詞性」parts of speech，而我們就用這些詞性來造句。詞性包括名詞 noun、動詞 verb、形容詞 adjective 和介系詞 proposition。

每個句子 every sentence 都需要一個主詞和一個動詞 need a subject and a verb，主詞 subject 通常是名詞 often a noun。名詞是代指一個人、一個地方或一件事的字詞。看看你的房間四周，所有你能想出名字的物品都屬於名詞。動詞 verb 描述的是動作 describe actions。想一想某些你所從事的活動，那些字都是動詞。

有時候我們還會使用其他詞性，像是形容詞 adjective，其作用在形容名詞和代名詞等其他單字 describe other words like nouns and pronouns：熱的、冷的、白色的、黑色的、風大的、下雨的、晴天的，這些字都屬於形容詞。

Words to Know

• **language** 語言　• **sentence** 句子　• **adjective** 形容詞　• **preposition** 介系詞
• **describe** 形容；描述　• **pronoun** 代名詞

There are / four types of sentences / in English. They are / **declarative, interrogative, exclamatory,** and **imperative** sentences.

Declarative sentences / are the most common. They are just statements. Use them / to state facts. You always end these sentences / with a period. All of the sentences / in this **paragraph** / are declarative ones.

An interrogative / is a question. Use this kind of sentence / to ask other people / about something. They always end / with a question mark. You know / what that is, / don't you?

Sometimes, / you might be / really excited / about something. Or perhaps / you are happy. Or maybe / you have a strong emotion. Then you use / an exclamatory sentence. You end / these / with an **exclamation point**!

Finally, / you might want to / give a person an order. Use an imperative sentence / to do this. In these sentences, / the subject is "you." But don't say that word. Instead, / just give the order.

英文句子分為四種 **four types of sentences**：陳述句 **declarative sentence**、疑問句 **interrogative sentence**、感嘆句 **exclamatory sentence** 以及祈使句 **imperative sentence**。

陳述句是最常見的一種，屬於說明性的句子 **statement**，用來陳述事實 **state facts**，在陳述句的句末要使用句號 **period**。本段文章的每個句子都是陳述句。

疑問句是一個問題 **question**，用來向他人提問 **ask other people about something**，在疑問句的句末要使用問號 **question mark**，你知道那是什麼吧？

有時候，你會對某事感到非常興奮 **really excited**，你可能很開心 **happy** 或是情感豐沛 **strong emotion**，此時你就可以使用感嘆句。在感嘆句的句末要使用驚嘆號 **exclamation point** ！

最後，你也許會想下一道指令 **give an order** 給他人，此時你可以使用祈使句。祈使句的主詞就是「你」，但是不需要講出這個字，只要下命令就好 **just give the order**。

Words to Know

- **declarative** 陳述的 - **interrogative** 疑問的 - **exclamatory** 感嘆的
- **imperative** 表示命令的 - **paragraph** 段落 - **exclamation point** 驚嘆號

Common Mistakes in English 英文常見的錯誤

Writing in English / is not easy. There are many **grammar** rules. So you have to be / very careful. Two common mistakes / are **sentence fragments** / and **comma splices**.

A sentence fragment / is an incomplete sentence. A sentence must always have / a subject and a verb. Look at / the following sentence fragments:

attends the school　　My father, who is a doctor

Neither of these / is complete. The first fragment / needs a subject. The second fragment / needs a verb. Make them / complete sentences / like this: / "Jane attends the school." "My father, who is a doctor, is home now."

Comma splices / are also common mistakes. These are / sentences / that use a comma / to connect two **independent clauses**. Look at / the following comma splices:

My brother studies hard, he's a good student.
I'm sorry, it was an accident.

Neither of these / is correct. The first sentence / **either** needs a period / **or** the word because: "My brother studies hard / because he's a good student." The second sentence / needs a period, / not a comma: / "I'm sorry. It was an accident."

英文寫作並不容易，有許多文法規則 grammar rule，所以必須小心謹慎。兩種常見的文法錯誤 two common mistakes 是片段的句子和逗點謬誤。

片段的句子 sentence fragment 是一個不完整的句子 incomplete sentence，一個句子一定要有主詞和動詞。讓我們看看以下的句子片段：

attend the school　　My father, who is a doctor

以上兩個例子皆不完整，前者需要一個主詞 need a subject，後者需要一個動詞 need a verb。完整的句子應該是：「Jane attends the school.」以及「My father, who is a doctor, is home now.」。

逗點謬誤 comma splice 也是很常見的錯誤，這些句子使用逗點 use a comma 來連接兩個獨立的子句 to connect two independent clauses。讓我們看看以下的逗點謬誤：

My brother studies hard, he's a good student.
I'm sorry, it was an accident.

以上兩個句子皆不正確，第一個句子要用句號或是 because：「My brother studies hard because he's a good student.」。第二個句子要用句號 need a period 而非逗號：「I'm sorry. It was an accident.」

Words to Know

- **grammar** 文法　- **sentence fragment** 片段的句子　- **comma splice** 逗點謬誤
- **neither** 兩者皆不　- **independent** 獨立的　- **clause** 子句　- **either . . . or** 不是……就是

Every language has / common sayings. People use them / in various **situations**. They are hard to **translate** / **into** other languages. But they **make sense** / in their own language.

English has / many common sayings. One is / "Better late than never." This means / it is better / to do something late / than never to do it. Another is / "Two heads are better than one." This means / a second person can often help / one person doing something. And "An apple a day keeps the doctor away" / is a common saying. It means / that eating apples every day / helps keep you healthy. So the person will not get sick / and won't have to see a doctor.

　　每個語言都有常見的格言 <u>common saying</u>，經常使用於各種情況。格言很難翻譯 **hard to translate** 成其他語言，但在原本的語言中卻通情達意 **make sense in their own language**。

　　英文中有許多常見格言，其中像「Better late than never.」（亡羊補牢 **Better late than never.**），意思是即使起步晚，也勝過什麼都不做；還有「Two heads are better than one.」（一人計短，兩人計長 **Two heads are better than one.**），意謂第二個人的幫忙通常有所效益。「An apple a day keeps the doctor away.」（一天一蘋果，醫生遠離我 **An apple a day keeps a doctor away.**）也是很通俗的諺語，它表示每天吃蘋果有助健康，不生病也就不需要去看醫生。

Words to Know

• **saying** 諺語　• **situation** 狀況　• **translate into** 翻譯成……　• **make sense** 合理；有意義

80 Primary and Secondary Colors 三原色和第二次色

There are / three basic colors. They are / red, yellow, and blue. We call these / three primary colors. You can make other colors / when you **mix** these colors together. For example, / mix red and yellow / to create orange. **Combine** yellow and blue / to make green. And you get purple or **violet** / when you mix red and blue together. We call these / secondary colors.

Of course, / there are / many other colors. You can make black / by mixing red, yellow, and blue / all together. You can also mix / primary and secondary colors / to get other colors.

基本顏色有三種，分別是紅色、黃色和藍色 red, yellow, and blue，我們稱之為三原色 three primary colors。把這些顏色混合在一起，就可以調出其他顏色。例如，把紅色和黃色混合 mix red and yellow 就能夠調配出橘色 to create orange。把黃色和藍色混合 combine yellow and blue 就能夠變成綠色 to make green。還有，混合紅色和藍色 mix red and blue together 就會調出紫色或紫羅蘭色 get purple or violet。這些顏色我們稱為第二次色 secondary colors。

當然，還有許多其他的顏色。你可以把紅色、黃色和藍色全部混合 mix all together 調出黑色 make black，也可以把三原色和第二次色混合變成其他顏色。

Art galleries display / the works / of lots of painters. There have been / many painters. Some of them / are very famous. Artists make / many different kinds of **paintings**. But they are all beautiful / **in their own way**.

Picasso was / a famous **modern** painter. Manet, Monet, Cézanne, and van Gogh / painted / more than 100 years ago. Leonardo da Vinci / was very famous / also. He painted / the most famous **portrait** / in the world: / the *Mona Lisa*. Rembrandt was a painter / from a long time ago. So was / Michelangelo. He painted / around 500 years ago.

畫廊 art gallery 展示 display 了許多畫家 painter 的作品。在這麼多畫家之中,其中有些非常有名。藝術家 artists 繪製了許多不同類型的畫作 make many different kinds of paintings,而每幅畫都有其難以言喻的美。

畢卡索 Picasso 是一位有名的現代畫家 famous modern painter,而馬奈 Manet、莫內 Monet、塞尚 Cézanne 和梵谷 van Gogh 是 100 多年前的畫家。李奧那多・達文西 Leonardo da Vinci 也非常有名,他畫了一幅全世界最有名的肖像畫 the most famous portrait:《蒙娜麗莎》*the Mona Lisa*。林布蘭 Rembrandt 也是很久以前的畫家,還有米開朗基羅 Michelangelo,他是約 500 年前的畫家。

Realistic Art and Abstract Art

82

「寫實派」與「抽象派」藝術

There are / two main kinds of art. They are / realistic art / and abstract art. Some artists like realistic art, / but others prefer abstract art.

Realistic art / shows objects / as they look / in **reality**. For example, / a realistic artist / paints a picture of an apple. The picture will look / **exactly** like an apple. Most art / in the past / was realistic art.

Abstract art / looks different / than realistic art. Abstract art / does not always look exactly like / the real thing. For example, / an abstract artist / paints a picture of an apple. It will not look like an apple. It might just be / a red ball. That is abstract art. **Nowadays**, / much art is abstract.

有兩種主要的藝術型態 **two main kinds of art**，分別是寫實派 **realistic art** 和抽象派 **abstract art**。有些藝術家喜歡寫實派藝術，有些則偏好抽象派藝術。

寫實派藝術呈現物體實際看起來的樣子 **show objects as they look in reality**。舉例來說，寫實派畫家畫了一顆蘋果的畫，那張畫看起來就像是一顆真的蘋果。在過去，大部分的藝術作品都是寫實派藝術。

抽象派藝術看起來就和寫實派不同了。抽象派藝術不會看起來就像實際的東西一樣 **do not always look exactly like the real thing**。舉例來說，抽象派畫家畫了一顆蘋果的畫，但那張畫看起來就不像蘋果，它可能像一顆紅色的球。這就是抽象藝術。現今，有很多的藝術都屬於抽象派。

Words to Know

· **realistic** 寫實派的　· **abstract** 抽象的　· **reality** 實際；真實　· **exactly** 確切地
· **nowadays** 現今

Architects have / very important jobs. They **design** / buildings. Some design / tall buildings / like **skyscrapers**. Others design / restaurants, hotels, or banks. And others just design / houses.

Architects need to have / many skills. They must be **engineers**. They must be / good at math. They must be able to draw. They must have / a good **imagination**. And they must work well / with the builders, / too.

Architects draw **blueprints** / for their buildings. Blueprints show / how the building will look. They are / very **detailed**. When the blueprints are done, / the builders can start working.

建築師 architect 的工作相當重要，他們設計建築物 design buildings。有些建築師設計像摩天大樓的高樓大廈，有些設計餐廳、飯店或銀行，而有些只設計房屋。

建築師必須要擁有很多本領 have many skills，他們同時也要是工程師、有很強的數學能力 good at math、能夠繪圖 able to draw、有良好的想像力 have a good imagination，還要能和建商合作無間 work well with the builders。

建築師會替建物繪製藍圖 draw blueprints，用來展示其樣貌 how the building will look。藍圖涵蓋複雜的細節 very detailed，當藍圖繪製完畢，建商便可以開始興建工程。

Words to Know

- **architect** 建築師　· **design** 設計　· **skyscraper** 摩天大樓　· **engineer** 工程師
- **imagination** 想像力　· **blueprint** 藍圖　· **detailed** 詳細的；複雜的

People often visit / art galleries and museums / to look at paintings. There are / many famous paintings / in places around the world. People call / the greatest paintings / "**masterworks**." What makes a painting great? There are / many different elements.

First, / the lines and shapes / that an artist uses / are important. Realistic artists make / their lines and shapes / **imitate reality**. Abstract artists do not. The way / of using lines and shapes / is the main difference / between realistic and abstract art.

Also, / the colors in the painting / are important. The colors should / **go well with** each other. Light and shadows / are important elements of paintings, / too. Light can affect / the way / you feel. The way / that artists use light in their paintings / can affect your **emotions** / as well. So some artists may use / a sharp **contrast** / between dark and light.

An artist should also have / a good **sense of space**. This means / that the painting should not be / too crowded or too **empty**. The painter should / always try to find **balance** / in a painting. That makes great art.

人們常常會到畫廊和博物館欣賞畫作。世界各地都有許多著名的畫作,人們將最偉大的畫作 the greatest paintings 稱為「名作」masterworks,是什麼讓這些畫作如此出色呢?這其中包含許多不同因素 many different elements。

首先,畫家所使用的線條和形狀 lines and shapes 是很重要的,寫實派畫家運用線條和形狀模擬真實世界,抽象派畫家則否,運用線條和形狀的手法正是寫實派與抽象派藝術之間的主要差異。

其次,色彩 colors 對於畫作也是很重要的,顏色必須要彼此搭配 go well with each other。光影 light and shadows 也是畫作的重要元素之一,光線和畫家運用光線的方式亦能影響你的感受,所以有些畫家會在畫作上使用強烈的明暗對比 sharp contrast between dark and light。

畫家也要有好的空間概念 good sense of space,意即一幅畫作不能顯得太過擁擠或太過空曠 not too crowded or too empty。畫家必須隨時掌握畫作的和諧 find balance,如此方能造就偉大的藝術。

Words to Know

- **masterwork** 傑作　・**imitate** 仿效　・**reality** 現實　・**go well with** 與……協調
- **emotion** 情感　・**contrast** 對比　・**sense of space** 空間感　・**empty** 空的　・**balance** 平衡

Most people think / that art is just painting / or drawing. But there are / many other kinds / of unique art.

For example, / some artists love / cold weather. The reason / they like the cold / is that they make ice **sculptures**. They take huge blocks of ice / and use saws, hammers, and **chisels** / to create sculptures. Of course, / when the weather gets warmer, / their artwork disappears.

Most people don't **think of** / **bed covers** / **as** art, / but others do. Many people make **quilts**. These are bed covers. But the quilt makers / put many designs / on their quilts. The designs can be simple, / or they can be very **complicated**. But no two quilts / are ever alike. Quilt making / is a popular form of **folk art** / in some places.

In America, / Native Americans have / many unique forms of art. Some of them / paint rocks. Others / make **tiny** sculptures / from rocks, wood, or bone. And some Native Americans / even use sand / to make art! This is called / sand painting. It can produce / many beautiful pieces of art.

大多數人都認為藝術就是指繪畫或是圖畫 painting or drawing，然而，其實還有許多其他類型的獨特藝術 unique art。

舉例來說，有些藝術家喜愛寒冷的天氣，如此便能創作冰雕 make ice sculptures。他們取用大型的冰塊 take huge blocks of ice，並以鋸子、鐵鎚與鑿子 use saws, hammers, and chisels 來創造冰雕。當然，一旦天氣轉暖，他們的藝術品也隨之消失。

多數人不會認為被單是什麼藝術，但對某些人卻不然。許多人製造床單 make quilts，也就是床罩 bed cover。這些床單創作者 quilt maker 將許多圖案運用 put many designs 在床單上，這些圖案可簡可繁，但幾乎不會重複，在某些地方床罩的創作是一種普遍的民俗藝術 popular form of folk art。

美國的印第安人 Native Americans 擁有許多獨特的藝術，有些人彩繪岩石 paint rocks，有些人利用岩石、木材或是骨頭 from rocks, wood, and bone 來製作小型雕刻 make tiny sculptures。有的印第安人甚至會利用沙子來創作藝術！稱之為沙畫 sand painting，可以創作出許多美麗的作品。

Words to Know

- **sculpture** 雕像　• **chisel** 鑿子　• **think of . . . as** 認為……是　• **quilt** 床單
- **complicated** 複雜的　• **folk art** 民俗藝術　• **tiny** 很小的

There are / so many kinds / of musical instruments. They **make** / many different **sounds**. So there are / also many kinds / of music. **Rock musicians** / often use / the guitar and drums. **Jazz** music needs / a piano and **saxophone**. And **classical music** uses / many various kinds / of instruments.

People often play / two or more instruments together. They do this / in a band or an **orchestra**. But the musicians must all play / at the same time. Many of them / read **sheet music**. This tells them / what **notes** to play. If they play well together, / they create a **harmonious** sound.

樂器有許多種類 so many kinds of musical instruments。由於樂器能夠製造出各種不同的聲音 make many different sounds，所以音樂分為許多種 many kinds of music。搖滾音樂家 rock musician 通常會運用吉他和鼓 guitar and drum；爵士樂 Jazz music 需要鋼琴和薩克斯風 piano and saxophone；古典音樂 classical music 則運用了許多不同種類的樂器 various kinds of instruments。

人們通常會一起演奏兩種或兩種以上的樂器，組成一支樂團或管弦樂隊 in a band or an orchestra，不過，這些音樂家必須同時間演奏 all play at the same time。他們大多數都會讀譜 read sheet music，這樣他們才知道要演奏哪個音符 what notes to play。如果他們同時都能夠演奏得很好 play well together，就可以創造出和諧的音樂 create a harmonious sound。

Words to Know

- **make a sound** 發出聲音　• **rock** 搖滾樂　• **musician** 音樂家；樂手　• **jazz** 爵士樂
- **saxophone** 薩克斯風　• **classical music** 古典樂　• **orchestra** 管弦樂隊
- **sheet music** 樂譜　• **note** 音符　• **harmonious** 和諧的；悅耳的

Popular Children's Songs 受歡迎的兒歌

What makes a song popular? There are / many factors involved. Often, / the simplest songs / are the most popular / with people. The words to the song / might be easy, / so people can / remember them easily. Or the **melody** is easy / to play or remember, / so people often **hum** / or **whistle** / the music.

Some songs are **well-liked** / by young people. *Bingo* / is one of these songs. *Old MacDonald* / is another, / and so are / *Twinkle, Twinkle, Little Star* / and *La Cucaracha*. Why do people like them? The words often **repeat**, / the words rhyme, / and the **tunes** are **catchy**.

　　一首歌為何會受到歡迎呢？有許多原因。<u>最簡單的歌曲</u> the simplest songs 往往會<u>最受歡迎</u> the most popular，因為簡單的歌詞容易使人記住 remember easily。或者是因為容易演奏或記住的旋律，讓人們可以經常哼出或用口哨吹出 hum or whistle 音樂。

　　有些歌曲相當受到年輕人喜愛，〈賓果〉*Bingo* 是其中一首歌曲，還有〈王老先生有塊地〉*Old MacDonald*、〈小星星〉*Twinkle, Twinkle, Little Star* 和西班牙文歌曲〈蟑螂〉*La Cucaracha*。人們為什麼喜歡這些歌曲呢？因為歌詞常常重複 the words often repeat、押韻 the words rhyme，以及曲調都很動聽且容易記住。

Words to Know

• **melody** 旋律　• **hum** 低哼　• **whistle** 吹口哨　• **well-liked** 受到喜愛的　• **repeat** 重覆
• **tune** 曲調　• **catchy** 動聽而易記的

People have / different **tastes** / in music. Some like / slow music. Others like / fast music. Some like / to hear singing. Others like / to hear musical instruments. So there are / many different kinds of music.

Classical music / **relies upon** / musical instruments. It has / very little singing / in it. On the other hand, / **folk music** and **traditional** music / use / both instruments and singing. Every country has / its own kind of folk music. It's usually fun / to listen to.

There are also / many kinds of modern music. Rock music / is one popular **genre**. So is jazz. Some people **prefer** / rap or R&B. **Overall**, / there is / some kind of music / for everyone.

人們對於音樂有不同的喜好 **have different tastes in music**。有些人喜歡輕音樂，有些人喜歡快的旋律。有些人習慣聽加上歌聲的曲子，有些人偏好樂器演奏，因此音樂有許多不同的種類 **many different kinds of music**。

像古典音樂 **classical music** 就是以樂器演奏為主，旋律中很少會出現歌聲。另一方面，民謠 **folk music** 與傳統樂 **traditional music** 同時使用了樂器搭配上歌聲。每個國家都有自己的民謠音樂，通常它們都富有趣味。

現代樂 **modern music** 也分為許多種類，其中的搖滾樂 **rock music** 很受歡迎，爵士樂 **jazz** 同樣也是。有些人則喜愛饒舌樂 **rap** 或節奏藍調 **R&B**。整體說來，每個人都能找到自己喜歡的音樂 **some kinds of music for everyone**。

Words to Know

- **taste** 愛好　- **rely upon** 取決於　- **folk music** 民謠　- **traditional** 傳統的　- **genre** 類型
- **prefer** 偏愛　- **overall** 整體說來

Some instruments / look alike / or have common characteristics. We can put / many of these instruments / into families. There are / some different families / of musical instruments.

Keyboard instruments / have keys / to press. The piano, organ, and keyboard / are in the keyboard family. The violin, viola, and cello / have **strings**. So they are called / string instruments. There are / two kinds of wind instruments: / **brass** and **woodwinds**. Brass instruments / include / the trumpet, trombone, and tuba. Woodwinds / are the clarinet, flute, oboe, and saxophone. **Percussion** instruments / are fun / to play. You hit or **shake** them / with your hands / or with a stick.

There are / many other kinds of instruments. **Apart**, / they make lots of sounds. Together, / they combine / to make beautiful music.

某些樂器看似相像,或是擁有共同的特徵。我們可以把這些樂器分門別類,樂器可分為幾種不同類型 some different families of musical instruments。

鍵盤樂器 keyboard instrument 有鍵 have keys 能彈,包括鋼琴、風琴和電子琴,都是這個鍵盤樂器中的一員。小提琴、中提琴和大提琴有弦 have strings,因此被稱為弦樂器 string instrument。管樂器 wind instrument 分為兩類:銅管樂器和木管樂器 brass and woodwind。銅管樂器有小號、長號和大號;單簧管、長笛、雙簧管和薩克斯風則是屬於木管樂器。打擊樂器 percussion instrument 演奏時很有樂趣,你可以用手或拿棒子敲擊、震動 hit or shake 樂器。

除此之外,還有很多其他類型的樂器。這些樂器分開 apart 演奏時,會製造出很多的聲響 make lots of sounds,但合奏 together 時,它們卻結合譜出美妙的樂音 make beautiful music。

Words to Know

• **keyboard** 鍵盤　• **string** 弦　• **brass** 銅管樂器　• **woodwind** 木管樂器
• **percussion** 打擊樂器　• **shake** 震動　• **apart** 分開

90 *The Nutcracker* 胡桃鉗

Every Christmas season, / people all around the world / go to the **ballet**. And many of them / see *The Nutcracker*. It is / one of the most famous and popular ballets / in the world. It **was composed** / **by** Peter Tchaikovsky.

In the story, / it is Christmas Eve. Clara receives a nutcracker / as a present. She **falls asleep** / in a room / with the nutcracker. Suddenly, / the nutcracker and the toys / grow big, / and they **come to life**. Then, / they battle an army of mice / and defeat them. The nutcracker becomes a prince, / and he and Clara go to his **castle**. They watch many dances / there. Then, / Clara wakes up / and learns / it was only a dream.

The music and dances / in *The Nutcracker* / are very famous. The music is beautiful, / and the dances **require** great skill. **Along with** the story, / they have made *The Nutcracker* / an important part of Christmas / for many people.

　　每年到了聖誕時節 **every Christmas season**，世界各地有許多人會去欣賞芭蕾舞 **go to the ballet**，其中很多人觀看《胡桃鉗》*The Nutcracker*，它是全世界最出名且最受歡迎的芭蕾舞之一。《胡桃鉗》是由彼得‧柴可夫斯基所創作 **composed by Peter Tchaikovsky**。

　　故事的背景為聖誕夜 **Christmas Eve**，克萊拉 **Clara** 收到了一個胡桃鉗 **receive a nutcracker** 禮物，她拿著胡桃鉗在房間裡睡著 **fall asleep** 了。突然間，胡桃鉗和其他玩具突然變大 **grow big**，而且有了生命 **come to life**，他們和一群老鼠軍團交戰 **battle an army of mice** 並將之擊敗 **defeat them**。胡桃鉗化身為王子 **become a prince**，並和克萊拉前往他的城堡 **go to his castle**，在那裡欣賞了許多舞蹈表演 **watch many dances**。接著，克萊拉突然醒了 **wake up**，並發現一切只是一場夢 **only a dream**。

　　《胡桃鉗》中的音樂和舞蹈都非常有名。它的音樂極為優美，舞蹈技巧也非常高超，加上動人的故事內容，使《胡桃鉗》成為許多人在過聖誕節時的一大要事。

Words to Know

- **ballet** 芭蕾　　- **be composed by** 由……創作　　- **fall asleep** 睡著　　- **come to life** 賦予生命
- **castle** 城堡　　- **require** 需要　　- **along with** 和……一起

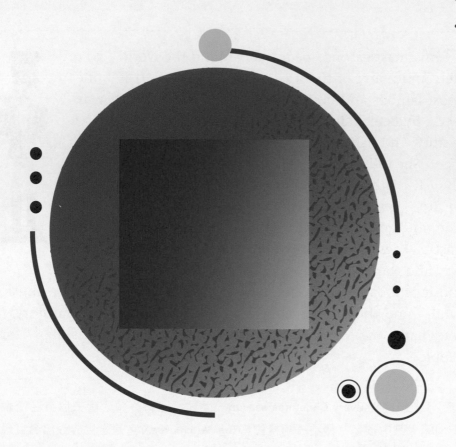

Answer Key

01 Good Neighbors 好鄰居

1 (b)

2 a. Neighbors b. privacy c. help, out

3 a. help out 幫助 b. community 社區
c. greet 迎接；問候

02 A Day at School 學校裡的一天

1 (b)

2 a. T b. T c. F

3 a. homeroom 學生接受導師指導的教室
b. cafeteria 自助餐廳 c. recess 休息

03 Christian Holidays 基督教的節日

1 (c)

2 (b)

3 a. believe in 基督教 b. celebrate 慶祝 c. dead 死的

04 Different Kinds of Jobs 不同類型的工作

1 (c)

2 a. People often look for jobs after they finish schools.
b. They are service, manufacturing, and professional jobs.
c. They are doctors, lawyers, and teachers.

3 a. manufacturing 製造業 b. training 訓練
c. service job 服務業

05 How Technology Helps People 科技如何幫助人類

1 (b)

2 a. advanced b. Internet c. medical treatment

3 a. vaccine 疫苗 b. advanced 先進的 c. invention 發明

06 The Leaders of the American Government 美國政府的領導者

1 (a)

2 a. The president leads the American government.
b. Each state has two senators.
c. They work in the Capitol in Washington, D.C.

3 a. senator 參議員 b. Washington, D.C. 華盛頓（哥倫比亞特區） c. bald eagle 白頭鷹

07 State and Local Governments 州政府與地方政府

1 (c)

2 a. The most powerful person in a state is the governor.
b. The legislature passes the bills.
c. They are called mayors.

3 a. governor 州長 b. represent 代表
c. state capitol 州議會大廈

08 The Jury System 陪審團制度

1 (b)

2 a. There are two kinds of juries.
b. It is a petit jury.
c. It decides if the defendant is innocent or guilty.

3 a. prosecutor 檢察官 b. evidence 證據 c. criminal 罪犯

09 Oceans and Continents 海洋與大陸

1 (b)

2 (b)

3 a. New World 新大陸 b. island 島 c. continent 大陸

10 What Is a Map 何謂地圖

1 (c)

2 a. Maps b. cities c. seas

3 a. detail 細節 b. land 陸地 c. border 邊界

11 National Parks 國家公園

1 (c)

2 a. Yellowstone National Park was the first national park.
b. The Grand Canyon is one of the world's largest canyons.
c. They tour, go hiking, and even camp in the parks.

3 a. canyon 峽谷 b. go hiking 去健行
c. preserve 保存；保護

12 Endangered Animals 瀕臨絕種的動物

1 (b)

2 a. F b. T c. T

3 a. hunt 追獵；打獵 b. set aside 留出；儲存
c. endangered 快要絕種的

13 American Geography 美國地形

1 (b)

2 a. Northeast b. Midwest c. Rocky

3 a. flat land 平坦的土地 b. hilly 多山丘的；丘陵的
c. feature 特徵；特色

14 The Southwest Region of the United States 美國的西南部地區

1 (a)

2 (b)

3 a. diverse 不同的；多種多樣的 b. plateau 高原
c. rich with 富含

15 The Civil Rights Movement in the Southeast Region 東南部地區的民權運動

1 (b)

2 a. Civil War b. separate c. Martin Luther King, Jr.

3 a. discrimination 歧視 b. segregated 被分離
c. guarantee 保證

16 Short Stories From the Northeast 東北部的短篇小說

1 (c)

2 (b)

3 a. upstate 州北部的 b. go off 離開 c. take place 發生

17 How Native American Tribes Came to America 印第安部落如何到達美洲

1 (b)

2 (a)

3 a. live off the land 靠農耕、狩獵等方式生活
b. nomad 遊牧者 c. herd 畜群

18 Three Great American Empires 美洲三大帝國

1 (c)

2 a. The first American came from Asia.
b. The Mayans lived in the jungle in Central America.
c. The Aztecs lived in North America.

3 a. temple 神殿；寺廟 b. defeat 戰勝；擊敗
c. capital 首都；首府

19 The Anasazi 阿納薩齊族

1 (c)

2 a. They disappeared.
b. They disappeared around 1200.
c. No one is sure why.

3 a. drought 乾旱 b. cliff 懸崖；峭壁 c. artifact 手工藝品

20 The Fall of the Aztec and Inca Empires 阿茲提克帝國和印加帝國的衰敗

1 (a)

2 a. They looked for god, silver, and other treasures.
b. The Spanish defeated the Aztecs and Incas.
c. They made the Native Americans slaves. /
They enslaved the Native Americans.

3 a. treasure 金銀財寶；珍寶 b. conquistador 征服者

c. cruel 殘忍的

21 More Europeans Come to the Americas 更多歐洲人來到美洲

1 (c)

2 (c)

3 a. colony 殖民地；移居地 b. voyage 航行
c. wealthy 富裕的

22 The English in America 在美洲殖民的英國人

1 (c)

2 a. Virginia b. Jamestown c. freedom

3 a. Jamestown 詹姆斯鎮 b. the Pilgrims（大寫）1620 年
搭乘五月花號（*Mayflower*）移居美國的英國清教徒
c. disease 疾病

23 Ancient Egyptian Civilization 古埃及文明

1 (c)

2 a. F b. T c. T

3 a. the Sphinx 人面獅身像 b. hieroglyphics 象形文字
c. pharaoh 法老

24 Early Indus Civilization 早期的印度河文明

1 (a)

2 a. It is the Indus Valley civilization or the Harappan
civilization.
b. They used copper and bronze. /
They made objects from both cooper and bronze.
c. They used one based on pictographs.

3 a. pictograph 象形文字 b. agriculture 農業；農耕
c. Harappan civilization 哈拉帕文明

25 Ancient Greece: Athens and Sparta 古希臘：雅典和斯巴達

1 (b)

2 a. Sparta b. Athens c. warlike

3 a. philosopher 哲學家 b. city-state 城邦
c. accomplishment 成就

26 All Roads Lead to Rome 條條大路通羅馬

1 (c)

2 (a)

3 a. invader 侵略者 b. emperor 皇帝 c. enormous 巨大的

27 The Spanish Conquer the New World 西班牙人征服新大陸

1 (a)

2 a. Aztec b. weapons c. Tenochtitlan

3 a. ally 結盟；聯合 b. the throne 王位 c. weapon 武器

28 The Reformation 宗教改革

1 (b)

2 (b)

3 a. excommunicate 把……逐出教會
b. thesis 論題；論點 c. reformation 改革

29 The French Revolution 法國大革命

1 (a)

2 a. Nobles and the clergy had good lives.
b. King Louis XVI and Marie Antoinette ruled France.
c. Napoleon Bonaparte ruled France.

3 a. oppressive 專制的；暴虐的
b. divine right 神賜予的權力 c. clergy 神職人員

30 The Great War 世界大戰

1 (c)

2 a. F b. T c. T

3 a. assassinate 暗殺；行刺 b. alliance 同盟 c. trench 戰壕

31 How Plants Grow 植物如何生長

1 (b)

2 a. T b. F c. T

3 a. soil 土壤 b. branch 樹枝 c. nutrient 養分

32 Roots, Stems, and Leaves 根、莖、葉

1 (b)

2 a. stems b. minerals c. Chloroplasts

3 a. sap（樹等的）汁；液 b. anchor 使固定
c. transport 運送；運輸

33 Places to Live 棲息地

1 (c)

2 a. F b. T c. T

3 a. habitat 棲息地 b. survive 活下來；倖存
c. temperature 溫度；氣溫

34 Living Things vs. Nonliving Things
生物與非生物

1 (b)

2 a. living b. water c. make

3 a. nonliving 非生物 b. shelter 庇護所 c. similar 類似的

35 How Are Animals Different
動物的相異處

1 (c)

2 (b)

3 a. feed 餵養 b. amphibian 兩棲類
c. lay eggs 下蛋；產卵

36 Warm-Blooded vs. Cold-Blooded
Animals 恆溫動物與變溫動物

1 (a)

2 a. Warm-blooded b. Mammals c. amphibians

3 a. internal 內部的 b. regulate 調節 c. soak up 吸收

37 An Insect's Body 昆蟲的身體

1 (b)

2 (b)

3 a. thorax 胸 b. exoskeleton 外骨骼；外甲
c. antenna 觸角

38 The Life Cycles of Cats and Frogs
貓和青蛙的生命週期

1 (a)

2 a. A baby cat is called a kitten.
b. It takes about one year.
c. They are born in eggs.

3 a. tadpole 蝌蚪 b. hatch 孵出；孵化 c. gill 鰓

39 The Life Cycle of a Pine Tree
松樹的生命週期

1 (b)

2 a. cones b. ground c. seedling

3 a. seedling 樹苗 b. pine cone 松果 c. sprout 發芽

40 Photosynthesis 光合作用

1 (a)

2 a. F b. T c. F

3 a. photosynthesis 光合作用 b. capture 捕獲
c. release 釋放

41 What Is a Food Chain 何謂食物鏈

1 (b)

2 a. plants b. bottom c. prey

3 a. bottom 底部 b. prey animal 獵物
c. relationship 關係；關聯

42 Fishing and Overfishing 捕魚與過度捕撈

1 (b)

2 a. The oceans help the earth stay healthy.
b. They catch fish and shellfish.
c. They are getting smaller (and smaller).

3 a. shellfish 水生有殼生物　b. fishing ground 漁場
c. overfish 過度捕撈

43 **How Animals Become Extinct**
動物如何絕種

1 (c)

2 (b)

3 a. woolly mammoth 長毛象　b. ecosystem 生態系統
c. pollution 汙染

44 **Staying Healthy** 保持健康

1 (a)

2 a. Germs　b. defeat　c. medicine

3 a. break down 故障；健康狀況變差
b. fight back 反擊；抵抗　c. germ 細菌

45 **Caring for the Five Senses**
關心我們的五種感官

1 (c)

2 a. T　b. F　c. T

3 a. sunburn 曬傷　b. blow your nose 擤鼻子
c. taste 嚐；辨味

46 **The Organs of the Human Body**
人體的器官

1 (c)

2 a. nerve system　b. heart　c. skin

3 a. pump blood 輸送血液　b. digest 消化
c. organ 器官

47 **Seasons and Weather** 季節與氣候

1 (b)

2 a. T　b. F　c. T

3 a. bloom 開花　b. season 季節　c. foggy 有霧的；多霧的

48 **How Can Water Change** 水如何變化

1 (c)

2 a. liquid　b. state　c. ice

3 a. boil 沸騰　b. solid 固體　c. freeze 結冰；凝固

49 **The Layers of the Earth** 地層

1 (b)

2 a. The earth is divided into three parts.
b. It is called the crust.
c. It is the mantle.

3 a. core 地核　b. surface 表面　c. layer 層；地層

50 **How to Conserve Our Resources**
如何保存我們的資源

1 (c)

2 a. Nonrenewable resources cannot be replaced easily.
b. They should turn the water off.
c. It can save natural resources.

3 a. recycling 回收　b. oil spill（油輪）漏油
c. conserve 保護；節省

51 **What Changes the Earth's Surface**
什麼讓地表改變

1 (b)

2 (a)

3 a. weathering 風化　b. topsoil 表土　c. break down 分解

52 **Fossils** 化石

1 (b)

2 a. remains　b. Minerals　c. fossils

3 a. imprint 印痕　b. rot away 腐壞　c. get buried 被掩埋

53 **Is Pluto a Planet** 冥王星是行星嗎

1 (a)

2 a. F　b. F　c. F

3 a. solar system 太陽系　b. distance 距離　c. object 物體

54 **The Phases of the Moon** 月相

1 (b)

2 (a)

3 a. phase 月相　b. crescent 新月　c. wane 月虧；月缺

55 **Measuring Food** 計量食材

1 (a)

2 a. The person is making cookies.
b. $\frac{3}{4}$ cup of brown sugar is needed.
c. $1\frac{1}{2}$ cups of chocolate chips are needed.

3 a. gallon 加侖　b. ingredient 食材　c. teaspoon 茶匙

56 **Benjamin Franklin** 班傑明‧富蘭克林

1 (a)

2 a. electricity　b. kite　c. key

3 a. get shocked 觸電　b. lightning 閃電
c. electric charge 電荷

57 **How a Magnet Works** 磁鐵的作用

1 (c)

2 a. A magnet is made of magnetized metal like iron or nickel.
b. They are the N pole and S pole.
c. They will repel each other.

3 a. magnetic pole 磁極　b. repel 排斥
c. magnetic field 磁場

58 The Invention of the Telephone
電話的發明

1 (b)

2 a. telephone b. electricity c. 1876

3 a. vibration 振動 b. transmit 傳送；發送 c. pulse 脈衝

59 Physical and Chemical Changes
物理變化與化學變化

1 (c)

2 (b)

3 a. compound 化合物 b. matter 物質 c. dissolve 溶解

60 Conduction, Convection, and Radiation
傳導、對流和輻射

1 (a)

2 a. Conduction b. convection c. radiation

3 a. convection 對流 b. particle 粒子 c. force 強迫；強推

61 Five Simple Shapes 五種簡單的形狀

1 (b)

2 a. F b. T c. T

3 a. pyramid 角錐形 b. oval 橢圓形 c. cone 圓錐形

62 Plane Figures and Solid Figures
平面圖形與立體圖形

1 (c)

2 (c)

3 a. sphere 球體 b. solid figure 立體圖形
c. rhombus 菱形

63 Polygons and Congruent Figures
多邊形與全等圖形

1 (a)

2 a. At least three line segments can make a polygon.
b. They are squares, rectangles, and rhombuses.
c. They are identical.

3 a. symmetric figures 對稱圖形 b. polygon 多邊形
c. congruent figures 全等圖形

64 Addition and Subtraction 加法和減法

1 (a)

2 (c)

3 a. minus sign 減號 b. difference 差 c. addition 加法

65 Making Change 換零錢

1 (c)

2 a. People buy goods and services with money.
b. One quarter is worth twenty-five cents.
c. 2 dimes and 1 nickel are worth the same as a quarter.

3 a. value 價值 b. dime 十分硬幣 c. bill 紙鈔

66 Greater and Less Than 大於和小於

1 (a)

2 a. after b. greater c. less

3 a. math term 數學術語 b. equal 相等的
c. less than 小於

67 Number Sentences 算式

1 (c)

2 a. number sentences b. plus c. addition

3 a. tally 計數 b. number line 數線
c. number sentence 算式

68 Time Passes 時間流逝

1 (b)

2 a. He arrives at school at 7:45.
b. He has four hours of class in the morning.
c. It finishes at 3:00.

3 a. a quarter 十五分鐘 b. until 直到
c. half past ……點半

69 Why Do We Multiply 我們為什麼要做乘法

1 (c)

2 a. equal groups b. 1 c. 0

3 a. factor 因數 b. multiply 乘；乘以 c. product 乘積

70 Solve the Problems (1) 解題（1）

1 (c)

2 a. T b. F c. F

3 a. count 計算；數 b. share 分享 c. plus 加上；外加

71 Solve the Problems (2) 解題（2）

1 (b)

2 a. kilometers b. tall c. kilogram

3 a. weigh 有……重量 b. scale 體重計
c. at a time 每次；一次

72 Reading and Writing Fractions and Decimals 分數與小數的讀寫

1 (b)

2 a. It is $\frac{1}{6}$.
b. You read it two point four five.
c. It is $\frac{1}{2}$.

3 a. fraction 分數 b. decimal 小數
　　c. the simplest form 最簡形式

73 *Aesop's Fables* 伊索寓言

1 (c)
2 a. F b. T c. F
3 a. lesson 教訓 b. moral 寓意 c. character 人物；角色

74 **The Greek Gods and Goddesses** 希臘眾神

1 (c)
2 a. Olympus b. Hera c. Ares
3 a. powerful 強大的 b. mythology 神話 c. hero 英雄

75 **A Friendly Letter** 一封友善的信

1 (a)
2 a. date b. questions c. capital
3 a. closing 結尾辭 b. capital letter 大寫字母
　　c. greeting 問候語

76 **Parts of Speech** 英語的詞類

1 (a)
2 a. It needs a subject and a verb.
　　b. They describe actions.
　　c. They describe other words like nouns and pronouns.
3 a. subject 主詞 b. adjective 形容詞
　　c. action verb 動作動詞

77 **Different Types of Sentences** 句子的種類

1 (c)
2 a. It is s declarative sentence.
　　b. It is a question.
　　c. It ends with an exclamation point.
3 a. emotion 情緒；情感 b. declarative sentence 陳述句
　　c. imperative sentence 祈使句

78 **Common Mistakes in English** 英文常見的錯誤

1 (c)
2 a. F b. F c. T
3 a. independent clause 獨立子句
　　b. comma splice 逗點謬誤
　　c. sentence fragment 不完整句

79 **Some Common Sayings** 常見的格言

1 (b)
2 a. F b. T c. F
3 a. make sense 有道理；有意義 b. saying 諺語
　　c. will 意志；決心

80 **Primary and Secondary Colors**
三原色和第二次色

1 (b)
2 a. yellow b. secondary c. Black
3 a. primary color 原色 b. secondary color 合成色
　　c. combine 結合

81 **Famous Painters** 著名的畫家

1 (b)
2 a. You can see them at art galleries.
　　b. Leonardo da Vinci painted it.
　　c. He painted around 500 years ago.
3 a. artist 藝術家；美術家 b. portrait 肖像 c. gallery 畫廊

82 **Realistic Art and Abstract Art**
「寫實派」藝術與「抽象派」藝術

1 (b)
2 a. Realistic b. Abstract c. red
3 a. still life 靜物畫 b. landscape 風景畫
　　c. abstract art 抽象派藝術

83 **What Do Architects Do** 建築師的工作

1 (a)
2 (c)
3 a. architect 建築師 b. detailed 詳細的
　　c. skyscraper 摩天大樓

84 **Elements of Painting** 繪畫的要素

1 (c)
2 (c)
3 a. masterwork 傑作 b. contrast 對比；對照
　　c. balance 平衡

85 **Unique Art** 獨特的藝術

1 (c)
2 a. They use blocks of ice, saws, hammers, and chisels.
　　b. It is a quilt.
　　c. Native Americans do sand painting.
3 a. quilt 被子；床罩 b. chisel 鑿子 c. folk art 民俗藝術

86 Musicians and Their Musical Instruments 音樂家和樂器

1 (b)

2 a. T b. T c. F

3 a. harmonious 悅耳的 b. orchestra 管弦樂隊

c. note 音符

87 Popular Children's Songs 受歡迎的兒歌

1 (b)

2 a. simple b. hum c. catchy

3 a. hum 低哼 b. rhyme 押韻 c. melody 旋律

88 Different Kinds of Music 不同類型的音樂

1 (a)

2 a. T b. F c. F

3 a. R&B 節奏藍調 b. rap 饒舌音樂

c. folk music 民俗音樂

89 Different Kinds of Musical Instruments 各種樂器

1 (b)

2 a. keyboard b. woodwinds c. hit

3 a. percussion instrument 打擊樂器

b. woodwind 木管樂器 c. characteristic 特色

90 *The Nutcracker* 胡桃鉗

1 (a)

2 a. Tchaikovsky b. Christmas c. prince

3 a. come to life 變得活生生；栩栩如生

b. battle 與……作戰 c. composed by 由……創作